THE LOST SON

by

Aidan Lucid

All rights reserved. No part of this publication may be reproduced, distributed, or transmitted in any form or by any means, including photocopying, recording, or other electronic or mechanical methods, without the prior written permission of the publisher, except in the case of brief quotations embodied in critical reviews and certain other non-commercial uses permitted by copyright law.

This is a work of fiction. Names, characters, businesses, places, events, locales, and incidents are either the products of the author's imagination or used in a fictitious manner. Any resemblance to actual persons, living or dead, or actual events is purely coincidental.

For permission requests, email the publisher, addressed "Attention: Permissions Coordinator," at the following email address: gary@garyrevel.com or the author, Aidan Lucid: thezargothiansaga@gmail.com

© Copyright Aidan Lucid 2019

Published by Jongleur Books 2019.

Book Design by Gary Revel

Front and back cover illustration by SMStudioinc
(https://www.fiverr.com/smstudioinc)

"The flow of this novel is such that I just kept on reading. There are some great fight scenes in this book, and some very well fleshed out interactions of totally believable characters. Give it a try; you will enjoy it, especially if you believe in magic."
- J.D. Warner, author of, *Hexa-tech*

"*The Lost Son*, is a unique fantasy novel that begins with a bang. This fast-paced adventure keeps the reader turning pages, while it offers a story that will keep you guessing."
- Brandy Alexander, author of, *Genesis*.

"The plot of the book is solid and engaging, exciting and well developed. All told, I believe Aidan shows promise in his story and I will keep my eye out for the next one."
- Scott Collins, author of, *Days' End*.

"*The Lost Son* was written by Ireland's own, Aidan Lucid, and let me tell you, he is going to be one of the shining stars in the literary world. From the first chapter, this story has it all…"
Randy Belaire, author of, *The Reckoning: Chronicles of the Shadow Chaser*

TABLE OF CONTENTS

Foreword – Pg 5

Acknowledgements – Pg 6

Character Pronunciation Reference – Pg 7

Prologue – Pg 8

Chapter One - A Mysterious Discovery - Pg 11

Chapter Two - A Whole New World - Pg 31

Chapter Three - The First Test - Pg 79

Chapter Four - A Glimpse Into the Past – Pg 116

Chapter Five - Preparing for War Pg 130

Chapter Six - No Turning Back – Pg 168

Chapter Seven - Last Fight for Freedom Pg 176

Chapter Eight - Meeting the Father – Pg 192

Chapter Nine - Homeward Bound - 204

Epilogue - 216

Foreword

As the acquisition editor for a science fiction magazine, and the judge of several writing competitions, I've encountered many thousands of stories. Many of them involved dragons and the Bermuda Triangle, but not at the same time. Many of them employed a talisman such as a coin but not in the way Aidan Lucid does in *The Lost Son*. Many stories have as their protagonist an everyday person to whom something extraordinary happens but not here. Look for that cusp moment, several times, dear reader and you'll not want to stop reading. The book on how to write young adult fantasy has to be rewritten to take into account this fascinating novel.

I first met Aidan Lucid's writing twelve years ago. The narrative was diamond, a little rough but I knew it was destined to shine and here it is.

Geoff Nelder FRMetS., MSc., Bed
Author of the *ARIA Trilogy*

Acknowledgements

Firstly, I just want to say a big thanks to SMStudioinc for the fantastic illustrations on the front and back cover.

Another special thanks goes to Geoff Nelder for his brilliant foreword; also for his help both with this book and my other works down through the years.

Tony and Gail at Jefferson Franklin Editing for their great suggestions on the second last round of editing. Also d_pamela from Fiverr.com for the last round of edits. From the bottom of my heart, thank you.

Patrick Kilroy, former pilot and owner of Kilroywashere.org, deserves a mention. The flight scenes in chapter one and two would not have been possible without his invaluable advice.

Many thanks to Leonardo Borazio for a dozen (additional) illustrations and to John Blackford for doing the illustration with the dragon attacking the plane in chapter one. Your talents are much appreciated. Also to Invader 000 for the illustrations of: Hannorah, Karina and Tracey.

My final thanks goes to you, the reader, for purchasing this book. If you enjoyed it, then please leave a review on Amazon, Goodreads etc.

CHARACTER PRONOUNCIATIONS

Aranok	Aaron-ach
Damone	Da-moan
Detrok	Dee-trok
Eranam	Err-on-am
General Fradar	Fray-dar
General Haynach	Hay-nach
Hamorin	Hammer-in
Hannorah	Han-nora or Han-no-rah
Hernacious	Her-nass-ee-us
Karina	Car-eena
King Argoth	Ar-goth or Our-goth
King Gronach	Groan-ach
King Mordoch	Mor-duck
King Zakarius	Za-care-ee-us
Nemus	Nee-mus or knee-mus
Orkinad	Or-kin-ad
Porok	Po-rock
Queen Cyren	Siren or Sigh-wren
Queen Eusaba	You-say-ba
Slyvanon	Sly-va-non
Tyram	Toy-ram
Verach	Ver-ach
Wernach	Were-nach
Xongrelan	Zon-gra-len
Zymbion	Zym-bee-on

PROLOGUE

Avran and Temrok, both Sadarkian, in their black armor, jumped as the throne room's double doors slammed shut. They knelt while their king's footsteps echoed as he approached them. King Zakarius's broad shoulders made his shadow wider, the low sun made it longer. An imposing figure in the flesh made more so by the light. Zakarius's long black hair fell just below his shoulders.

Avran and Temrok dared not look at him until they were given express permission.

Zakarius sat on his throne and fixed his gaze on the two guards kneeling before him. The Sadarkian yellowed skin tone contrasted as his hand stroked down the length of his black beard. It was neatly and cleanly shaved, groomed to pointed perfection. Over his head was a large portrait of his predecessor, King Mordoch.

Mordoch was revered for being a fair and just king. Zakarius had always hoped to be better than Mordoch and in his opinion, he surpassed all of his predecessor's accomplishments by winning more wars than him.

"Stand up." His clear voice cut the silence of the room.

Avram and Temrok stood holding their helmets underneath their right arms. They stared at Zakarius, his eyes sharp with intelligence, calculating. "Then you understand eradication is the only option?"

"We do, sire," Temrok said.

"Very well. But before you go, understand this." Zakarius walked down to look into their eyes.

They looked up at him.

"This mission is important. If you fail, I will burn each and every one of your children and make you watch. Understood?" Both soldiers nodded nervously.

"I said, *understood*?" Zakarius barked.

"Yes, sire!" Avram and Temrok answered in unison.

"Dismissed."

Avram gave his salt and pepper haired friend a nervous glance before each put on their helmets and left.

ZAKARIUS'S THRONE

Zakarius passed the columns lining each side of the throne room as he walked to the window to his far left. Shadows cast by flames on the candles danced on the marble floors. Each candle was in a candle holder attached to every column. Over both sets of columns were balconies that had rows of seats where the Senate would sit whenever he had a meeting with them.

Zakarius stood by the window, gazing down at the dragons. Large black chamfrains covered their heads; their lower bodies were protected by black armor, which blended seamlessly with their skin. They sat with their wings tucked in by their sides.

Ladders rested against each dragon, Zakarius watched as Avram and Temrok climbed onto them. When they were seated, the ladders were taken away.

The dragons spread their great leathery wings. As they headed east, a sound like cannon fire exploded behind the clouds. A large, velvet-colored spinning hole opened. Both beasts banked to the right and flew into the portal. Momentarily it expanded and then collapsed, closing after the riders.

Zakarius chuckled, imagining the smell of his enemies' blood wafting into his nostrils.

Chapter One

A Mysterious Discovery

November 5th, 1945

JOHNSON   MACCALL

Many thousands of feet above the Bermuda Triangle, the TBF Avenger disturbed the blue sky's silence. Captain Edward Johnson, age 40 and his friend, Sergeant Conor MacCall, 37, crewed the dark blue Torpedo bomber. They flew without a bombardier/belly-gunner because they did not expect any action. This was a routine patrol for the Naval Air Station in Fort Lauderdale near Miami.

"It's a good morning for flying. The one thing I haven't missed these last two years is the miserable weather back home," said Conor in his strong Glaswegian accent.

"I agree with you on that one," Edward replied in his Oxford drawl, his brown eyes surveying the area around him. He had dark-blond hair and a blond moustache.

Sitting in the rear of the plane, controlling the turret gun and radio, Conor pushed back his carroty hair and turned his green eyes towards Edward.

"Do you ever think about home?"

"All the time."

"What do you miss the most?"

Edward thought for a moment before answering. "I miss my parents. Every Sunday, Sandra and I would take the kids and visit my folks, staying for a few hours. Sandra loved Mum's baking. Mum always fussed over the kids."

"I suppose you miss her baking too, sir, eh?" Conor chuckled as he asked this.

"Well, I suppose I do. But there're better opportunities over here so we had no choice but to move."

"Aye, I'll second that. I miss meeting the lads on a Saturday for a wee game of footie and then the few pints after. I'll tell you this much, one thing I don't miss is shooting down Germans over London."

"True, true." Edward surveyed the area once more, satisfied that there was no present danger. "I suppose we'll head back," Edward said. "Radio the station to all clear the area."

"Aye, sir. I'll get right on it."

Twenty minutes from base, a brilliant white light exploded out of nowhere, engulfing the sky as far as they could see. Sound burst around them, ricocheting with memories of bombing raids, flak and fire, the uncertainty of survival, deafness isolating each man in his real and recalled fear, never knowing if they would make it back. The light intensified, burned their retinas.

Shielding their eyes didn't help much.

As suddenly as it arrived, the light disappeared.

"What in blazes just happened?" Conor said, blinking his eyes, readjusting to normality.

"Your guess is as good as mine," Edward replied.

Both Conor and Edward's headphones suddenly burst with static as they received a transmission from base.

"Fort Lauderdale to FT-4, do you read me?"

"This is Fox Tare Four to Fort Lauderdale; we read you loud and clear. What's the problem? Over," Conor replied.

"You got two unidentified bogies closing in on your position. Three o'clock."

Conor shook away the last of the retina burn and looked again. When paying a second glance, he saw the bogies approaching. "Roger that, Lauderdale. Bogies spotted. FT-4, out." His headphones crackled as Lauderdale was cut off. "Sir, I know this may sound strange, but they don't seem to be planes coming towards us."

"Of course they are. What else can they be?"

Conor shut his eyes and squinted, focusing harder. On second glance, he became slack-jawed.

"I think they're..." he swallowed the unreality of the thought. "They're... dragons. Black dragons. And there's someone riding them."

"This is no time for jokes."

"I'm not joking. They're gaining on us. Break left!"

"Don't be daft. There's no such-" Edward stopped in mid-sentence as he too saw what Conor had seen. "My God!" he exclaimed in awe. "Bloody hell, how's this even possible?" Edward snapped out of his momentary, shock-induced paralysis. "Hold on!" The TBF Avenger swooped down.

The dragon followed. Opening its large mouth, it belched fire and narrowly missed the TBF Avenger's tail.

"It's big, ugly and just blew fire at us. That's a dragon in my book!" Conor cried. He unleashed a wave of bullets from the turret gun but the dragon swerved, evading them.

Edward again performed an Immelmann Turn, beginning as a loop, then while upside down at the top of the loop, rolling the plane over, ending right side up, higher and going in the opposite direction. When the captain had finished the maneuver, Conor continued firing.

The dragon turned upside down and again blew fire upon them. The flames licked the cockpit's Plexiglas, cracking it. The glass had also been blackened a little. Fumes from the flames leaked through the cracks.

Conor yelped with fright. "That was close, sir. If we don't lose it, we're toast."

Their large pursuer flew over the plane. The dragon's tail was inches from the cockpit. From Conor's position, he could see the scales on its stomach trailing down to its tail. All of its upper body was covered in black, shiny armor. He caught a brief glimpse of its rider's hideous face.

"I don't know what's uglier, that creature or the big dragon," Conor said, hands trembling, sweat trickling down his forehead.

The dragon leaped higher, twisted and turned, leveling at the frightened airmen's six.

"By my estimation, it's only four to five inches from our tail."

"Hold your fire and tell me when the monster is about to open its mouth," Edward replied.

Conor glanced at the dragon. Its bright yellow eyes alight with a volcanic orange glow. "I think it's ready to blow," he warned, hysteria tingeing his voice. He stared back at the jet-black monster and gulped.

"Hold on. Be ready to fire."

"Aye, sir."

Edward pulled up, briefly soaring into the air and banked left. The dragon flew over them and dropped right down in front of the TBF Avenger. Edward opened fire using the guns at the front of the plane.

The black-armored rider abandoned his dragon and fell to the sea. The onslaught of fire ripped through the monster. Its right wing shredded as bullets found their mark.

"Bull's-eye," Edward shouted.

"Good shooting, sir. Phew, that was close." The Scot wiped his brow, moist from perspiration.

"Yes it was. I'm glad we made it. I can't believe what just happened. How on Earth did that dragon get here? Anyway, we're alive and that's all that matters."

Another dragon dropped down so close to the plane; its bellowed war cry reverberated through the metal skin.

The TBF Avenger banked left, just about evading a burst of fire.

The second beast increased altitude until it was beyond their line of sight. It seemed that the threat had gone.

Unfortunately, it reappeared behind them.

"I'll try and hold it off again." Conor's hands vibrated with each shudder of the weapon while firing.

Edward made the plane climb but couldn't shake off the beast. When that failed, the plane plunged into a three hundred and sixty degree spiral and then shot up again. That failed, too.

"It's too good for us. We mightn't be able to shake it off," Conor admitted.

"Don't worry; I've got one more trick up my sleeve. Hold on tight."

"Are you sure you know what you're doing, sir?" Conor asked, looking at the sea below rising up to meet them. He returned to firing at the creature, but it dodged the turret gun's bullets.

"Yes, MacCall," Edward answered.

The plane began to shudder, became harder to control. The water was perilously close.

Cold sweat gathered as Conor's heart thumped, his breathing quickened, he was on the verge of hyperventilating. He took a deep breath to control the danger. "Altitude four hundred feet and closing," the Scot announced with a quiver creeping into his voice.

"I know what I'm doing."

"Three hundred feet, sir." *What the hell is he up to?* "Two hundred." There was still no response from the pilot.

"One hundred," Conor squeaked, feeling death was now imminent. He began to question his captain's mentality. "Fifty feet. Pull up, Captain. Pull up!"

Gravity seemed to shift as the TBF Avenger pulled up, narrowly missing the impact. Water rippled as they passed over it.

The dragon and its rider splashed into the ocean. Relief washed through Conor. Edward's crazy maneuver had actually worked.

"They're gone. I thought we were done for," Conor shouted, relieved.

"I can't believe you doubted me," Edward said. "Have faith, old boy."

"Aye, sir, but try tellin' my underwear that." Conor tried to catch his breath. "First there was that blinding light and then we got attacked by two dragons. What a day! Where in God's name did they come from?"

"I wish I knew but I think it's best if we don't tell Lauderdale the truth."

"What will we tell them, sir?"

"Radio back and inform them that—" Edward was cut short - the radial engine stopped working. "Dammit."

An eerie silence surrounded them. For the first time, they could hear the wind blowing across the canopy. The engine's comforting vibration gone.

Conor knew Edward would lower the nose to establish a glide. Both men remained calm as there was still time to regain control. Their plane, at eight thousand feet, was now descending.

"I'll try to switch the fuel," Edward said. This was done by manually switching fuel between the tanks by rotating a lever in the tanks' direction.

Nothing happened.

"I'll try to restart the engine."

From his time in training, Conor understood that in order for Edward to restart the engine, the pilot would first reach his hand over to the throttle, moving it back and forth while adjusting the prop with the lever next to the throttle. As Edward did this, his right hand was on the stick and trimmed it up.

"The engine won't restart." Edward's calm was the opposite of Conor's emotion.

"That's just bloody great," Conor mumbled.

The TBF Avenger was now at one thousand seven hundred feet above the glittering ocean.

Continuing his efforts to get the engine started, Edward said, "Radio the base and tell them we need help."

"Aye, sir," Conor said, returning to the radio. "Mayday, mayday, this is Fox Tare Four to Fort Lauderdale. We need help. We're going down. I repeat, we're going down!"

"Fox Tare Four, this is base. We did not receive your full message. Please repeat. Do you copy?'

Edward sighed his displeasure. "Dammit."

"Base, this is Sergeant Conor MacCall from FT-4. Our engine has stopped and we're going down fast. We need your help. Over."

"Base to FT-4, there's interference in your signal. We can't receive your full transmission."

"Aw, to hell with it! There's no use radioing Lauderdale, sir."

"I don't understand why they're not receiving us fully."

The plane was still gliding over the water, now less than nine hundred feet.

"In what direction do you think the breeze is blowing?" Edward asked.

"I'm not too sure, sir, but I think it's north westerly."

"Thank you."

The TBF Avenger was now moving north west to head towards land. Conor's flight suit became even more drenched with sweat, his breathing more rapid. He gulped as he watched Edward's hands tremble as they gripped the throttle.

Edward now had to admit defeat at four hundred feet.

"Four hundred feet and closing," Conor announced.

"I know. Parachuting from this height would be pointless. It looks like we'll have to ditch. I've tried everything and the engine won't restart. Tighten your seatbelt and shoulder harness as much as you can."

Conor had trained for a situation like this but it was his first time performing an actual ditching.

They were thirty seconds away from hitting the ocean.

"We may flip, so remember your Dilbert Dunker training," Edward advised.

Conor tightened the strap across his lap.

"If we do die, then it was an honor serving with you."

"The honor was all mine, MacCall."

The ocean was rushing up to greet them, Conor could see the water beyond Edward's helmet.

Then both men gasped as the waters separated and a black, menacing hole appeared, the TBF Avenger heading straight for it.

"What the bloody hell is that?" Conor shouted in panic.

Edward's voice trembled as he replied, "I don't know. But whatever it is, it doesn't look good. I'm too low to turn away and it seems to be going down at our rate of descent. Brace yourself!"

Both men screamed as their plane nose-dived into the hole. It fluctuated inwards, creating a winding violet pathway.

* * *

In the darkness of his chambers, Zakarius's face was visible only in reflected luminosity. The light from the revolving object highlighted his gritted teeth, his disappointment and disgust as the magic ball showed him the failure of his two riders. He cursed as the metallic beast and all the dangers it held reached the portal. Zakarius left his chambers, slamming the door behind him.

An hour later, he walked into the courtyard. After he watched the riders fail their mission, he immediately ordered Avram and Temrok's children be dragged out of their homes along with their mothers to the courtyard. As he entered, soldiers positioned all around the white walls stood to attention. Both mothers wept as they wriggled in vain to break free from the soldiers' tight grip.

Each set of children were tied to two poles that were hammered into the ground. Below them lay a mound of straw. Avram's little boy and girl, aged six and seven, whimpered, tears streaking their pale faces. Temrok's two girls, both 13 and 14, cried also.

"Please spare them," begged Avram's wife, her long brown hair partially covering her face as she continued to struggle to break free.

Zakarius ignored her pleas, turning instead to his soldiers looking on, awaiting his orders. "Their fathers were the best dragon riders in my army and they failed. So let this be a lesson to any of you who do the same." He nodded to a guard standing beside the children. The soldier poured a large clay jug of oil over them.

"No, please," Avram's little girl cried as she saw him take a lighted torch from the wall.

Soon cries of agony filled the courtyard as flames ravaged the children. Soldiers covered their noses as the stench of burning flesh invaded their nostrils.

Zakarius watched as the flames' reflection danced in his eyes. But he still wondered how he would deal with the threat of the two men on the metallic beast and what dangers they would present.

He turned his attention to his middle-aged general, Haynach. Zakarius motioned with his head for Haynach to come to him. He had confided in him earlier about the humans coming through the portal.

"Send a team out to the forest to scout it. If those men arrive, I want them killed immediately. Bring me their heads."

"Yes, sire." The general nodded before departing.

Zakarius smiled as he returned to watch the flames lick the children's flesh before devouring them completely.

* * *

Present Day - Harleyville, America

TRACEY

Seventeen-year-old Henry Simmons walked with his head lowered and hands stuffed in the pocket of his green combat trousers. A little puff of wind blew through his brown hair as his blue eyes stayed fixed on the ground. Today had been an emotional rollercoaster. He experienced the euphoria of passing Mr. Smythe's dreaded biology summer exam. This was soon followed by bitter disappointment. He had stared into Tracey Maxwell's sky-blue eyes hid behind her red-rimmed spectacles as he asked, "Hey, Tracey, um…I was wondering if you'd like to be my date for the prom Friday night?"

    He'd never forget her smirk as she placed a hand on Henry's shoulder. "You're a nice guy, Henry, but I'm not going to be your date. Sorry." The constant replaying of those words darkened his day, and his mood. It had taken him two weeks to pluck up the courage to ask the most gorgeous girl in school out, then she'd gone and torn his heart out, dumping it in the trash.

Tracey Maxwell, although a "nerd" like him, was hot and interesting in her own way. The fact that she was the top Fortnite player in his school only attracted more boys to her. Henry liked Tracey for two years, even before she changed her hair color and shed a few pounds. She favored long brunette instead of her former short, spiky blonde hairstyle. Other boys began noticing her more too after her transformation, including Brad Thompson, captain of the football team. Henry felt that he didn't have a chance of being with Tracey given the strong competition. Still, every time she'd pass him in the hallway, he'd receive a whiff of her strawberry perfume and his stomach would flutter. So taking his chances, he decided to ask her out but Henry knew he was hoping for too much when he asked her to the dance. Deep down, he knew it was worth a try besides always wondering 'what if'. Never did he realize that a rejection would be this hurtful.

"Hey, Henry," a voice called out. "Hold up."

Henry turned around to see his best friend, Joey Arnolds, running to him. Joey was taller and physically leaner than Henry. He removed the blue New York Knicks baseball cap, smoothing down his red crewcut before putting the baseball cap on again.

"Are you heading home?" Joey asked.

"Yeah, I don't feel like having lunch now."

"But what about the rest of your classes?"

"I think I'll give them a miss. Don't you have PE after lunch?"

"Uh-huh, but I'm just gonna skip it. I've practically made the lacrosse team."

Henry chuckled at his friend's remark.

"Won't your parents be home now? Your mom will freak if she thinks you're skipping classes," Joey said.

"Nah, Mom and Dad are away on business for the day and if she finds out, I'll just say I didn't feel well or something."

"I guess Tracey wouldn't have anything to do with you skipping lunch?" Henry didn't answer. "I knew it. You've had a crush on her for like, years now, dude. Time to forget her," Joey said.

"Yeah, I know, but it's just... so hard to. I never thought being turned down by her would suck so much."

"Yeah sorry, bro'."

Henry sighed and decided to change the subject. "How's your grandma after her hip op'?"

"Grandma's grandma: cranky as hell but she's getting round pretty good. May as well go there now until Mom picks me up after her shift at the precinct."

"Your grandma won't rat you out?"

"As long as she can watch Dr. Phil in peace, she don't care who's there or why."

Henry was unsure whether or not to ask his next question but decided to anyway. "Do you ever, like, think about your dad?"

"Nah. He can't be bothered to call me or Mom so why should I?"

A car honked twice behind them. Henry turned around and groaned as he recognized the three boys in it.

"Oh no," Henry grumbled.

"What's wrong?"

"That's Brad Thompson and his guys."

"Wait a sec, he's not still pissed with you over busting his bike light, is he?"

"Uh-huh."

"But that was a year ago."

"Try telling him that."

Brad Thompson was a guy most boys wanted to be like and most girls wanted to be with. Henry had to admit, but never openly, that Brad was good looking with his dirty-blond hair gelled back and 1950s Elvis type sideburns. He pulled in a short distance from where Henry and Joey stood, turning off the ignition.

Brad, and his two friends, Tom Robinson and Richard Moran, got out of the blue Sedan. Brad and his cronies all wore denim jeans and Letterman football jackets with yellow sleeves.

"Look, don't worry. I got your back," Joey said.

"Well, well, well, if it ain't Fatso and Simmons," Brad said with a menacing grin. The other boys spread out, blocking Henry and Joey's path. "Maybe you need to get your eyes checked, I'm not fat anymore, Thompson," Joey replied. Joey, although still a little pudgy, had lost 20 pounds by taking up jogging, playing lacrosse and reducing the amount of junk food.

"Just let us pass, okay?" Henry said.

"I will… but you gotta give us something first…you know, as payment," the football captain replied.

"Like what?" Henry said.

"Oh I don't know… your lunch money, any candy you have on you or that nice cell I've seen you using, Simmons," Brad answered.

"And what if we don't wanna give you anything?" Joey asked.

Brad stepped forward, put his face right up to Joey's. "If you don't, then me and the guys here are gonna make sure you regret it."

"Joey, let's just give them what they want," Henry said.

Brad stood straight and said, "I'd listen to your buddy there, Fatso."

"Again, I'm not fat and no, I'm sick and tired of jerks like you pushing guys like me and Henry around." Joey put his bag on the ground. "You want our stuff, come get it."

"Joey, come on," Henry pleaded. "There's three of them and only two of us."

"You really wanna do this?" Tom asked.

"Hell, yeah," Joey shouted.

"Get 'em," Brad ordered.

Tom and Richard were on top of Joey but he fought back, kneeing Tom in the crotch. Joey managed to push Richard to the ground but soon fell from Tom's sucker punch to the stomach. Tom and Richard pinned Joey down.

Henry charged at them, shoving Richard off. Brad snuck up behind Henry and put him in a headlock. Henry tried to wriggle out of it but couldn't escape the tight grip.

"You should've just given us somethin'," Brad said. "Then we wouldn't have had to do this." Brad nodded to his friends. The boys got Joey to his feet.

Joey managed to push Tom away but Richard delivered a hard punch to his stomach before he could react.

"Stop it. Leave him alone!" Henry roared. Brad released his hold, throwing Henry to the ground.

Joey doubled over moaning. Henry could see through his friend's clenched fist and gritted teeth that he was trying hard not to cry.

"All right, guys, that's enough." As soon as Brad said this, the other boys stepped away. "Just so you know, this little beat down was courtesy of Sid Connors. He says Tracey's his girl. A friend of his saw you ask her out so he sent me a text to send you a message. Next time you go near her, we'll tune you up real good."

"Since when do you care about Sid?" Henry asked.

"Since he promised me $100 to do this. See ya later, bitches."

Brad kicked Joey's school bag, sending it rolling down the road a little before he got into his Sedan with his friends and drove off.

Sid Connors had been a thorn in Henry's side for the last three years. Henry had defeated him in the final of the local Call of Duty tournament and Sid could not let it go, taking every opportunity of making Henry's life miserable. He would send taunting messages online, leaving notes calling Henry "dickweed" or "cheater" wedged in the side of Henry's locker, occasionally spitting at him but only when Henry was alone and Sid wasn't.

Henry helped Joey up. "Are you okay?"

"What do you think?" he shot back, a little embarrassed. "Come on, let's go home," Henry said.

* * *

Jasper sniffed the chunks of cat food in his dish and turned away in disgust. He was a gray American Bobtail with an unusual acquired taste for a cat.

He would only eat a piece of steak, or some of Mrs. Cleary's lasagna. Mr. Anderson, Jasper's owner, had gone to a poker tournament for senior citizens leaving his cat in the care of Mrs. Williams, a mean elderly lady. Mrs. Williams detested cats, and because of this, Jasper was evicted from the house while she stayed there.

While Jasper sat on the grass, plotting a dreadful and scratchy vengeance for Mrs. Williams, the breeze began to blow. He looked up, sniffing the air, his eyes narrowed. The wind grew. Palm trees began to rustle as it swept through their leaves. Jasper's fur stood on end. His instincts told him that something peculiar was in the air. The little feline's green eyes widened with amazement as a black dot appeared in the sky, which then broadened into a whirling tornado, gray in color. A golden coin was thrown from the tornado.

Overwhelmed with curiosity, Jasper took a few steps closer to investigate. The coin spun on the ground and had a pulse-like glow. Jasper ventured closer to the glowing spinning object.

Just as the cat was almost beside it, the tornado spun quicker than before. He tried with all his might to run away, but couldn't. The cat clawed the air and screamed as he was sucked into the vortex.

HENRY FINDS THE COIN

Henry was near his house when he saw Mr. Anderson walking around searching for something. The old man wiped his eyes with a piece of tissue. To Henry, it looked like he had been crying.

"Are you all right, Mr. Anderson?" Henry asked, but the man never answered. "Can I help you?"

"Jasper's gone. My little baby's gone," he cried, his hands raised in despair.

"Where'd he go?"

"I don't know. The lady minding him said that there was a terrible wind and it must have scared him off. He was outside for a few minutes only."

"I'm sure he's around here somewhere."

Putting his bag down, Henry helped Mr. Anderson search for the cat by climbing the small stepladder and combing the gardens on either side. Then he searched in the old man's shed. The cat was nowhere to be found.

Mr. Anderson wept a little, dabbing his eyes again.

"Thank you, Henry. I'm sure he'll show up later. You better go home in case your mom's looking for you."

"Sorry I couldn't find him for you. If I see him, I'll let you know, okay?"

Mr. Anderson nodded and went inside.

Picking up his bag, Henry unbolted the front gate. He was about to lock it again when a shiny object glittering under the bush caught his eye.

Bending down to investigate, he found withered leaves had covered the object. Clearing them revealed a shiny, golden coin with unusual, engraved inscriptions. At first glance, and from the many Discovery Channel documentaries on ancient civilizations Henry had watched, it appeared to be Aztec in origin, bearing similar shapes and drawings, but he quickly dismissed that idea.

Anyway, even if it were an Aztec coin, what would it be doing around here? Henry thought.

The gold appeared to have no blemishes, scratches or rust. In the center on one side of the coin was something that looked like two hooks positioned back to back under a half-circular code of letters. Henry didn't understand what they meant.

This could be worth something, he thought. I'd better keep it safe for a while.

The coin and his curiosity weighed heavy in his pocket as he entered the house.

First thing, he fed Cody, their bulldog. Henry reheated the meal his mother had left him in the microwave and burped upon finishing it. The lamb chops were tender and mint gravy poured over them added a delicious flavor. Henry loved his mother's mashed potatoes because she always made them so soft and creamy.

After cleaning and putting away the dishes, he went up to his bedroom, the attic room. It had pine wooden flooring and a slanted timber ceiling. In the middle of the room was a king-size bed with a Captain America duvet. A 32inch television set and a game console were in the corner near a window. Posters of Jennifer Lawrence were on his walls, along with a few posters of some WWE wrestlers such as John Cena and Dwayne "The Rock" Johnson. On the locker to the right of Henry's bed was a tower of Marvel comic books. Cluttered on his dressing table were family photos including him as a little kid. In one he as a baby being bounced on his grandpa's knee as grandma looked indulgently on. Even though he loved his space and privacy, there were times he wished that he had a brother or sister for company.

From the bedside locker, Henry took an Iron Man comic, climbed into bed and began reading.

Sometime later, Cody's barking woke Henry from a deep sleep. The comic that lay across his chest was returned to the locker as he moved to his desk.

He wondered about the coin, twisting it under the table lamp on his study desk. Its golden color seemed to radiate an aura. The strange sigils were unlike anything he had seen before. He put it in his pocket and got started on his homework.

Henry was in the middle of studying the Renaissance when a door being closed downstairs startled him. At first, the panicky thought of burglars breaking into his house crossed his mind. He immediately searched for some form of weapon, but a look at the clock revealed that it was 9:45 pm and his parents were home. They were literary agents. Today they had a meeting with a publisher.

The door creaked as Suzanne, his mother, opened it slowly.

"Hi, honey," she said as she placed her hand on his shoulder. "Did we scare you?"

"Yeah, I thought someone was trying to break in."

"Oh I'm sorry. How was school today?"

"Ah you know, same as usual. How was the meeting with the publisher?"

"Boring. Your father fell asleep halfway through and I had to wake him up. Thank God no one else noticed."

Henry laughed. "Guess I better go to bed. I can do the rest of this in the morning."

"Okay, baby. Just make sure it's done." She kissed him on the forehead and left the room.

Heavy raindrops pounded the windowpane as thunder crashed down. Flashes illuminated the jagged outline of the far off mountains. Henry placed the coin on his desk and changed into checkered pajamas.

Having climbed into bed, he found the cold sheets sent a chill throughout his body, but it soon passed. Henry laid his head on the pillow but the persistent rain kept him awake.

"I wish it would stop raining already," he grumbled.

Just as Henry was about to close his eyes again, a golden aura surrounding the coin caught his attention. The golden object's glow intensified and the rain outside stopped.

"Whoa. Did you...do that?" Henry said as he approached the coin, cautiously. At first he reached out to touch it, and then withdrew his hand. He gulped before attempting to take it again. The coin felt warm in his palm; the inscriptions still glowed like the dying embers of a fire.

"This is crazy. What am I thinking? There's no such thing as magic coins," he scoffed. Still, his curiosity was piqued. Could it be that this small gold coin stopped the rain? He decided to put it to the test.

"I know I'll look stupid doing this but I'm gonna see if you really are magic." He thought about all the things that he could wish for and decided on something that would be easy to grant.

"I wish for a packet of chocolate chip cookies." He waited for a packet of cookies to appear…but nothing happened.

"Yeah, I knew I was gonna look dumb asking for that." Henry put the gold object back on his desk. "Magic coin, my ass," he said, shaking his head, still feeling a little silly for believing the coin had some powers in it.

Just as he was about to climb into bed, Henry stopped in his tracks as an eerie chill invaded his room. The curtains billowed; the light from the lamp on his bedside locker began to flicker.

"What the hell?" Henry got out of his bed and retreated to the window, to stay as far away from the coin as possible. His desk shook. A cloud of purple smoke materialized above the golden object. The coin's markings glowed once more and from the smoke popped out a packet of chocolate chip cookies. Once his wish had been granted, the smoke disappeared; the room temperature returning to normal. His desk stopped shaking.

Once he felt it was safe, Henry approached the desk.

"Wow," Henry said as he picked up the packet. "I don't believe this." He opened the wrapping and tried a cookie. "Mmm," he moaned with pleasure as the chocolate chip melted on his tongue. The cookie itself was crunchy – just the way he liked it. "So this really is magic," Henry whispered in awe as he held up the coin, inspecting it.

Maybe if I wish tomorrow for Tracey to be my prom date it might come true. Then he remembered the beating Joey had got and for a moment he hesitated.

"Maybe going with her to the prom isn't such a good idea." But being in Tracey's arms and kissing her outweighed the negatives of making this wish.

Man, if I got just got one kiss from her, it'd be worth it. Henry put the coin back on the desk and went to bed, closing his eyes, dreaming of being with Tracey.

* * *

The school bell rang, ending English class. Henry ran to the bathroom. Seeing that a cubicle was free, he went in, closing the door. He rubbed the coin, shut his eyes and pictured Tracey in his mind. "I wish for Tracey Maxwell to be my date for the prom."

A wave of light washed over the coin. It was time to test his wish.

Henry emerged from the toilets with the bag on his right shoulder and walked confidently down the hallway to his locker. Henry shut the locker door after taking the books he needed.

Tracey came around the corner, heading straight for her locker. As she passed Henry, a faint whiff of strawberry perfume assailed his nose for a few seconds before the scent faded.

Time to make my move, Henry thought. "Hi, Tracey."

"Hey, Henry," she replied not stopping to meet his gaze. "Got something on your mind?"

"Well, I was wondering if you'd like to be my date for the prom."

She shook her head as if in a short daze and then looked at him. This time her red lips broadened to a warming smile.

"Yeah, sure," she said, "see you tomorrow night at eight."

Henry's heart leapt with joy. "Cool, see you then," he said, walking away, grinning like the Cheshire cat.

* * *

Suzanne's car stopped outside Harleyville High. She turned off the engine. Henry held a bouquet of flowers meant for Tracey. Suzanne got them from a nearby florist after school earlier that day.

"Well, honey, this is it," she said. "Enjoy your night and remember—"

"Home before midnight," Henry repeated what he had been told all week. "Yeah, Mom, I know."

"Good. Now, have a great time." She kissed him on the cheek and let him go to meet his date.

Pushing open the main hall's double doors, the heavy thumping of techno music greeted him. In the far right corner, a teacher guarded a table full of cola drinks. On the wall behind the teacher was a banner that read, 'Harleyville High Prom 2019.' The lighting was muted, only the lights on stage shone down.

Joey rushed over to Henry. Excitement bubbled in his voice. "Hey, Henry, the guys are all talking about you. How the hell did you manage to get a date with Tracey?"

"I guess it was just my lucky day, and she had a change of heart."

Before Joey could respond, the doors opened wide framing the girl of Henry's dreams. As she entered, it seemed the world stopped spinning and a thousand angels sang a heavenly chorus as she walked towards Henry in slow motion. Henry thought Tracey looked hot in her red, tight-fitting dress. Her hair flowed naturally behind her as she walked.

"Sweet," Henry said in astonishment.

Tracey stopped before Henry, eying up both him and his tuxedo. "Love your suit. Did you pick it out yourself?"

"Yeah," Henry said and then introduced his friend. "This is Joey."

"Hey, Joey," She shook his hand. "You don't look half bad either."

Walk the Moon's 'Shut Up and Dance' pumped out through the speakers. Tracey grabbed Henry's hand.

"You wanna dance, Henry?" she said.

"Um...sure," Henry replied, more than a tad nervous.

"Come on, it'll be fun," Tracey said, dragging him onto the already crowded dance floor.

Joey was left holding a bunch of flowers meant for Tracey, as the two headed away. Tracey danced a little too fast for Henry, he found it difficult to keep up with the rhythm of her moves. Then in a sudden unexpected movement, Tracey wrapped her arm around his waist, pulled him in and they kissed.

At first, Henry's eyes opened wide in shock, but he gradually got the knack of kissing. It was the sweetest moment of his entire life.

"You liked that, huh?" Tracey asked, holding his hands.

"Totally," Henry answered, still stunned by the amazing kiss.

"Cool. You wanna catch a soda?"

Henry felt the cell vibrating in his pocket. "Can you excuse me for a moment?"

"Yeah, sure. I'll be over by the soda stand."

Henry had gone outside before answering the call that showed only the words 'Unknown Number' on the display screen.

"Hello?"

"Hey, Simmons," returned a voice laden with scorn. It was not on the phone but right behind Henry. It was instantly recognizable.

Sid Connors shut his flip-phone, sliding it inside his tuxedo jacket. The tall, lanky boy's slick quiff seemed out of place, betraying his whole geeky look as the glare of the streetlight reflected on his glasses. Little patches of acne were spread across his face.

Henry wondered what Tracey ever saw in this guy, who, in Henry's opinion, looked like a 1950s butler trying too hard to be cool.

"What's wrong, did Brad up the price this time?" Henry quipped.

"Ha, ha, very funny." Sid took two steps closer. "But you really should've listened to him. Did you not get the part about Tracey being *my* girl?"

"Last time I checked, Tracey wasn't your girl anymore."

"Well I'm telling you she is," Sid took another step closer. Henry could smell Sid's cheap cologne, "and you had no right to ask her out." Sid smacked the phone out of Henry's hand.

"No," Henry cried as the expensive electronics smashed to pieces. "Dude, that is a $300 phone. I saved hard for that!"

Sid stepped on the phone's cracked screen, glass crunching under his right foot. "Guess it's worth nothing now."

"This is getting really old. Screw you, I'm going in." Henry was about to walk past but Sid put a hand on his chest.

"You're not going anywhere 'til we settle this."

"I'm not gonna fight you, so get lost."

"You mightn't wanna fight…but I do."

Before Henry could react, Sid threw a hard right, landing it square on Henry's jaw. He followed up with two other lightning quick punches: one to the stomach and another to the face.

Henry cried out and sank to his knees, both arms wrapped around his stomach.

The second quick blow knocked Henry to the ground, where he split his forehead on a sharp stone. Sid kicked him twice in the stomach before spitting on him.

"That'll teach you never to mess with me," Sid said. As he was about to return to the hall, the side door opened. Tracey came out into the yard.

"Oh my God, Henry!" She rushed to him and squatted at his side. "Are you okay?"

"I'm…I'm fine."

"Why did you do this, Sid?" She glared up at him. "I told you we were over."

Sid frowned, his jaw momentarily clenching. "Come on, Tracey, what do you see in *him*?"

"God, you can be such a jerk sometimes!"

"Whatever," Sid sneered then stormed inside.

"I'm so sorry about this, Henry." Tracey helped him get to his feet.

"Thanks." He winced as he straightened and touched the bleeding gash. A coppery taste filled his mouth, he spat out blood.

Suddenly he worried that the golden coin might have fallen out of his pocket when he fell. He patted his tuxedo jacket, finding it still in the inside pocket. He took it out, relieved.

"What's that?" Tracey asked.

"Oh, it's just my good luck charm."

Almost in slow motion, a droplet of blood crept out of the cut on Henry's head and fell onto the intricate disc. Henry watched as it slithered into the engraving of the two hooks.

Henry winced and recoiled, dropping the coin as a yellow beam shot up from it, far into the sky. Tracey jumped back. She looked up as thunderous clouds gathered to block out the moon. A mysterious wind howled. Both Henry and Tracey took another few steps back from the coin, frightened by what was happening all around them.

"I… think I'm gonna head back inside," Tracey said.

A tiny sparkling of light appeared above both teenagers and transformed into a large, swirling hole.

Tracey screamed. "That's it, I'm outta here." Tracey fled to the side door but it wouldn't open. She banged on it. "Somebody let me in," she screamed. Nobody answered. The girl began to cry, rooted to the spot in fear.

Henry's hands began to tremble and he almost abandoned the coin when a thundering voice spoke telepathically from the hole:

"DO NOT FEAR, CHILD. I WISH YOU NO HARM. I HAVE WAITED A LONG TIME FOR THE MAGIC IN THIS COIN TO BE ACTIVATED."

"Activated?" Henry asked, puzzled, approaching the portal with caution. "What do you mean?"

"YES, ACTIVATED BY THE BLOOD OF SOMEONE WORTHY OF THE COIN'S POSSESSION."

"Me? I'm worthy?"

The coin's beam vanished. The magical object flipped into his palm. It felt warm like a beating heart. Though he was full of self-doubt, he was both intrigued and flattered.

"YES. COME, YOUNG HENRY. YOUR DESTINY AWAITS."

Both teenagers screamed as they were sucked into the portal.

JOHNSON AND MACCALL'S TBF AVENGER

Chapter Two

A Whole New World

Another strong gust buffeted the TBF Avenger out of the portal. Edward hadn't felt anything like it since getting caught in the tail of a hurricane that took an unexpected turn into his flight path.

Suddenly the external forces stopped which itself required a ton of manual adjustments to fly by wire. A check of the altimeter showed ten thousand feet.

Through the window they could see a different moon in a cloudless sky over a forest, the trees of which stood tall and straight, no hint of wind in their serene reach.

"Night time?" Conor said in disbelief. "How long were we in that thing? Where do you think we are, sir?"

"Don't know," Edward glanced at his instruments, same heading, "but it's nowhere near Florida. Radio base, let them know we're okay."

"Not possible, sir. All I'm picking up is static. I think we're too far out of range."

"Bugger." Edward adjusted slightly to compensate for running on one engine. "Engine's still not working. Try Lauderdale again."

"There's no use. All I'm picking up is static. The radio must've been damaged while we were in that… thing."

"We'll have to land, and now. Look for somewhere."

"Aye, sir, but these trees are a problem." Conor searched the landscape.

"Clearing, two o'clock. But I'm not too sure it's safe for landing."

"It's worth a try. I'm taking us down."

Pulling back the canopy, Edward banked their plane to the right and followed the clearing. Gliding the plane perilously close to the treetops, he lined it up.

To Edward, the trees looked like spikes ready to impale the aircraft.

"We're going too close to the trees, sir. Pull up!"

"We'll make it."

When the treetops were about to touch the armored bottom of the TBF Avenger, the pilot gave it full flaps.

"Come on…come on," Edward prayed under his breath.

The plane lifted just enough to clear the trees. They were now going down again to land.

Edward concentrated on what was in front of him, more than a hint of concern crept into his voice as he said, "There's a cliff up ahead, MacCall."

"What?"

"There's a cliff up ahead."

Edward guessed Conor had seen the cliff beyond the narrowing trees as the Scot grew quiet. Darkness and the forest had hidden this danger as they were going down.

"Can't change course but those two big trees at the end will clip our wings off and slow us down," Edward said. He moved the throttle forward making the TBF Avenger descend faster at a safe speed.

The TBF Avenger wobbled as it neared the trees.

"Brace for impact!" Edward landed, bouncing and bumping on the uneven ground as the plane skidded into the trees. As predicted, the wings were clipped.

Both men covered their heads as the wings ripped away, somersaulting into the air. With a heavy thud, the TBF Avenger dug into soft earth but thankfully didn't flip. Momentum jerked and juddered them forward. Ahead was the cliff. Even though the TBF Avenger slowed down, it continued towards the edge, towards their doom.

"Do you think she'll stop?"

"It should."

"I bloody hope so," Conor said.

Sparks flew from the remainder of the wings. Dirt and earth piled up underneath the landing gear as the TBF Avenger gouged the ground, leaving a deep trail in its wake.

"I don't think we're going to make it!" Conor yelled.

"Stay calm," Edwards yelled back, "it might make it. We're losing speed."

Twenty five feet to go and the arching trees on either side looked like menacing creatures as they passed them. The plane still screeched as it ploughed through the dirt, the edge was seconds away.

"Fifteen feet," Conor screamed in a strained voice.

"We'll make it," Edward replied but not with the amount of confidence he had aimed for.

Both men gripped their seats hard, breathing heavily. They knew that bailing out now was not an option, even though it seemed more pleasant than going over a cliff.

Conor mumbled, "I can't watch."

With nine feet to go, Edward warned, "Hold on."

Both men blessed themselves as the plane slowed, drawing nearer to the edge.

Within an instant, it came to a screeching halt with its nose and a little of the upper body teetering on the cliff's edge. The tail lifted precariously as it stopped. It took a moment for both men to open their eyes and realize that they were still alive.

"You did it, sir," Conor said, relieved. "The plane stopped."

"You doubted me, yet again?" Edward joked, relief flooding through him.

Both men knew that they were not yet out of danger. They were precariously balanced, so the next obstacle they had to overcome was getting out of the plane without tipping it over.

"We'll have to be careful getting out," Edward warned.

"You don't have to tell me that, sir."

"I'll get out first." Edward released his harness. As soon as his weight shifted, the plane rocked. He gulped, remaining still.

"For Christ's sake, don't move. The plane could tip over. " Conor ordered despite rank. "I'll get out the back and then you can do the same." Conor unharnessed, picked up his canteen. With the canopy already pulled back, he stepped out onto the wing, sat on it and slid onto the ground. Conor climbed onto the tail, straddling the fuselage. The craft felt more stable now. He called for Edward to follow.

Edward, with the canteen in his hand, stood on his seat and moved to the rear of the plane. But just as he was about to climb out the side, he lost his footing, falling back.

The TBF Avenger's rear lifted. Conor tried with all his might to hold it down.

"Quick, sir, get up. I don't know if I can hold this much longer!"

Tipping forward, the nose pointed downwards.

"Get out. Jump. I'm losing balance," Conor cried.

Edward stood on his seat and bounded from the falling plane. He landed, rolling a few times before stopping.

Conor, now watching the TBF Avenger dive forward, clambered to safety, landing on the grass.

The aircraft creaked and whined as it went over.

Both men ran, diving as the plane plummeted to its destruction with a loud crash, a boom echoing from underneath them. Smoke drifted from the flames into the night's sky.

"Are you all right?" Edward asked.

"Aye," Conor answered, panting. "That was close."

"Yes, too close for my liking. The main thing is we're alive." Both men sat for a moment, trying to catch their breath.

Edward rose to his feet, walked to the edge of the cliff, peeking over it at the flames and rubble below. "We better head off into those woods," he said eventually. "The people around here mightn't be friendly."

Leaving their helmets behind, they picked up their canteens and set off.

Carefully trekking through the woods, they ran from tree to tree, surveying through the darkness to see if anybody was about. The moonlight provided enough light for them to make their way through the forest. Edward noticed that each tree trunk was not brown but black instead. Leaves were not the customary green but pale blue. An orange liquid oozed from some of the trunks. Birds resembling magpies flew over their heads but when they were in direct contact with the moonlight, marigold orange feathers were where black ones should be.

Where the hell did we crash? Edward thought.

"Funny-looking forest, sir. Never seen anything like it," Conor said, puzzled. Edward could see from Conor placing a hand on his pistol that the Scot was nervous but did not want to admit it yet.

As they walked on further, Edward stopped, hearing at last a familiar sound. He placed a hand on Conor's shoulder to prevent him going farther.

"Shh. Can you hear that?"

"No, sir," Conor replied.

"It sounds like a river to our far left. Follow me."

Conor followed Edward as he ran among the maze of trees.

After running for what seemed like a few minutes, they arrived at a stream; Edward had been correct. The water glittered as the moon gazed down upon it. Dipping his hands into the water, Edward splashed some onto his face. It washed away the dirt from the tumble.

"Sweet Jesus above. Now everything makes sense, sir," Conor said, staring up at the sky.

"What do you mean?"

"The trees, birds, everything here. It all makes sense now." Conor's face had grown ashen.

"What are you talking about, MacCall?"

"Look over there, sir. There's one moon."

"Don't tell me you haven't seen a moon before," Edward joked, a grin now under his blond moustache.

"Aye, I've seen one but not two."

"Are you sure you didn't bang your head?"

"No. Look for yourself." Conor first pointed to the right and then to his left at the second moon.

"My God." Edward's jaw dropped as he saw the two moons. He spun on his heels to return his attention to Conor. "But that can't be."

"But it is." Conor's hands were on his hips; a worried expression on his face.

"No. There must be… must be some logical explanation."

"How, sir? Last time I checked, there's only one moon where we come from."

"Maybe while we were in that thing, it did something to our eyesight."

"Come on, Captain! Get real. Look around, does this look normal to you?"

"No," Edward conceded reluctantly. "But how… why? This doesn't make sense."

"Aye. *That* I agree on."

"So… this means we're on a different planet." Edward's face was now blanched.

"My thoughts exactly, Captain. That thing under the water must have been a door of some kind to another world. Maybe that's how the two dragons came to attack us. And if this is another planet, there's no telling what's 'round here." Then he paused for a moment. "And if we're stuck here, that means I'll never see my sweet lass, Ailish, again or any of my family. We have to go back to where we arrived. I can't stay here forever." The Scottish airman started running.

"MacCall, wait!" Edward gave chase. "Slow down." He followed Conor between the trees and finally caught up with him, tackling and bringing his friend to the ground.

"Get off me. We can't stay here."

"I know that. I'm scared too." Edward gripped both of Conor's shoulders. "But we have to think logically. We flew God knows how many miles from that door to here. It would take us a few days to get back there. Anyway there's no guarantee that the door will be there to take us home. Even if it does, don't forget we were mid-air. Without a plane, how would we get high enough?"

"What are you suggesting? We wait around here for some creature, some other dragon to kill us? If you want to do that, fine. I won't sit around and die. Now get the hell off me!"

Conor threw a punch, but the Englishman blocked it.

"Keep your damn voice down, man, or we'll get caught. I'll get off when you're calm."

"Calm down? We're on a different planet and you want me to *calm down*?" Edward saw his friend study his expression, which was reinforcing Conor to remain calm otherwise Edward would keep him pinned. "All right, all right. I'll be calm."

As Conor said this, Edward got off. Both men sat down.

Edward said casually, despite his own growing concern. "I know you're scared, Conor, but don't you think I feel the same way too? We have to think this through. Treat it like falling behind enemy lines."

"With all due respect, sir, the longer we sit around here thinking about this, the longer we'll be in this place."

"I understand that, but we can't just run off into the woods like a pair of idiots. We must think this through. There has to be a way back, I'm sure of it."

"And what if there's no door when we arrive there?" Conor asked.

"Let's just hope that won't happen."

"What will we do in the meantime?"

"Let's go back to the river, fill our canteens, one thing we're bound to need is water and we don't know where we might find the next source. Then we'll find a place to camp for the night. In the morning, we'll start the journey back. I guess you're right. If we came through there, then there's a chance we might get back home. But we have to be careful. Come on, let's get the water."

Conor and Edward remained silent, thoughts of doom and gloom hovered around them as they walked back to the river. The leaves in the trees rustled as a breeze began to pick up. The wind whistled around them. It brought back memories of scary stories read and told in impressionable childhood years. Both men knew things weren't right and each had a hand to their pistol.

Moving back from the running water, they picked a place to camp. They collected a few dry fallen branches and started a fire, sitting in front of it warming their hands.

Edward spoke to break the awkward silence. "You know, in all our time flying together, you never said much about Ailish."

"There's not much to say really, sir. I just fell in love with her."

"Nobody just *falls in love*, MacCall. Where did you meet her?"

"Two months before the war started, I was at a dance and I saw her 'cross the floor. I was too chicken to ask her to dance so one of my friends did for me."

"I bet that went down well with her."

Conor chuckled before answering. "Oh, aye. Teased the hell out of me she did. We just had something… don't know how to describe it."

"So when did you see her again?"

"The next day. We met for tea at a café and hit it off ever since. During the war I wrote to her and she sent pictures."

"Oh yeah? What kind of pictures?" Edward asked with a mischievous grin.

"Not the kind you're thinking of, just ones of her and some other lassies. What about you and Sandra? How did ye meet?"

Edward took another drink from his canteen, corking it when finished. He wiped his mouth before continuing. "I carried a friend of mine to the hospital. He broke his arm. She tended to him and like you and Ailish, we had something special too when we first met."

Without warning, the force of the wind grew stronger, almost quenching their fire. Rain fell as thunder rumbled in the sky. Clouds smothered the moon. Flashes of lightning could be seen behind them. Both men ran under a large tree for shelter.

"What's going on?" Conor said, reaching for his .38 again.

Lightning bolts seemed to hit a short distance from the two men. It appeared to be striking in a peculiar circle. Little ripples formed in the air, like that of shimmering water.

Edward saw a look of recognition washed across Conor's face. "The door…I think it's opening again."

* * *

With forces pummeling them within the swirling violet portal, screaming was one of the few things they could do. Henry and Tracey spun out of control, light and sound crashing about them; Henry tried to shield his ears as he frantically looked for Tracey. She was tumbling closer, then suddenly away, he reached out, but she wasn't there. He called her name, but the winds took the sound. A flash of red caught his eye and he snatched at her, grabbing her hand to bring her closer to him and fighting against the forces trying to pull them apart.

"Hold onto me," Henry said as he tried to protect her from the lightning that flashed around them.

We gotta get outta here, he thought. "Whoa," he said as a golden bubble formed around them. *How did that happen? Maybe the coin did it.* Henry looked at Tracey, her eyes were squeezed shut. She was trembling against him, too afraid to look at the vortex. The bubble softened the blows as they were thrown around inside the portal like a ball in a pinball machine. His body was sore as he hit off either side of this mystical gateway.

"What the hell is this, Henry?"

"I don't know. Some kind of portal, maybe."

"A Portal? That's crazy!"

"Well look at it. What else is it?"

"You're right. Oh my God…that means…" Her voice trailed off. Henry saw a look of despondency in her eyes as she grew quiet.

The thunder grew louder; lightning struck more frequently.

As they bounced off the violet wall once more, Henry stared down a steep decline with an opening at the end.

"I think I see a way out," he yelled.

Both teens were thrust forward towards the opening.

As they were ejected from the gateway, the golden bubble vanished. Henry and Tracey were sent sliding and tumbling along a soggy surface. The portal behind them had sealed itself shut. Henry grimaced as his body ached.

"Ow!" Tracey said, sitting up. She looked down at her knees first. Apart from a few scrapes and bruises, there was no damage done to them. She then looked at her dress, Henry recognized that look – disgust. There was a large mud stain on the front of it. "Ugh! My dress is ruined and so's my hair." She pulled leaves that were caught into her dark auburn tresses. "Are you okay?"

"Yeah… think so," his answer lacking assurance.

Tracey turned to him and yelled, "Just what the hell has that coin gotten us into, Henry and where are we?"

"Beats me." Henry tensed as he spotted what appeared to be two men approaching, one of them holding some sort of gun Henry didn't recognize. He realized Tracey had noticed them too as she became quiet.

"Hold your fire, MacCall. The last thing we want is for things to get out of hand," he heard one say.

"Don't hurt us," Henry said.

"Don't worry, we won't," the man had a British accent. He turned to the other man. "Put away your gun."

Henry saw the second person holster his weapon.

"Where are we?" Henry asked.

"We don't know. Somehow you came here the same way we did. What's your name?"

"My name's Henry, Henry Simmons and this is Tracey Maxwell. We were at our prom when this big hole or portal appeared and sucked us in. How did you guys get here?"

"First of all, my name's Captain Edward Johnson and my friend here is Sergeant Conor MacCall. We were flying back to our base and our plane, just like you said, was sucked into a hole."

Henry looked at their clothing; their uniforms were similar to the old Air Force pictures his grandfather had up on the wall.

"Where was your base?" Henry said.

"Fort Lauderdale, Florida," Conor replied.

"But you don't sound American. How come you're in American Air Force suits?"

"We transferred from the RAF after the war," Edward said.

"After the war? You said your base is in Florida? My grandpa told me that place closed down in the '40s. Your flight suits look old. What year are you from?" Henry queried, with a great deal of curiosity.

"Nineteen forty five," Edward replied. "Why? What year are you from? Your clothes seem different," he added, looking at Tracey's dress. "The girls back home don't wear dresses like that."

"We're from twenty nineteen."

"Twenty nineteen?" Conor asked, astonished.

"You're from the future? That's amazing," Edward said.

"I hate to interrupt," Tracey interjected, "but we need to figure out how to get back home…and fast."

"Yeah, Tracey's right. We need to find a way to open the portal again."

"Well, how do we do that, Henry?" Edward asked.

"Do you guys have a knife?" Henry asked.

"I do. Why?" Edward replied.

"I need it to cut myself because my blood got us here," Henry showed them the coin. "Do you see this? This brought us here. A drop of my blood fell onto the coin from this cut." He pointed to his forehead.

"It's gone," Tracey gasped pulling his attention and looking at him in wonder. "Henry the cut… it's gone!"

Henry touched his forehead. "It is gone," he said surprised. "Weird." He thought about all the other aches and pains. There were only the ones from their fall from the vortex.

He looked back to the airmen. "Anyway, a drop of blood fell on the coin and next thing I know, we're here with you guys. I need a knife to cut myself."

"Hold on a minute, young man," Edward replied in a stern voice. "We're not going to give you a knife to harm yourself."

"Yeah, Henry. I want to get back too but don't you think that's a bit drastic?" Tracey asked.

"Look, I know it sounds crazy but I'm talking about a little nick not slashing my wrists. Using my blood will work. I promise." Dried blood now covered his cut. "Maybe if I pick it some blood will drop onto the coin." Henry was about to pick at the dried blood when he saw Conor tense up.

The Scotsman tapped Edward on the shoulder. "Sir, I think there's something in the bush over there."

Before Edward had a chance to speak or reach for his gun, a creature emerged with a crossbow trained on them.

Tracey shrieked, hiding behind Henry.

"What kind of creature are you? I saw one of your kind before," Conor said, looking at the beast's sheer size. He appeared to be seven feet tall.

"As if you do not already know, human," the soldier replied, pronouncing every word with a snarl.

As the soldier came closer, they could see that he wore black armor and his skin was yellow. On its hands were warts.

"I am of the Sadarkian, sworn enemy to your kind."

Edward took upon the role of negotiator. "We mean you no harm," he said. "My friends and I are lost."

"I have orders to take you all back to my king." With his crossbow raised, the soldier took a few steps forward, eying the pilots' guns. "Throw your weapons to the ground." He curled a finger around the crossbow's trigger. "Do it now," he barked.

"All right, we'll do as you say." Edward opened the holster and extracted his gun, placing it down on the soil. "Do as he says, MacCall."

Conor threw down his pistol.

"I hope King Zakarius will allow me to tear the flesh from your bones later tonight." The soldier laughed sinisterly and began to pull the trigger, when a cry came from behind.

"Over my dead body you will!" An agile, gray and black furry animal launched itself at the Sadarkian, landing on the tall beast's back, clawing at its neck.

In the midst of the confusion, the soldier fired the crossbow with lost aim and the bolt hit a tree.

"Get off me," he roared, dropping his weapon, using both hands to wrestle the attacker off of him.

"Jasper?" Henry exclaimed, baffled to see the cat, slightly more baffled that the cat was talking. "How the hell are you talking?"

The guard quickly rearmed the crossbow, lining up another bolt, removing it from the others he had strapped to his right thigh.

"What ugly beasts have your kind joined with now?" he asked, staring at the cat in disgust.

"Hey, who are you calling ugly, mustard-face?" Jasper retorted.

"First the trees, then the moons and now talking cats? Just what exactly is this place?" Edward said.

"Shut up! You are beginning to give me a headache so get moving or I will put you all out of your misery right now." The soldier gestured to them with his crossbow to walk ahead of him.

A whirring sound coming from behind him, caused the guard to lower his weapon and glance at the bushes. A knife flew in his direction, embedding in the giant's throat. He pitched forward.

Tracey gripped Henry's arm while she gasped as two figures emerged from the bushes. Although his jaw dropped a little, he tried hard to hide his shock at their appearance. One dressed in a cream tunic and black trousers, was a humanoid, Henry guessed a little over six foot, bald and with peculiar green eyes. His skin was orange and his ears pointy. The male carried a crossbow in his left hand and quiver over his left shoulder. The other was a short, pudgy creature, perhaps a meter or so tall, garbed in a dark salmon colored tunic, brown jerkin and matching pants, came out from his hiding place and picked up the knife. The creature had two horns on its head and no ears. Parts of his bushy, red beard were braided. The small being moved over to yank the blade from the still gargling throat of the dying Sadarkian. He wiped down the blade with a large leaf, clearing the pink blood from it.

"Eww," Tracey said, wrinkling her nose.

Conor, Edward, Jasper, Henry and Tracey, watched the robust man sheath the dagger back into its scabbard.

"Thank you, Mr...?" Edward's voice trailed off in uncertainty.

"No need to thank me. The name is Xongrelan and I am a Jenorme. My friend here is Damone. He is a Volark." Damone nodded at them. "We saw you and your friends come through the hole in the sky. Come, we better hurry. More Sadarkians will be along soon."

"Wait, where are you taking us?" Henry asked.

"To a safer place than this. Please, we really must hurry." Xongrelan and Damone ran but stopped when they heard no footsteps behind.

All five stood their ground.

Henry could see from the Jenorme's rigid stance that Xongrelan was beginning to grow impatient.

"We're grateful that you saved us, my wee friend, but how do we know we can trust you?" Conor asked.

Xongrelan sighed before responding. "I understand your skepticism but please, you have to trust us. I promise you will not be harmed if you follow us."

"Um, Henry, I think we better go with them," Jasper said, sounding worried.

The hairs on Jasper's back were starting to stand, his tail puffing up. Even his ears were pulled back. The teenager recognized those signs.

In the far off distance, he could see flickering flames from torches, more Sadarkians running amongst the trees. He was still unsure of trusting Xongrelan and Damone, but Henry knew he didn't want to encounter other soldiers.

"Okay, I can't believe I'm about to say this but I'm with Jasper on this one, Henry," Tracey said.

The airmen picked up their weapons.

Xongrelan opened up a pouch attached to his belt. He threw some sparkling dust into the air. A luminous blue orb appeared, lighting up the area around them.

"Whoa," Tracey said in amazement while staring at the glowing orb.

Henry could see that both pilots' jaws hung in awe too.

"What's that?" Henry asked.

"This will guide us to where we need to go." The orb moved ahead, turning each tree trunk's dark brown into a pale, aquatic blue. Xongrelan waved at the others to follow him as he walked ahead. "Come on."

"Where are you taking us?" asked Henry as they hurried to catch up with Damone and Xongrelan.

"You will find out soon enough, boy," Xongrelan replied.

"Wait," Henry said, catching Xongrelan's arm. "Where exactly are we going? We need to know."

"Henry's right," Edward added. "With the greatest of respect, how do we know we can trust you?"

Damone now spoke, each word firm and insistent. "Look, if we wanted you dead, you would have been left there with the Sadarkian. We are taking you to the town where we live. You will be safe there. I promise."

Henry looked at Tracey; Edward looked at his co-pilot for a moment before nodding to Henry in confirmation. He took this as a sign that it was safe to trust their rescuers.

"Let's go," the boy said.

Following them, the group came to the cliff where the plane had been lost. The damaged TBF Avenger was still ablaze.

"It's a dead end," Tracey said looking at the large gap between the two cliffs.

"How do we get across?" Edward questioned.

"Watch," Xongrelan replied with a grin. Xongrelan reached once again into his pouch, he cast dust over the cliff's edge, closed his eyes, and shouted, "Kanach brustun!"

A bridge wavered into view like a stack of dominoes knocking each other over. The red-bricked bridge reached the other side. For a brief period the five visitors were amazed, admiring the way it had built itself. When Xongrelan yelled them out of their shock, they ran across the bridge, turning back to watch it disappear again.

"Won't the Sadarkians cross the bridge too?" Conor asked.

"No, we are two of only a few people who know it exists so the Sadarkians cannot follow us," Damone replied.

All seven moved into the forest, their surroundings illuminated by the orb. Xongrelan's and Damone's trousers were dirty, as if they had been lying down in mud. On Xongrelan's, a black belt fitted with a little scabbard, went around his large waist. Although he was small, muscles bulged in his arms inside the salmon-colored tunic. His red hair was wet but Henry guessed it was from a combination of sweat and rainfall.

"So where exactly is this town?" Henry asked.

"Not far from here. We are taking you there because you will be with your own kind – humans. I am the only Jenorme there. Damone is a Volark from a different realm."

"What other creatures are there?" Edward asked.

"You will see."

"Do you have a leader?" Conor asked.

"Like I said, you will see that you will be safe there. I promise. We got to keep moving. Hurry."

Henry's heart raced, his eyes darted from tree to tree as he and the others walked through the eerie silence of the forest. Each tree had different colored leaves. A sweet aroma like that of honey wafted past them and to the boy, it seemed to be coming from every treetop. Birds chirped a song only known to them. Fireflies, normally with a burning yellow glow, seemed to be enveloped in a teal light, as they zipped to and fro. Although this place looked serene, Henry feared, and almost expected something or anything to leap out in front of them at any second. Tracey held onto his arm tight. Birds flew out from underneath the branches, causing Henry to almost jump back and Tracey scream.

"Relax, boy," Damone told the teenager. "Nothing to fear in these woods." He continued to lead them.

Henry knew that the airmen were nervous too, because they kept their hands on their holsters.

"Who goes there?"

They jumped at the sound of the voice. The airmen automatically drew their weapons. Xongrelan raised his hand in hail to the soldier in the tall watchtower hidden within the trees. Henry looked up, saw the bow and arrow the soldier had aimed at them.

Henry looked around, he spotted another watchtower on their other side; the lookout there had obviously seen them too. He trained a bow at them also.

"Lower your weapons, men. It is us, Xongrelan and Damone." The lookouts didn't relax. Xongrelan turned and looked at the airmen. "Whatever those are, put them down." Only when the airmen holstered their pistols did Xongrelan turn back to the man in the tower. "These are my friends. They are lost and looking for somewhere to rest for the night."

"Sorry, sir, you may pass." The soldier waved him on.

The group moved forward.

Xongrelan and Damone eventually came to a stop. "We have arrived," Xongrelan said.

"Where?"

"Our home," Damone replied.

"But there's no building here," Henry said, seeing only more tall trees.

"It might look that way but our home is here."

"Why is this place invisible?" Edward asked.

"So that the Sadarkians cannot see our town and attack it," Xongrelan replied this time.

"But if they can't cross the bridge then they wouldn't be able to attack," Henry returned.

Xongrelan studied Henry's face before answering. "My dear boy, they have dragons that can destroy our homes."

Tracey leaned in close, her breath a little shaky with disbelief and dread when she whispered in his ear. "Did he just say dragons?"

"Uh-huh," Henry replied.

"Great," Tracey said, her tone dripping with sarcasm laced with concern.

Xongrelan reached into his pocket and held up what seemed like a diamond that sparkled under the moonlight. "Would all of you mind standing back over there?"

"Why?" Henry asked.

"I need to get us into the town but only I and a few others know the words to reveal it. And I want to keep it that way for the safety of the people here. So, if you do not mind…?"

"We understand," Edward replied. They walked away from Xongrelan and Damone until they were out of earshot.

After Xongrelan muttered some words they could not understand, a bubble instantly surrounded them and then a large stone wall built around a village, appeared. From the outside, to Henry the village looked like it was one and a half times the size of the baseball stadium he lived close to. A road lead up to and beyond an iron gate. Henry had guessed that trees were cut down to make room for this place but it was a magic illusion that made people think this was one continuous large forest.

"Wow," Tracey and Henry chorused as they smiled in amazement while gazing at the town.

"Xongrelan is back. Raise the gates!" someone inside shouted. The iron gates were raised. Staring around in wonder, hardly able to believe it, Henry was the first of the strangers to enter. Jasper still had a fluffed up tail.

"Come inside. No need to be afraid," Xongrelan said.

"Wow," Henry said, soaking in all their surroundings, marveling at the village, as the gates were lowered. Most of the townspeople stopped in their conversations. They stood staring at the new arrivals. Most of the men wore white shirts and trousers. Some women wore long flowing dresses, and some dressed like the men.

Once inside, to Henry's left, there was a log cabin that acted as a gatehouse. A guard could be seen inside a window, winding a handle to lower the gate. To Henry's right, stood a guard tower made out of enduring bamboo with a thatched roof tapering to a point. A little bell hung off a wooden rafter going across the length of the roof. In front of them was also a well similar to ones Henry had seen in his history text books when studying the medieval period. It was made out of different color stones, its rim wet from recent use. A little levy was used to lower a bucket into water. Directly behind this well were many rows of single storey thatched houses with ten in each row. Each house was painted in white. These reminded him of the old Irish style cottages he had seen in paintings. Between gaps in the houses, a rope going from one to another, acted as a clothesline as he saw dresses and tunics hanging from them. Behind these homes was another watch tower similar to the ones at the gate. A few feet away from this tower were market stalls. Some contained what resembled flour or grain. Others also had meat-hooks dangling at the end of a piece of string, which was attached to the top of the stall.

To Henry's far right were stables holding many types of horses with him only recognizing black stallions. Gates with iron bolts on them kept each horse inside. Beside the stables were what appeared to be little shacks used by blacksmiths. He saw a middle-aged man hammering on a red hot blade placed over an anvil. Beside this was a large training area surrounded by a pine fence. Two soldiers had a mock sword fight with wooden swords. Archery targets were also in this training area. Its ground was covered in sand. Another watch tower was placed beside this.

To Henry's immediate left was a four-storey building, equivalent in size to the mansions owned by millionaires back home. Its exterior was painted in a pale cream and its roof was slated. Henry noted that it seemed out of place with the other buildings that were here and assumed it belonged to someone of importance, possibly a king or their leader.

But a king is in a castle. Who could this be? he thought. Beside the mansion was a long, rectangular stone building with two heraldic shields of a lion and eagle outside its double doors. Henry thought this was a barracks of some kind as there were a constant flow of soldiers and knights coming in and out of there.

The bubble had disappeared. Three soldiers, one in front with two walking behind him, wearing chain mail and white surcoats with diamond emblems in the center, stepped forward, carrying long swords. They appeared to be human, as were most of the people here, except for Xongrelan and Damone. The soldier in front scrutinized clothes the strangers wore. He looked them over with suspicion.

"Xongrelan and Damone," he said, "who have you brought with you?"

"We found these strangers abandoned in the forest, Sir Dreyfus," Xongrelan answered. "They would have been killed by the Sadarkians if we had not found them."

"Where are you four from?" Sir Dreyfus asked Edward.

"We're not from here. It's… hard to explain how we arrived," Edward answered.

The knight's hand gripped the sword's hilt. His tone was a little harsher. "If you are not from these parts, then where do you come from? Your clothes look…strange."

"I understand we look out of place but we're from-" Edward said.

Damone butted in, "They are from far north of here. Their horses were stolen by thieves."

"What is that beast you bring with you?" Sir Dreyfus pointed to Jasper.

"He is a rare animal used for hunting," Xongrelan explained.

Sir Dreyfus considered then nodded, believing Xongrelan and Damone's lies. "You know the laws as well as I do, Xongrelan and Damone. These visitors must be brought to the king and queen and it is up to them if they will let them stay."

"Of course," Damone agreed.

Henry and the others looked around them in unease but let themselves be led to the big house, all the while being stared at in amazement and fear by the townspeople.

Two soldiers followed behind them. Guards at the entrance stood to attention, saluting Sir Dreyfus by beating their chest with their right hand twice and raising it in the air with a closed fist. Holding spears in their left hands, they stood aside and let the group walk in.

Inside, the house was much larger than it had appeared outside. Its interior was decorated with soft, colorful stylish carpets and its walls were painted in elegant colors, with some rooms painted in coconut white, amber or a light calming cream. The lower storey contained many rooms. The velvet curtains over the windows were closed. Floors were covered in unusual colored hardwood. Of course, they were shiny and clean like everything else in this house. Henry recognized this type of timber as his uncle worked in a hardware store that also sold timber for flooring people's houses. Each room was provided light from little lanterns hanging from the ceiling.

Servants inside the large building, like the people outside, stared at these strangers, making a corridor for the new arrivals as they passed them. Henry noted that male servants and ushers wore a lilac under tunic, with a strawberry red gown, and gray tights with matching long-toed shoes. Maids wore silky magenta tunics over a white chemise.

Henry thought that the chambers to the left were kitchens as pots and pans could be heard banging from inside its ajared doors. An aroma of some homemade soup slipped from the kitchen out into the hallway. On the right was a large hall that had three doors – a double door and another door five inches to the right.

Several feet away from the strangers was a set of stairs leading up to the next level.

"This way," Sir Dreyfus said, indicating to them with his right hand.

The stairs spiraled upward but Henry was relieved that they didn't spiral too far, for his legs were tired. He felt weak after the long journey. Tracey groaned as she made her way up the stairs. He and the others reached the second storey and were now in a long hallway with more lanterns hanging from the ceiling. Windows were on the left, opposite the lamps. The hallway had many doors on both sides but Sir Dreyfus stopped at the very end.

"Wait here a moment, please," the knight said as he opened a door and shut it again.

"Where's he going, Xongrelan?" Henry whispered.

"He is going to tell Queen Cyren you are here."

"Where's the king?" Henry asked.

"He is sick. Now when we go inside, you must kneel before Her Majesty if she speaks to you or your friends."

A minute later, Sir Dreyfus beckoned the new arrivals to enter the throne room.

Henry, the airmen, Tracey and Jasper walked into the throne room, which he guessed was the same size as his gym hall back in Harleyville High. Henry stared at the dark cerise colored carpet that was like a pathway leading up to the golden carved chairs where the queen sat. The king's chair was empty. On each side of the room, on mini-pedestals, were marble busts of various men. Henry deduced they were past kings from the crowns on their heads. The walls in the throne room were decorated with various crested shields.

Henry's eyes widened in frightened amazement at the Volarkun woman sitting on one of the chairs in the throne. Just like Damone, her skin was orange but her pupils were an eerie yellow. Long purple hair flowed down past her shoulders, falling onto her emerald green dress. A brown belt with a silver buckle was around her waist. A gold ring was on her left index finger. Although her appearance proved frightening to Henry, there was something oddly attractive about her. He noticed the others pretending not to gaze too much at Cyren as they kept lowering their eyes to the floor.

She waved at the party to approach. They moved forward, kneeling before her as they reached the steps leading up to the throne. They stood only when she granted express permission.

Cyren first addressed Xongrelan. "I have been told by Sir Dreyfus that you and Damone brought these strangers from the forest."

"Yes, Your Majesty. They would have been killed otherwise."

"That was very brave of you both to bring them here but you know my husband and I do not grant amnesty to just anyone. We would have to have a special reason to allow them to stay. Can you give me one?"

"With your permission, Your Majesty, I would like the sorceress Karina to be here while I explain why I saved them."

Cyren thought for a moment and granted his request. She motioned to a guard with her right index finger to approach.

"Please bring Karina to me at once."

"Yes, Your Majesty," said the guard with a bow.

KARINA

"No need," a strong female voice said as a wooden door opened from the right of Cyren.

Karina, along with a young boy and girl, all human, walked into the room. Henry guessed she was a little over six feet and in her early 50s. Her long coffee brown hair was plaited and her gray eyes bore an unusual gleam. Karina's clothes elicited a smile from both Henry and Tracey who stood beside him. Karina's bright pink shirt was inside a white jerkin and trousers were cucumber green. A thin, brown belt held her trousers up. She wore sandals that had a dark red leather strap on them.

"Looks like someone needs to get a mirror," Tracey whispered into Henry's ear.

The girl was much shorter than Karina, pretty with long, silky smooth black hair. To Henry, she looked like some of the Goths in his school. Her lips were dark red. The boy, around the same height as Karina, was broad-shouldered with flaxen hair. His gray eyes roved over Tracey and the others, studying them.

Karina continued to speak, "I saw these people arriving from my window."

"Thank you for joining us. Continue, Xongrelan," Cyren said.

All eyes now lay on him.

"We were out hunting when we saw the two men come through a black hole in the sky on a flying beast. Then the boy and girl came later through the same hole but in a different place. We could not believe our eyes. These people may have..." Xongrelan paused, as if to carefully choose his next words, "a special purpose here."

Henry, judging from Xongrelan's posture, saw that he was uncomfortable with what he was saying.

"Permission to speak privately with you, my Queen?" Xongrelan asked.

"Yes, please step forward."

"I think Karina might want to hear this also."

Cyren gestured with her head for Karina to step forward too.

Henry watched Karina and Xongrelan huddle around Cyren, whispering to one another. After a minute or so, Karina turned to study the new arrivals.

Henry felt an unusual thumping sensation in his head, almost as if something was inside it. He noticed that Edward, Conor and Tracey rubbed their foreheads too. They began shaking their heads. Were they feeling the same thing?

"I know what you are feeling now is uncomfortable but please do not be afraid," Karina said, "This is just a test."

"What kind of test?" Edward asked.

"She is sensing if you are telling the truth or if you are a danger to us," Cyren said.

"Are you saying you're reading our minds?" Edward replied sounding annoyed.

"Yes I am," Karina answered softly. "I am not trying to pry but as my queen said, I need to see if you are a threat."

Henry knew by the tense expressions they wore, none of them were happy about someone reading their thoughts. Neither was Henry, but it seemed they had no choice.

"Well, Karina, what did you find? Are they a threat?" Cyren asked.

"Right now I do not think they are." Another short bout of whispering began. When it was finished, Karina walked towards Edward and Conor.

Henry watched Karina, in fact all the locals, with a strong sense of wariness. There was no certainty on how this would play out.

"Did you come through the hole on a flying beast like Xongrelan said?" Karina's pupils stared at the airmen's flight suits. "I sense you are soldiers. Which one of you is in charge?"

Edward spoke up. "I am, ma'am, Captain Edward Johnson. This is my crewmember Sergeant Conor MacCall."

"Where is your flying beast now?" Karina asked.

"After we came through the hole, our plane, what you call a beast, didn't work properly and we crashed. My friend and I were able to escape before it went over the cliff, but the plane is a wreck. It went down close to where that invisible bridge is."

"I see. I am going to put my hand on your forehead and that will tell me if you are lying or not. Is that all right with you?"

"Do we have a choice?" Edward asked.

"By not letting her do this means you are hiding something, Captain." A harshness crept into Cyren's tone.

Edward sighed before replying, "All right. Do it."

"It will not hurt." Karina placed her left hand on top of Edward's head and then lowered her own in concentration. Raising her head again, she faced her queen.

"Do these men speak the truth?"

"Yes, Your Majesty, they were brought here against their will."

"What about the children? Please test them too," Cyren ordered.

HANNORAH

Karina beckoned the black haired girl to approach her. "Hannorah, I want you to do to the girl what I have been doing so far. She might not be so afraid of you."

"Yes, mistress."

Hannorah stood in front of Tracey. Henry could see that she looked at Hannorah with wary eyes. It was difficult to trust in that moment. As Tracey stared into the girl's green eyes, Henry offered her a small encouraging look. She reached for his hand and his fingers intertwined with hers.

"This will not hurt. I promise," Hannorah said. "What is your name?"

"Tracey."

"This won't take long, Tracey."

While Hannorah reached out as Karina had, Karina studied Henry; her mouth broadened into a warming smile. "And what is your name, sir?"

"Henry Simmons."

"How did you arrive here?"

"I was at my prom dance with Tracey when-"

"Prom dance?" Karina said, bewildered.

"Yes, it's a special celebration where we come from. Anyway, I was attacked. I fell to the ground and cut myself. When some of my blood spilled onto a gold coin—"

"Wait, did you say gold coin?"

"Yeah, and a voice spoke to me from inside the hole. The next thing I knew it's night time and me and Tracey are in some forest."

Karina touched Henry's head and looked down. When finished probing his mind, she opened her eyes, her gaze boring into Henry. "Where is the coin now?"

"It's here." Henry took it out of his tuxedo pocket, putting it in Karina's smooth palm.

"Hannorah?"

She looked at Karina and replied, "I think what Henry said is true. This girl came with him." Hannorah looked at Tracey with sympathy. "They are lost and afraid."

"Good work. Thank you," Karina said. She then walked to Cyren and presented the coin to her queen.

Cyren inspected the object, holding it up to the light. Karina leaned in, whispering something to Cyren. At once the queen stopped examining the coin, giving the sorceress a look of surprise. She listened further to her, nodding in agreement.

Karina straightened and approached Henry. Standing in front of him and with an amiable grin, she stared down at the teenager. "Would you come with me? Do not worry, you are not in any trouble. We just want to perform a test."

"Wha- what kind of test?" Henry stammered, instinctively leaning away from the woman.

"I will explain as we go. This will be painless, if that is what you are worried about."

"Wait a second," Edward said as he stood in front of Henry. "I don't mean any disrespect, but we want to go with him to see this…test. We all stay together."

"I understand your feelings," Karina said. "You are lost and afraid and not sure of whom to trust, but you have my word, Captain, none of you will be harmed here."

"Thank you, but I still want to go with you."

Karina looked to her queen for guidance.

"Very well," Cyren agreed, "but your friends and the strange animal must stay here."

Karina spoke gently again to Henry, "If you would not mind coming to my room."

"Okay," Henry agreed, gulping.

Tracey grabbed Henry's wrist and said in a low, fearful but insistent voice, "Henry, please don't leave me alone."

Xongrelan approached Tracey. "You will be fine and so will he."

"You stay with Conor. It'll be okay." He hoped more than he believed as Tracey's eyes became watery but there was nothing he could do, even as Conor stepped closer to her in mute support. Henry felt guilty leaving her there.

"Sorry," he mouthed as he moved towards Karina.

Cyren stood up. "Come along. Let us go and perform this test."

"Your Majesty, can I speak with you a moment?"

"Yes, Karina," Cyren said.

Karina stood close to her and talked in a hushed tone, but Henry could still hear the sorceress. "I think we should go to my room without any guards. Our guests are still afraid. If they become even more fearful then the boy may not do the test."

"Understood."

Karina turned to face Hannorah and the boy who stood with her. "Hannorah, Daniel, you stay here."

They nodded and watched Henry walk with Edward, Cyren and Karina from the throne room. Three guards moved to go with them, but Cyren signaled them to stay.

KARINA'S ROOM

WITH ALL HER MAGIC SPELLS

As Henry went into Karina's room, he was reminded of a fortune teller's caravan that he was in at a county fair a few months ago when Joey dared him to get a palm reading. Opposite the door was a wide window. Underneath it was an oak table. In the center of the table was a cloth over a rounded lump he assumed to be a crystal ball on a stand. To the right, a large bookshelf stood against the wall, containing volumes of bulky books. On the left was a large chest with strange carvings of animals. When the door was shut, Henry saw a big neatly made bed that looked comfortable and bouncy.

"Please sit, Master Henry," Karina said, indicating the end of the bed.

Henry sat. He had guessed right. The mattress was bouncy and comfortable. He untied his bow tie and undid the top button of his shirt.

Karina took the coin from her pocket. "Hold out your hand. When I put this coin in your palm, you must close your eyes and concentrate."

"On what?" Henry asked.

"On the coin," Karina said, placing it in Henry's palm. "Now close your eyes, cover the coin with your fingers, and squeeze it tightly."

Henry did as he was told. The pulse he had felt in his own world returned, it had a soothing effect, calming him.

Karina's words now had a tranquil effect, each one sounding as relaxing as the next.

"Feel the pulse of the coin. Let it guide your senses. You have nothing to fear."

The magical object put Henry into a hypnotic state; his head fell lifelessly to his chest. Henry heard Karina walking to his right, followed by the sound of something being opened.

"A knife?"

When Henry heard Edward's worried exclamation, he wanted to snap out of this trance, open his eyes but they refused to comply.

"If I am correct, then this should not have any effect on him," Karina answered.

"I can't let you hurt him," Edward said.

Whoa, he's standing up for me again... and we only just met, Henry thought. I guess he is a cool guy after all.

"He will not be harmed, I promise you."

"But you just said if you were correct, which means you're not too damn sure!"

"Please, calm down. I know you only want to protect him but you have to trust me. I would never do anything to harm him."

There were some movements that Henry didn't know how to interpret. But he was sure that sound was someone dragging in an annoyed breath. "All right," Edward finally agreed, "but if he's hurt in any way, I'll make you pay."

"I understand, but trust me, he will not be harmed." Henry sensed Karina was close again. "Hold out your other hand, Master Henry. Palm up."

When Henry held out his palm, Karina made a slight incision. The young teen felt a sharp moment of pain but it was nothing compared to what Sid could do to him. The discomfort eased almost immediately. He curled his fingers over the spot, but felt nothing unusual.

"Good God," Edward said in both awe and confusion.

"Does this test prove that he is the one we have been waiting for?" Cyren said.

"It does. It is time to wake him up."

"Wait. Before you wake him up, Captain, I must insist that you keep what has happened here to yourself. Only you, Xongrelan and I can know about this. Henry will know in time why he is here... just not now."

"Why can't everyone else know and why are MacCall and I here?"

"The time is not right yet to tell you everything. When it is, all will be explained. So please, keep this a secret," Cyren said.

"I must wake Henry now before he is too deep into the trance." With her right hand on Henry's shoulder, Karina spoke again. "The coin's pulse is weakening. Can you feel it weaken?"

"Yes," Henry replied.

"Good. Now, open your eyes and awaken."

Open your eyes and awaken, repeated and reverberated around Henry's mind like a recurring echo. He rubbed his eyelids before staring at Karina, Edward and Queen Cyren.

"Well, did I pass the test?"

"Yes, you passed," Cyren answered with a smile. "Let us return to the throne room. Lead the way, Henry." She extended her arm towards the door. When the queen sat down on her throne, she beckoned Xongrelan, Tracey and Conor forward. Edward, Jasper and Henry stood beside them.

"I understand you have no place to stay, so you may stay here until further notice. Xongrelan will show you to your quarters when they are prepared."

Edward spoke up. "Thank you. Can I ask a favor of you, Your Majesty?" Cyren nodded and Edward continued. "Could you lend us some men tomorrow to go and see if there's anything salvageable from where our plane crashed?"

"Of course, we shall do that tomorrow. Xongrelan will show you to your rooms when they are ready. Goodnight."

"Thank you," Edward said with a bow.

"Good night, Your Majesty," Henry said and others bid her a good night also.

As they were being led away by Xongrelan to their quarters, Henry said, "Captain Edward?"

Edward stopped and waited for Henry to walk beside him.

"Thanks for having my back in there." The English pilot stared at him with confusion. "I mean in Karina's room. Thanks for standing up for me."

"Oh, that. Don't worry. I just didn't want to see you get hurt."

"I know and I appreciate that," Henry replied with a smile of gratitude.

* * *

SLYVANON

Slyvanon, hunched due to a crippled back, and holding a candle in a metal candlestick holder, dressed in clothing made of animal fur and with little hair on his head, was bent slightly over the dead soldier. His thin, nimble fingers rested on the Sadarkian's forehead. The wound on the soldier's throat was covered with leaves. "Yes, Tyros, you saw something and soon we will see what it was," Slyvanon mumbled.

The door creaked as it opened. Slyvanon jumped, the silence in the room felt deafening as Zakarius and Lieutenant Serak walked in.

Slyvanon faced his king and bowed while holding the candle over the dead body.

"I am told you sensed something from him." He pointed to Tyros.

"Correct, Your Majesty." Slyvanon spoke with a slightly high-pitched tone. He moved aside for Zakarius to inspect the body. "Only you can see what it is."

The king placed a hand on Tyros's forehead, closing his eyes in deep concentration. Sliding his fingers down to Tyros's eyes, Zakarius said, "I shall see what you saw."

Flames from the candles in the room became more intense and brighter in their blaze, as the events this soldier had seen were now played out in Zakarius's mind. He told Slyvanon and Lieutenant Serak what he saw.

The vision started with Tyros hunting in the forest. Then he saw the thunder and the humans' flying monster coming through the gateway.

"The Foretold Ones are here," Zakarius said.

The vision continued. Tyros saw the dark blue metallic beast crash. Running to its crash site, he found no humans. He ran through the forest in search of the airmen and found them. As he was about to pounce on them, the gateway opened again, a boy and girl were thrown from it.

"Another? But he is just a boy," Zakarius remarked.

The vision skipped to when Tyros was hit with a dagger. "That is a Jenorme's dagger," the king said as he snapped out of the vision. Zakarius leaned up against the wall and rubbed his eyes, feeling drained after connecting with the soldier's mind.

"Are you all right, sire?" asked Slyvanon. Zakarius looked at Lieutenant Serak. "Leave us."

Serak bowed and left.

"So the Foretold Ones are here, sire?"

"Yes, they are and now in Argoth's care. A Jenorme killed this soldier. We must find and destroy them."

"But that will be hard because we do not know where Argoth and his people are," the old Sadarkian said while circling his king. Slyvanon stopped as Zakarius presented him with a fiery gaze.

"I thought by sending those dragons through the doorway Hernacious created, they would stop the Foretold Ones but they failed. Now they are in

Argoth's care and are probably planning an attack already. I swear I will find wherever Argoth's hiding…even if it means using every last soldier I have."

Slyvanon stood by a window, shooting a fleeting glance into the night's sky. "That may not be necessary. I think I know a way of finding them."

* * *

Henry awoke to the glare of daylight breaking through the tiny slit between the drawn curtains. It shone on his face and rescued him from a nightmare he had about the guard they had seen in the forest. Despite the hard wood proving to be far from cozy and caused his back to ache a little, Henry slept throughout the night from sheer exhaustion. He was thankful that there was a small bunch of straw which acted as a mattress. This softened the hard base of his bed but not by much. The rest of his room was almost bare except for a large, round wooden chest by the door, which he guessed was used for storing clothes because there was no wardrobe.

Jasper, who had asked to stay with Henry for the night, stretched his paws and arched his back. He began licking his paws before moving to cleaning his face.

"Hey, Jasper, how did you sleep?"

Jasper stopped grooming to answer, "As good as a cat can sleep. What about you?"

"Damn bed is hard, but I slept okay, I guess. Man, I still can't believe I'm talking to you like this. It feels so weird." Jasper licked his legs while Henry dressed.

As the boy buttoned up his shirt, a gentle knock came to his door. A young woman's sweet voice could be heard from outside it.

"May I enter?" she asked.

"Hold on a sec'." Henry quickly finished buttoning his shirt before opening the door.

The young servant held in her arms a bundle of clothes consisting of tunics, belts, undergarments, trousers and several pairs of leather strapped boots. "My name is Miralda. Queen Cyren sent these for you to wear."

"I'm supposed to wear *those*?"

"Yes, sir, by orders of the queen herself."

"No way," Henry replied, shaking his head.

"But, sir, you must. Both her and the king will be offended if you do not."

"Oh…okay." Henry took the clothes.

"Good day to you, sir." Miralda curtsied.

"Bye, Miralda," Henry said in an embarrassed tone as he shut the door. *I can't believe I have to wear these.* He looked at them, feeling uncomfortable even by just staring at them.

Jasper chuckled as Henry put on a lavender colored tunic, gray trousers and leather strapped boots. "Guess who looks like an idiot?" He fell to the ground in laughter.

"Shut up, Jas'."

* * *

In the banquet hall an hour later, Henry had just finished eating his breakfast while Tracey in a lilac dress sat staring at hers. In front of her was a bowl of porridge.

"Word of warning, this tastes worse than it looks," she said.

"Thanks." He eyed the bowl of porridge Miralda had set down upon him with a great deal of suspicion. "Guess we have no choice but to eat it, though."

Tracey shoved her bowl away. "Maybe but I've enough. So, how did you sleep?"

"Not too bad, surprisingly. You?"

"Do you not see the dark circles around my eyes?" Tracey answered with a half grin.

"That good, huh?" he replied and both laughed. Henry saw beneath Tracey's laughter, a scared look in her eyes that she was unsuccessful in hiding.

"Kept thinking about my dad all night," she said.

"Yeah…kept thinking about my folks too."

"Hey look at the bright side; at least now I get to live out my *Lord of the Rings* fantasy." Again both teens laughed but as soon as Tracey's laughter abated, she stared at the table in front of her for a few seconds before asking,

"Do you… do you think we'll get back home?"

"I hope so." Henry changed his answer immediately as a flash of even greater fear washed over her face. "I mean, yeah, sure. We have to, right?"

"I know… it's just that," her eyes welled up, "I- I wanna go back home. My dad must be freaking out by now." Tears ran down her cheeks.

"I'm so sorry about all this. I-"

"Sorry, Henry, I- I got to get some air." She left the banquet room in a quick stride.

"Tracey, wait." Henry wiped his face with a napkin and went after her, trying to keep up. "Wait."

After running up the stairs, she reached her room. She went in, shutting the door. Henry knocked twice and said, "Tracey, open the door, please. I want to talk to you."

"I just want to be on my own for a while, okay?"

"Look, I'm sorry. I-"

"Please, Henry, just leave me alone."

Henry knew it would be a waste of time in trying to talk her round right now, so he let her be.

Just as he was approaching the steps, he saw the boy that was with Hannorah in Argoth's throne room.

What was his name again? he thought. Danny… Denis… Daniel… yes, Daniel!

"You are the one Hannorah could not stop talking about last night," Daniel said. "My Aunt Karina thinks you are important."

"Daniel, is it? Nice to meet you." Henry extended his hand to shake Daniel's.

"Yes. Yours is Henry?"

"Yeah it is," Henry answered, still waiting for his hand to be shaken.

"Well, Henry, I cannot see anything special about you and I will not shake the hand of a peasant." Daniel, with his head raised high, brushed past Henry, continuing down the long hallway.

What's his problem? Henry wondered before walking down the stairs.

Henry met Edward, Conor, Karina, and Hannorah along with some of Argoth's guards at the stables. Jasper stayed behind feasting on a juicy steak.

Tracey was still in her room. Three mares were saddled and ready. Conor and Edward wore bearskin coats covering their tunics, Conor with a dark cream trousers and Edward a black one.

"Glad you could join us, Master Henry," greeted Karina. "I trust breakfast was suitable?"

"Yeah, it was great, thanks," Henry lied.

"You men ready to leave?" Karina directed her question at the airmen.

"Aye, we're good to go, lass."

"Very well. Let's ride out," Karina replied.

"Wait a second, won't the Sadarkians be out?" Henry asked.

"No, not during the day. The sun affects their eyes almost blinding them," Karina said. "That is why they stick to coming out at night instead."

"Oh, okay. Good."

The group mounted their horses and began their journey to the cliff.

**

Edward and Conor rode along behind Henry, Karina and Hannorah. There was a large cart brought with them in case there would be a lot to bring back.

Autumnal colored leaves were on the trees and blanketed the ground. Everything around Edward seemed so beautiful but he wondered if danger lurked somewhere in this forest, if some Sadarkian would jump out again to attack. Paying a quick glance to Conor who rode beside him, he knew from the Scot's uneasy demeanor that his friend was nervous.

"First time on a horse?" Edward asked.

"No, but I don't like them."

"Why?"

"When I was a wee lad, I saw a man trampled t'death by one. He was trying to bring the horse under control an' it knocked him down. The rest is history." The English pilot caught Conor looking at him, studying his posture. "You seem calm enough."

"My uncle used to own a horse. Every time I called, he let me ride it. Ivanhoe."

"Beg your pardon, sir?"

"That was the horse's name: Ivanhoe."

"Ah... aye, right."

"My uncle was a member of the Fourth Royal Irish Dragoon Guards in the Great War."

"Oh, I see. Bet he had a few stories to tell then, eh?"

"Maybe. He didn't tell us, though. Now I understand why." Edward let loose a nostalgic sigh as he gazed into the horizon, recalling a happy memory. "But when I used to ride Ivanhoe, it was just us. Nothing else mattered when we rode together."

"All your problems faded away. I can relate to that." Conor looked around before leaning towards Edward. "Do you think we can trust them, sir?"

"We've little choice really. If they wanted to kill us they would've done so already, I suppose."

"Maybe." Both men rode on in silence for another few minutes until Conor broke it with another question. "D'ya think we'll find anything that'll be usable?"

"Don't know until we get there but if I'm to guess, there'll not be a whole lot left to use. Maybe the turret gun could be salvaged. It might come in useful against the Sadarkians."

"My thoughts exactly, sir."

"We'll find out soon enough, won't we?" Edward replied, the cliff drawing ever closer. By his estimation, another ten minute ride.

They rode on in silence, taking in even more of the forest's beauty with pink flowers sprouting from some tree stumps. Edward smiled at the occasional pink butterfly with black dotted wings that fluttered around him as they continued through the forest. The sound of rivers running in the far off distance coincided with the chorus of songs sung by birds.

Ten minutes later, they arrived at the cliff. A smell of burnt metal greeted them.

"Everyone dismount," Karina ordered. She got down from her stallion, as did Hannorah, Tracey, Henry and the soldiers that accompanied them.

"Prepare the ropes to drop to the bottom of the cliff," Karina said.

The soldiers set about unfurling ropes that were attached to their saddles.

Karina approached Edward and Conor. "Are you both ready to be lowered down, Captain?"

"Yes, we are."

"Good. We will tie the ropes around you and make sure they are secure before you go down. Try not to worry, nothing will happen to you." Edward saw that she directed a comforting smile towards Conor who looked a shade paler than he did while riding his horse.

"Aye," Conor said in a shaky voice, her smile not having its desired effect.

Fifteen minutes later after they climbed down the cliff to the crashed plane using a rope, they had surveyed everything from the wreckage. Although the turret gun was damaged from the fire, both men figured that maybe Karina's magic might be able to restore it.

As Conor looked upon the TBF Avenger, his words were laced with hurt and sadness. "She served us well, eh, Captain?"

"That she did, MacCall. I don't think there's anything else for us to take?"

"Nah, sir. Nothin'. Everything's too burned."

"I agree. We best be heading back up." Edward shouted to Karina, "We're coming up."

When Conor had successfully reached the top, they dropped down a rope for Edward. Just as he was halfway up, without warning he was dropped two steps down by the rope.

"What's going on up there?" he shouted, his voice echoing the question towards the cliff's apex. His heart began to beat faster.

The rope now became loose, its material separating.

"Quick, guards, hold onto the rope. Pull him up!" Edward heard Karina shout.

He saw two soldiers rushing to grab it.

Sweat broke out on Edward's back and forehead. "Karina, help me!"

"We are trying, Captain Edward," Karina yelled.

The soldiers held onto the rope, heaving Edward upwards.

"Harder, men, harder! Put your backs into it," Karina barked.

Even with two soldiers pulling the pilot up, the rope now severed from the tree.

"Arrgghh!" Edward cried as he fell. He feared that he too would become part of the wreckage.

"No," He heard Karina roar. She cast out her right hand and the Englishman found himself stuck in mid-air.

"Oh, thank God," he said in relief.

Edward found himself being pulled up at a slow pace. He could hear Karina grunting loudly, almost in pain as she held onto him.

Edward gasped again as he stopped in mid-air before falling again, picking up speed with each second as he plummeted to his doom.

"Do something!" Edward heard Conor shout.

Edward saw Karina shake her hand twice before splaying her fingers while reaching out to grab him with her magic.

He closed his eyes just as he was a few feet from the plane, ready to be impaled by the wingtip. Edward was about to let loose a curse when he found himself stuck in mid-air, two inches from the right wing. He closed his eyes and opened them again, thanking whatever god was here for helping Karina save him from certain death…at least for now.

"Hannorah," Karina called out, "come quickly. Use your magic with mine to help bring him up."

The girl soon appeared at Karina's side. She took her mentor's left hand in her right and cast out her left hand. Edward guessed that they combined their powers because as she concentrated on him, from the distance he was at, he could make out a faint teal-colored aura around Karina's fingertips. If Karina and Hannorah were to let go now, Edward's fall would break his back or neck.

Almost immediately, Edward found himself floating back up towards the cliff's apex. As he got closer and closer to the cliff top, he could see how much strain was on Karina and Hannorah's faces. Both their hands trembled as they brought him up.

"Guards, get ready to grab him," Karina ordered just as he was within reaching distance of the clifftop. Two guards reached out their arms and caught him, pulling the pilot onto the grass.

"Thank you, lassies," Conor said to Karina and Hannorah. He then rushed to Edward's side. "Oh, thank God you're all right, sir," he said, helping Edward to his feet.

Karina and Hannorah winced as they rubbed their aching arms.

"Are you sure you are all right, Captain?" Karina asked.

Edward caught his breath before answering. "Yes, thank you." Looking at Hannorah he said, "Thank you both. I thought I was a goner there."

"I'm glad you're okay, Captain. I was really worried there for a second," Henry said.

"You and me both, Henry," Edward replied.

"Do you trust us now?" Karina asked with a warm smile.

"Yes, yes I do," Edward replied, winded. "I owe you my life, Karina and Hannorah."

Karina surveyed items from the wreckage. "Have you everything you need?"

"We do," Edward said, once more sweeping the salvageable items with his gaze.

"Then if there is nothing else to get below, we will return to the town." Karina gestured for some soldiers to help the exhausted Englishman mount his horse.

Soon, all of them saddled up and rode home

* * *

Later that evening Henry and Jasper wandered around the large mansion they were staying in. As they passed one room, Henry saw various colored hues creeping out from underneath the door.

I wonder what's going on in there. As the door was opened a crack, he peeped inside. Hannorah was staring at three orbs levitating in front of her. The orbs altered their color and shape. Some bobbed up and down like beach balls on water.

"Wow, that's cool." The words just slipped out as he stared on, awestruck at Hannorah's magic.

"You betcha," Jasper said also.

Henry knocked on the door.

"Come in," she said and he entered. Her room was like Karina's, but with more books which were everywhere: on her bed, table and a chest that was placed near the door. On her shelves were glass jars. Inside them were what looked like herbs along with other ingredients for potions.

"That's a neat trick," Henry commented.

When Hannorah clicked her fingers, the orbs vanished. She turned around. "Thanks. Please, sit down."

Henry paid a quick glance around the room. The only place he could sit was on her bed. "So how long have you been doing… that?"

"Five years. I am Karina's apprentice."

"Wow, it's really cool what you can do. So how did you get your powers? How long have you been here?" Henry asked.

"My father was a healer and my mother was a witch so-"

"A witch?" Henry butted in.

"Yes, a witch. Why are you surprised?"

"Where I come from witches are kind of bad."

"My mother was a witch of the light. Her powers do not come from dark forces. She heals people with her magic. During the war, we moved around a lot. When we found out about this place, we moved here. Karina saw me one day healing an animal and I guess I must have impressed her because she made me her apprentice. But I had to take an oath."

"What kind of oath?" Henry asked.

"I promised to use my magic for good and to heal people, not to harm them. If I break it, Karina will take away all my powers."

"I see. Can you do another trick for me?"
"Sure."

* * *

Tracey sat on her bed, wiping her eyes which were red from crying. She had been walking after Henry left to clear her head but when he came back, she went to her room to avoid seeing him. It was then that the homesickness had hit her in the solitude of her room.

I can't stay here. I can't live like this forever. If I can't get home, then maybe I can send some kind of message to my dad to let them know I'm okay. I could send one to Henry's parents too. A tear managed to find its way down her cheek. She wiped it with her sleeve. *There's got to be a way to do that. That Karina woman…she's some kind of… witch and they have magic, right? So maybe she has some spell I can use to send a message. I got to find her room. Look through her spell books. She's bound to have a spell book, they all do.*

Tracey dipped her hands into a basin of water that was by her bed and washed her face. She dried it with a cloth.

As Tracey entered the hallway, she saw a teenaged male servant in a purple uniform. He had short dark hair and his face was flushed from what she thought was a lot of walking as the boy was panting.

"Excuse me. Karina said she wanted a spell from a book. Where's her room?"

"Go down… the hall, up the stairs and… it's the first room on the right."

"Thank you."

She followed the directions, soon arriving outside Karina's room. She knocked twice but no one answered. Tracey was in luck, the door was unlocked. She looked in both directions before sneaking inside.

The girl breathed a sigh of relief when she closed the door. *I gotta work fast before she comes back.* She scanned the volumes of bulky tomes on Karina's shelf, noticing two books were pushed out a little further than the rest. Standing on her toes, she was able to see that a large book was concealed behind the others. She removed the two books and took out the hidden one.

"Maybe this is what I'm looking for," she said as she began flicking through its pages. Her heart sank upon looking through the book. She could not understand any of Karina's writing. It was written in a language alien to her.

Crap, what am I going to do now? Guess I better leave it. Tracey put the book back on the shelf, putting the other two tomes in front of it.

Closing the door, she saw the servant who helped her earlier. *Maybe I can use him to help me.* "Excuse me, sir. Can I borrow you for a second?"

"Certainly."

"I'm new here and Karina wants a spell brought to her. Problem is, I can't read her writing. Could you come in with me to just help me make sense of it?"

"Certainly," he replied, eying her with suspicion.

Tracey and the servant entered Karina's room. She took down the book where the spells were. "I, I mean Karina's looking for a spell to send a signal to someone. Can you read through this and see if you can find one?"

"Sure." Just as he thumbed through three pages, he stopped. "Are you sure Karina sent you here to get a spell?"

"Yes, of course!" She gave a nervous smile while batting her eyes, hoping her charm would convince him.

"Okay," he said, not fully convinced but still helped her. He continued to flick through the pages before stopping at a spell that looked like it was written centuries ago, with its page a dark yellow with ink blotches on certain lines, making it even more difficult to decipher.

"I think I found what you are looking for."

"Is it a signal spell?"

"At least that is what it says on top of the page."

"Okay, can you read it out to me?" The spell was only one sentence long so it would be easy to remember.

"Yes. It says say three words four times, 'hanya, oraktar, stedoolus'."

"Do I need any ingredients?" she asked. *Guess all those years of reading Harry Potter books paid off.*

"No, just say the words."

"Gotcha, thanks." He nodded and left.

Tracey placed the book down on Karina's bed. She recited the words that were to be chanted, "Hanya, oraktar, stedoolus." She repeated these words several times until the pages started to flip back and forth. Karina's large spell book floated and closed itself shut. The window, which was open, slammed closed by itself. Tracey swallowed hard when an orange light appeared to her right, flickering like a flame on a candle. It expanded into a large swirling vortex like the one she came here in. Karina's instruments, her potions in glass jars, were scattering about in the wind being generated by the portal.

Shielding her eyes from its almost blinding glare, Tracey gasped as a terrifying guttural growl was heard from within the portal. The strong glare lessened a little allowing her to see the dark figure of a hideous monster approaching. Boney spikes jutted out from the creature's back. Its hands were misshapen like a Gargoyle's claws, with nails falling down over its fingers.

"Oh no, what have I done?" she said.

The monster slinked towards the portal's opening, its growling growing louder.

* * *

Hannorah wiggled her fingers and the little shooting star spun around faster. Henry's eyes widened, mesmerized by her magic as the star spiraled upwards and then down again before rising once more. The shooting star left a glittering mist as it continued rising and falling.

"That's friggin' awesome," Henry remarked.

Hannorah stopped and her shooting star vanished. She groaned as she massaged her forehead.

"What's wrong?" Henry asked.

"Something is wrong in Karina's room. We got to hurry."

Hannorah raced out the door, Henry and Jasper ran close behind.

They were soon at Karina's room. Just as she was about to turn the handle on her mentor's door, Tracey swung it open, bumping into Hannorah as she tried to make a hasty exit.

Dread spread across Hannorah's face. "What did you do?"

"I don't know. I was just trying to-"

Hannorah shoved her aside and walked in. She saw the large book still levitating, recognized it, and knew straight away what type of creature was trying to emerge.

"Canoras," Hannorah said. The book landed in her hands. She thumbed through its yellowed pages to find a spell to close the portal.

Tracey shrieked as the creature's arm emerged from the portal. She could see its face more clearly now. Its skin was a citrus color. The beast had three glowing pink eyes that were just as menacing as its skin and long nails.

"Whoa. I thought Mrs. Williams was ugly," Jasper joked.

"Hannorah, I think now would be a good time to do something," Henry said.

"I am trying!" Her eyes were glued to Karina's book. She didn't see the head of the beast emerge. It opened its mouth, the monster's tongue flapping about as it looked upon the three teens and Jasper.

Tracey stood behind Henry as they retreated further out the door. "Oh my God, it's going to kill us," she cried hysterically.

"You are not helping," Hannorah said in a sing-songy tone before finally finding the page she was looking for. "Hena, mortita, cryanus!"

The beast bellowed a mournful roar before being pulled back into the portal, which was then reduced to a sparkling, pin-prick of light before disappearing. Everyone breathed a sigh of relief.

Suddenly Tracey became the center of their attention, shame and guilt washed through her. She couldn't meet the shocked gazes of Henry and Hannorah.

"I'm sorry, guys," she said.

"Do you have any idea of what could have happened if I was not here?" Hannorah asked. "That was a Gryon demon. He could have killed a lot of people if he came out through that...that thing!"

"I'm sorry."

"Sorry would not have stopped the demon if he had come through."

"Okay, I get it, all right? I just wanted to send a message to my dad that I'm okay. If it worked, I was going to come back and do the same for Henry. I miss daddy... my friends." Her lips trembled; there was a quiver in her voice as she spoke. "I just want to go home." She ran crying to her room. Henry looked at Hannorah, almost seeking her permission to go after Tracey.

"Everything is fine here. Go," she said, her tone a little more understanding now. Jasper remained with Hannorah.

Henry ran after Tracey and walked into her room. She was curled up in the fetal position on her bed.

"I said I was sorry."

"It's okay. I'm not here to give you a hard time. Look, Tracey, I'm sorry for bringing you here. I never meant for any of this to happen. We'll figure out a way to get back."

"But how? You don't even know for sure if we will. Do you know how to work the coin?"

"Well... not really, no."

"Well then. And I did mean it when I said I would've come back to tell you about the spell so we could've sent it to your parents too. I just don't want my dad to be worried about me."

"I know, and I'm worried about my parents too but maybe Karina can help us get back or something. No matter what it takes, we're gonna get back home."

"Okay." Tracey nodded and wiped her eyes again.

"So... are we cool?"

"Yeah, we're cool."

Hannorah knocked on Tracey's room door. "May I come in?"

"Sure," Tracey replied.

Hannorah along with Jasper came in. "So, did you two kiss and make up?"

Henry detected a hint of mischief in the cat's voice. "Shut up, Jas'," Henry replied, his cheeks scarlet.

"I apologize for shouting at you back there, but what you did was dangerous," Hannorah said.

"I know and I'm sorry," Tracey answered. "I just thought it would send a message back home."

"That spell is to be used outside. If you do not do it properly, it could summon a demon. They can see all signals sent and could follow the magic wherever it is used," Hannorah informed them. "That is why I was angry. Only a sorceress like Karina is allowed use it, only if they really, really have to."

"Are you going to tell her about this?" Tracey asked.

"Even though I should… I will not. She will know something was wrong anyway but I will tell her it was me who did a spell that went wrong."

"Thanks." Tracey offering a little smile to Hannorah.

"How did you know something was wrong in Karina's room?" Henry asked.

"When she made me her apprentice, she gave me a connection to her magic, and that included her spell books. That way if she was out and someone was using one of the spells when they were not supposed to, then I could be there to stop them."

Henry filled Tracey in on how long Hannorah had been here and how she became an apprentice.

"Do you have any brothers or sisters?" Tracey asked.

"I have a brother," Hannorah answered with a slight frown. "But he moved away after the war. He does not want anything to do with my family or our magic."

"Sorry to hear that," Tracey said, regret filled her expression for asking the question.

Henry then asked Hannorah something that had been bothering him since his first encounter with Daniel. "I met that Daniel dude earlier. He totally blew me off. What's his problem?"

"What do you mean by *blew you off*?" she replied.

"It's like he totally dismissed me. He thinks he's better than me. Why's he like that?"

"Daniel thinks that because his father is a knight and his aunt is Karina, he is above everyone else. Try not to let him get to you. I think he is kind of jealous of me too."

"What makes you think that?" Tracey said.

"I caught him saying once to his friend that he wished he had my powers. He is mean to me sometimes too, but I ignore him."

"Can you show Tracey some of your magic like you showed me earlier?"

"Certainly." Hannorah closed her eyes and meditated for a moment. A shiny ball appeared in front of her. She then turned her palms upwards and the orb transformed into a small, white butterfly with purple dots on its wings. It was still for a moment until it began to flutter.

"Wow," Tracey said as she watched the butterfly flutter around the room before leaving through the opened window. "That's amazing. Can you do something else?"

"You can't wish me up a nice piece of steak, can you?" Jasper asked.

"We are not allowed to feed animals in our rooms but I can do another trick." Hannorah smiled at them as she performed more magic.

* * *

Left shaken after her spell mishap, Tracey went to walk it off around the royal gardens at the rear of King Argoth's mansion. Even the bright colors from various roses and dandelions could not shake the guilt or take her mind off of what happened.

Daniel, who she remembered Henry talking about back in Hannorah's room, walked in her direction but never looked at her. She noted that for a boy his age, he was in great physical shape, with bulging muscles and broad shoulders seen inside his crimson tunic. Most girls around here may have found him attractive, she figured, but not her. She knew the personality behind the good looks and personality meant everything.

"Excuse me," she said to him. Daniel stopped.

"Yes."

"You're Daniel, right?"

"I am. Why do you ask?"

"I believe you talked to Henry earlier."

"The new boy Hannorah is always talking about? Yes. So what if I did?"

She arched an eyebrow, her hands now on her hips, unimpressed with his attitude. "Why did you talk to my friend like that?"

"Pfft, he is a peasant and not deserving of my time," Daniel scoffed.

"Oh really? And just who is?" Her arms were now folded, her voice becoming even firmer.

"What do you mean?" Annoyance creeping into Daniel's.

"You walk around here thinking you're better than everyone."

"I am actually…well, better than most boys my age. I am the son of Sir Dreyfus, Argoth's best knight."

"And that makes you special because…?"

"Because he is the best soldier Argoth has," Daniel replied in bewilderment.

Tracey read Daniel's condescending expression, as if thinking that the girl in front of him was stupid. The anger bubbled within her even more. "I see guys like you all the time, thinking you're so better than everyone else. Guess what? It doesn't end well for people like you."

Daniel's demeanor shifted to one of seriousness, his right fist clenched. "Are you threatening me, girl?"

"No, I just know you'll grow up without any friends because nobody likes people like you. So I don't care what you think of me. A word to the wise though:

talk to Henry like that again and next time I won't be so polite." Tracey spun on her heels and walked away, leaving Daniel to reflect on what she just said.

* * *

Henry had requested a candle in his room; he hated the dark. Now, he watched the flame dance and flicker on the wick.

A knock came to his door.

"Yup?" Henry said.

"Master Henry, may I come in?" Karina asked from outside the door.

"Yeah, sure."

Karina walked in, closed the door and pulled up a chair. "Are you all right? I sensed some sadness in you while you were eating this evening."

"I kind of wish you'd stop doing that," Henry replied.

"Doing what?"

"Reading minds. I find it creepy and annoying. Do you do it all the time?"

"No; only when I see my friends in trouble." Karina grinned as she finished.

"Well please don't do it on me again without asking, okay?" Karina nodded. "Thanks. Will you be honest with me if I ask you a question?"

"Of course. I will always be honest with you."

"Do you think the guys and I will ever get back to our own worlds?"

"I believe you will but only when a certain task is completed. I cannot tell you now but you will be told when the time is right."

"Why can't you tell me now?"

"Because it is not yet time for you to know."

"Okay." Henry tilted his head to the right as he thought of another question to ask, one that had been burning away in his mind since he came to Zargothia. "There's something that's been bothering me and maybe you can answer it. Why are you and the Sadarkians enemies?"

"Now that is something I can tell you, Master Henry." Karina sat back in the chair with folded arms.

Henry glanced into Karina's eyes. In them, the boy could see a sense of nostalgia.

"For many years there was peace between us and the Sadarkians until thirty three years ago, one of their kings – Gronach – captured some of our people and sent their heads back to Argothos – Argoth's father. A war broke out and for ten years we fought them. Argoth lost some of his family during the war, including his son, Aranok."

Karina held out her hand. An image wavered into view of Aranok's corpse lying on a stone slab with his hands clutching the pommel of his sword. He was a handsome young man with long, raven-black hair and with a broad build. He looked to be no more than eighteen. Henry could see who he guessed was a sorrowful Argoth and a weeping Cyren in a dimly lit tent. Argoth looked like an older version of Aranok but with shorter hair and chestnut brown eyes. The candle's flame glinted in them. The king and queen's grief matched the night's darkness.

"The Elders were not happy about us and the Sadarkians fighting so they called on our god, Zymbion and the Sadarkian god, Hernacious – to come together and sign a peace treaty."

Another image appeared, this time with Argoth and Karina inside a white diplomatic tent, sitting opposite a stern but pallid looking Sadarkian wearing a silk black robe with gold trimmings. Henry guessed that this had to be the Sadarkian king. Beside him sat an equally tall and fearsome looking soldier with eyes that could strike dread into a person just by glancing at them.

"Twenty years ago, Argoth, now king after his father's passing, and I, King Mordoch and his general, Fradar, met in the forest of Egorthinia and signed the treaty. We got back most of our lands but Mordoch and his people were allowed keep some. One of the rules was that neither human nor Sadarkian could cross the new border. If we did, they could imprison us and if one of their kind crossed over into our side, we could do the same to them.

"Not everyone was happy about the treaty. A man named Marcus sent a spy to keep him informed. His spy sent a message to him telling what we lost to the Sadarkians. Marcus was furious and decided to ambush Argoth. He gathered his friends and other men who were also angry about the treaty."

In a smoky mist, another image shimmered before them. Henry could see Marcus, a man of medium height and sandy-colored hair, lying in wait in some trees, as did his men, some with bows while others had swords or axes holstered in their belts. Once Argoth's carriage and army entered the forest, Marcus roared, his own soldiers unleashing arrows on Argoth's and descended on them.

"They ambushed Argoth and his soldiers at another forest as we were coming back from Egorthinia. We fought Marcus's men and beat them. He tried to run away but we caught him. Argoth banished him from Zargothia forever.

"Seven years later, I rode one day to the River Balonia. I saw two Sadarkians – a boy and his father - fishing on our side of the border. Their names were Turnaz and Nemus. I warned them not to come on our side of the border again. I did not think I would meet them again until one day I was on my own when I was about to be attacked by a vicious dog. As I fell off the horse, I hit my head on a tree and was knocked out. I would have been killed by that dog if it were not for Turnaz. Lucky for me he was on our side of the border when he found me. He secretly took me to his house to treat my wounds. From that day, we became great friends. I liked his son Nemus a lot too.

"Six months later, Turnaz's wife died and he was left to look after Nemus on his own. After several months of having little luck hunting for food, he sent me a letter begging to look after Nemus because he had no aunts or uncles. Argoth reluctantly agreed. So I took Nemus in and treated him like the child I never had. I used to take him to see Turnaz once every month but one day I found Turnaz dead in his bed. It looked like he committed suicide. His throat was cut. With his father gone, I was the only one Nemus had left."

A murky image wavered in the smoky mist of a hunched Sadarkian standing in a circle of other Sadarkians who seemed to be meeting in secret in a dark alleyway. Only the moon's rays from within the image provided enough light for Henry to see who was there.

"Shortly after Turnaz died, Slyvanon and a few others plotted to get rid of King Mordoch. It was also around this time that Mordoch was given the gold coin by Zymbion because Zymbion thought he was the fairest king that the Sadarkians ever had. Zymbion knew Mordoch would keep it safe. Ten years later, we had a secret meeting where he gave me that coin. He told me it would protect my people in the future.

"Around the same time, I was having strange dreams of my dead husband, Roylin. They were bothering me so I decided one day to go for a stroll to clear my head. Nemus came with me. We went to the River Balonia. I thought I saw my husband running in between the trees in the forest. I ran after him but never realized I had crossed the border. Nemus tried to warn me but I was so busy trying to catch up to Roylin, I did not listen. He disappeared and next thing I know, Nemus is caught in some trap. He was dragged away by two Sadarkian guards. I tried to help him but they hit me with some sleeping dart. I later realized I was tricked and someone made me see my husband to distract me while Nemus was kidnapped."

"What did Argoth do?" Henry asked.

"There was nothing he could do. I begged him to go after Nemus and bring him back but he could not risk another war. I hoped Mordoch would allow him to come home but they have a custom: if one of their own spends too much time with us, they kill them because they think that person could be a human spy. Nemus's head was sent back to me ten days later."

"I'm sorry to hear that," Henry said.

"Not half as sorry as I was at the time." Karina stopped for a moment. Henry saw the sorrow in her face. Karina cleared her throat and continued. "Three years later after Mordoch gave me the coin, he was killed and Zakarius was crowned king. He attacked our castle and caught us by surprise. We lost it to him and that was when I first met Zakarius. I could not believe it because he was actually Nemus."

"No way," Henry said, stunned.

"Yes, he is. Slyvanon had used some magic to make the head that was sent to me look exactly like Nemus's. That wretched bastard filled the boy's head with lies and turned him against us. He could not bear to call himself Nemus. He did not want anything to do with me. I tried to tell him I was tricked and was not aware he was alive but he would not listen. He thought we left him to rot in a cell in Mordoch's castle."

"Wait, so you're saying he took over the castle and didn't kill you?"

"Yes. We were lucky he had some ounce of kindness left in his heart. He told us the only reason he left Cyren, Argoth and I live was because Argoth allowed him stay in Zargothia after his father died. He threw us out of the castle and warned if we came back, he would kill us."

"So how were you able to bring the coin with you?"

"I snuck it out in my clothes. For months afterwards we lived in the forests, moving from place to place, hunting and killing whatever we could to eat. Soon we met Damone and Xongrelan because they were sent by their kings to protect us. A short while later, we met my brother, Sir Dreyfus, who managed to flee from the castle. He was one of the lucky few to escape because Zakarius slaughtered the vast majority who lived there. Dreyfus took us to a secret village where he and some others hid from Zakarius's soldiers. We lived there for two years until Zymbion appeared one day to tell us about Little Zargothia. He told us how to get here and gave us the powder used to cross the bridge to Argoth.

"We could not believe our luck when we arrived. Zymbion told us that he built this place to protect us from Sadarkians. When we arrived, we found the diamond that keeps this place invisible. We also found a scroll on the throne in the room where you met Cyren and it told us about events that will happen in the future."

"Wow, can I see it?" Henry asked, his voice bubbling with excitement.

"Not yet. You will get to see it when the time is right."

"Oh…okay," Henry replied, his chin fell to his chest in disappointment.

"Cheer up, you will see it soon. Eight months after we arrived here, I decided it was time to tell Argoth about the coin."

"Why didn't you tell him about it before that?"

"Mordoch said Zymbion told him I was to tell no one about the coin until I knew the time was right, so I kept my word. One month after I told Argoth about it, I received a message to go to a mountain called The Mount of Lilies to send the coin from there through something you referred to as a portal. That is how you came to find it and how the others from your world came here too. Hernacious was angry that Zymbion helped us and put a curse on Argoth-"

"What kind of curse?" Henry interrupted.

"He gets sick for a few months every year. Hernacious thought that with Argoth ill, Little Zargothia would be vulnerable but Cyren is a strong queen. She is one of the best warriors I have ever seen. But Argoth was not the only one to be cursed. He also turned some of the unicorns into dragons and dracorns."

Once again, the familiar mist formed above Karina's palm. In it could be seen beautiful, white unicorns grazing on a hillside. Suddenly dark clouds rolled in and thunder cracked around the peaceful creatures. Two threatening turquoise eyes glowed in the clouds and a yellow beam struck a unicorn. Soon it had transformed from white to acorn brown, its feathery white wings now matching its dark skin. Other unicorns were struck, suffering the same transformation. Others turned into dragons which were half the height of a mountain, with scaly black skin, smoke billowing through their nostrils.

"Poor things. So what's a dracorn?" Henry asked.

"It is a unicorn that is unable to make himself invisible, can breathe fire and is now brown instead of white. The unicorn queen, Eusaba, ordered her kind to go into hiding before more of them would be hurt by Hernacious. I feel sorry for them because they did not fight in the Great War against the Sadarkians. Hernacious was just angry and took it out on them too."

"Wow, that's an amazing story but I feel sorry for the unicorns. How did you and Argoth meet?"

"When I was about your age, I trained with a monk called Orkinad from The Order of Onosis. They were monks given knowledge by Zymbion himself. Orkinad taught me how to use magic properly. I was with him for five years. One day he came to Argothos' court and helped us to heal one of his lords. I must have made a good impression because Argothos wanted me to stay on. I was afraid to because I did not feel ready but Orkinad said I was. Since then, Argoth and I have grown close."

"Cool. He's lucky to have you on his side. Where are these monks now?"

"They are gone, wiped out by a Sadarkian garrison during the war."

"Oh… sorry to hear that. But there's one thing that's bothering me: Xongrelan is a Jenorme but he's the only one I see around here. Where did he come from?"

"He comes from Nevarom. During The Great War, a wizard named Skareon, one of Cyren's kind – a Volark – opened a portal at a place called, 'Hallow's Point'. He came to Zargothia through it. Argothos found him and he returned him to his king, Duvrona. Argothos and Duvrona became allies. They gave us food during the war but did not fight."

"Why not?"

"They feared being invaded by the Sadarkians but unfortunately, Zakarius found the portal. He invaded the queen's world Eviranna and Nevarom. Both Jenormes and Volarks are great allies but also have doors to each other's worlds making it easy for Zakarius to invade both."

"Where is King Argoth?"

"He is confined to bed most days."

"That's a shame." Henry yawned as a wave of tiredness washed over him. He stretched his arms. "Man, I'm beat."

Karina now unfolded her arms, placing both hands on her knees. "I think it is time for me to go to sleep. You should do the same."

"What've you got planned for me tomorrow?"

"Would you like to go hunting with Xongrelan and Damone?"

"Yeah, that would be awesome. Will I be able to use one of those cool crossbows?"

"Umm…we shall see. I do not want you to get hurt."

Henry's excited smile turned to a frown.

"But I am sure Xongrelan and Damone will take care of you."

Henry's smile returned, but then a gruesome thought crossed his mind. "Wait, I won't have to carry any dead animals, will I?"

"Oh no," Karina chuckled. "Now if you will excuse me…"

"Sure, Karina. See you in the morning."

Chapter Three

The First Test

The next morning, Xongrelan and Damone met with Henry to teach him how to throw a spear. Damone watched with folded arms while Xongrelan instructed the boy. Xongrelan explained the type of spear they were using was a pilum.

"Aw shoot. I'm never gonna get this," Henry shouted, after what seemed like twenty minutes of many misses.

"Focus, Henry. Just stay calm and focus," Xongrelan said, while picking up the pilum. It was embedded in the soggy grass just below an archery target.

"Xongrelan is right," Damone added. "It takes time and practice and you will be getting plenty of that," Damone said with a grin.

"It might be easy for you guys 'cause you've been doing this a lot longer than me. I just hope I've enough time to get it right."

"Everyone has to start somewhere. Even the best spearmen are not good on their first attempts. Here, try again." Xongrelan handed Henry the pilum. "Now concentrate, boy. First grab it in the middle of the shaft. Bring your arm back beyond your head with the tip of the pilum just behind your ear. Concentrate on whatever ring you want to hit but if you can, try and aim for the gold circle in the middle."

Henry stared at the colored rings, directing all his concentration on the bullseye.

"When ready, throw the spear wherever you want it to go, but not too hard."

"Okay, Xongrelan. I'll give it a shot." Henry then fixed his sights on the gold circle in the rainbow of rings and let the pilum soar. For the few seconds he watched in eager anticipation. *Please let it land right! Please!*

It did.

"Well done! We will make a master spearman out of you yet," Xongrelan said.

"Gee thanks. Maybe it was beginner's luck."

"You have to give yourself more credit than that," a female voice said from behind.

Henry spun around to see Karina standing there with a smile of approval. "What do you think, Karina? Will I make it?"

"With a little more practice you will be bringing back more catches than Xongrelan and Damone. Xongrelan, could young Henry go hunting with you and Damone today? It would give him a chance to put into practice what he has learned."

"Certainly, ma'am. We will teach him how to hunt with a bow."

"Be careful when letting him use it. We would not want any accidents to happen."

"We will take good care of him," Damone replied.

"Cool. When do we leave?"

"As soon as Xongrelan and Damone are ready. Do as they say at all times. Is that understood?"

"Yeah, sure. I understand."

"Good. Carry on with your training and good hunting."

"Thanks, Karina."

The woman waved goodbye as she turned and left. Henry picked up the spear again.

"So how long have you been doing this?" Henry asked Xongrelan.

"What, teaching people to use the pilum?"

"No, being a soldier."

"Ah, about thirty years now."

"You Damone?"

"Since I was twelve. We are conscripted into the army at that age in our world and have to serve and train until we are eighteen."

"Man, that must be tough."

"It was but I am stronger because of joining."

"Do you ever regret it?" Henry put the question to Xongrelan.

"Being a soldier? Had no choice really."

Henry threw the spear; it landed just underneath the red circle. "Damn it," he yelled, disappointed.

Xongrelan picked it up.

"Hard luck. You are getting there, though," Damone said.

"What did you mean, you had no choice?" Henry asked Xongrelan. *Wait, maybe I shouldn't have asked that.* "You don't have to tell me if you don't want to."

Xongrelan gave the pilum to Henry again. "No, it is fine. I have come to terms with it. I was unfaithful to my wife. In Nevarom that is a crime."

"So, you were sent to the dungeon?"

"No, I was given two choices: the dungeons or join the army and let me tell you, even the toughest Jenorme would not last a month in those cells. Rats as big as boars run around the place and eat you alive."

"Oh, okay." Henry shivered at the thought of meeting a rat from Nevarom. He stared ahead, sizing up the shot.

"In hindsight, it was the best thing that happened. I made some good friends and I appreciated my wife more. So let that be a lesson to you: never break the heart of the one you love."

"Got it." Henry threw the pilum. It landed in the bullseye. "Yes," he roared, punching the air.

"Well done, Henry. Want another try?" Xongrelan asked.

"Sure do. I'm feeling lucky."

* * *

DANIEL

Tracey closed her chamber's door. While turning a corner down the hallway, she bumped into Daniel.

"Oh sorry," she said. Tracey was at the top step of the stairs when Daniel called.

"Tracey, is it?"

"Yeah," she replied.

"Can I talk to you?"

"Sure, if you don't get all snobby on me again."

"Sorry for the way I spoke to you a few days ago. I am not usually like that to a lady."

"Are you really sorry?" Tracey replied sarcastically.

"What do you mean?"

"Well according to you, you're better than most boys, right?"

Daniel rolled his eyes before sighing. "You are not going to make this easy for me, are you?"

Tracey's unimpressed expression never shifted.

"Look, I am sorry, really but if you do not want to believe me, then fine."

Tracey's tone softened, her gaze became more amiable. "Okay, I believe you."

"Thank you. I will try and change. It will not be easy."

"My dad says change never is. Don't be a jerk to people anymore...and you never know, girls just might like you then."

"Well, I *am* handsome." Tracey glared at him once more. "Sorry. I will try not to speak like that anymore."

"It's okay to be confident but speaking like that doesn't impress anyone, least of all girls. Take my word for it."

"I know... and I appreciate that. Thank you. I will take my leave now." He bowed before going down the stairs, taking two steps at a time.

* * *

On horseback they rode through the forest of Egorthinia, which was an hour from town. Henry had Jasper behind him on the saddle. The cat being a natural hunter had insisted on joining them. Trees in this forest were larger than but not as beautiful as those in other forests. Many were bare with only thin, skeletal branches. Those that were fortunate to have leaves, however, had luminous colors of green, gold, orange, and yellow. Vines creeped up and around some trunks. Mushrooms sprouted from the bottom of some tree trunks but Henry didn't dare try one of them in case they were poisonous. Bushes were plentiful too in Egorthinia and Henry wondered if it was safe to travel as there was ample room for an ambush. Then he remembered what Karina had told him about sunlight temporarily blinding Sadarkians if they ventured out by day.

"So this is the famous forest where the treaty was signed, huh?" Henry asked, looking about him in wonder.

"Indeed it is," Xongrelan said softly.

These trees must have witnessed it all, Henry thought.

"Xongrelan, do you know where exactly the signing took place?"

"Not too sure but it may have been somewhere to our right. Now please be quiet, you might scare away our dinner."

All four dismounted. They tied the horses' reins to a tree.

"Watch your step. Any noise you make might scare the animals," Damone advised quietly. "You will need this."

Henry was given a round wooden shield. It was heavy and cumbersome.

"What do I need this for?" Henry raised it while asking.

"For protection from any wild animals that might be about." Damone sniffed the air for any scent of an animal.

"Do you smell anything, Damone?" Xongrelan asked.

"Yes, I do. Over there."

"Yeah, I'm picking up something too. My sense of smell seems to be better here than it is back home. I know more stuff too," Jasper added. "I guess this place made me smarter. Now I'll be able to get the better of the dumb mutts at home. If we get back there."

The tranquillity of the forest was suddenly rent by a piercing cry.

"What was that?" Henry said startled.

"Not too sure," Xongrelan answered while glancing around.

"It sounded like a boy," Damone said. "I think I know where the scream came from. Follow me."

Without making too much noise, all four ran to where the cries had originated.

Damone suddenly dropped to the ground, motioning with his right hand for the others to do the same. Crawling military fashion, Henry soon saw why they moved low. Ahead of them were two burly men taunting and slapping around a boy. One was a little taller than the other. Henry guessed that they were brothers as they bore a similar appearance. They each had a sword in a scabbard.

"We will enjoy teaching you a lesson, eh, Kamak?" the brother on the left said.

"Damn right, Xaz. I am going to enjoy slitting your throat, boy."

"Damone, we gotta save him," Henry said.

"We will but I need your help."

"Er… but I don't have enough training yet."

"You can put what you have been taught so far into practice," Damone replied.

"But I'm not ready," Henry said, this time a little firmer.

"Now is not the time for doubting yourself. Take Xongrelan's pilum and you throw it when I fire an arrow."

"Wait, shouldn't Xongrelan do that? I don't want to miss or hurt that boy."

Xongrelan handed Henry his pilum. "No. Damone is right. Time to put your training to use."

Henry eyed the pilum nervously as he took it.

"I will aim for the one on the left and you aim at the one on the right," Damone said. "Just remember what Xongrelan taught you. You can do it. Are you ready?"

Henry nodded. He put the shield flat on the ground. The pilum was positioned behind his head as he'd been shown.

Damone nocked an arrow on the string. Pulling it towards his cheek, he gave one look at Henry to see if he was prepared and with a gulp, Henry nodded. Damone trained the sights on the bow on Kamak and released the arrow. It struck his target in the chest. Xaz turned, searching for the person who killed his friend.

Henry had not yet thrown the pilum. He froze, now even more afraid as their position was discovered.

"What are you waiting for? Throw," Damone barked.

Henry was still frozen.

Xaz reached for his sword. He grabbed the boy's neck.

"Do it!" Damone shouted.

The heavy pounding of Henry's heart drowned out Damone's orders.

Sweat leaked through the teen's pores.

The captured young boy stared at the sword, whimpering, as it was half drawn from the scabbard.

"Throw it, Henry," Damone yelled as the thug's weapon was now fully drawn.

"I can't. I'm scared."

"Now is not the time for fear!"

In his peripheral vision, he could see Xongrelan's right hand almost ready to grab the pilum.

Pointing his blade at the boy's throat, Xaz raised the sword, ready to thrust it into the young boy.

"Now, Henry, *now*!" Damone said.

Henry's lips quivered as he threw the spear with a little too much force. It did not hit Xaz's chest as he had intended, but it did land on the arm holding the weapon. Xaz cried in pain and dropped the sword, trying to yank the spear from his arm, the boy was no longer a priority.

Damone lined up another arrow, sending it sailing to Xaz's forehead.

On one knee, the captive boy coughed and breathed in some air. Damone, Henry, Xongrelan and Jasper ran to him.

"Are you okay?" Henry asked, helping the boy to his feet.

"Yes, thank you," he replied hoarsely.

"What were you doing in these parts on your own?" Damone demanded sternly. "This area is dangerous."

"I was with my parents. We were traveling through the woods when those men stopped us. We gave them all our money but they killed my mother and father." He became a little choked up, finding it hard to speak amidst the sobbing but he composed himself and continued. "I ran as fast as I could but they caught me."

"What's your name?" Henry asked.

"Thomas," the short, raven-haired boy replied. Mud was smeared across his right cheek. His right eye sported a bright red bruise. A cut was on his left cheek.

"How far are your parents' bodies from here, Thomas?" Damone said.

"I am not too sure, sir. I just ran and ran and did not look back."

Henry had thought about asking Damone if they could bring his parents' bodies back to be buried but he feared that those brothers could have friends and they would be killed.

"Can we take him back to the castle? He's got nowhere else to go," Henry said.

"Yes. We will take you to King Argoth. We cannot exactly leave you here alone," Damone replied.

* * *

Two hours later, Henry went to check on Thomas. A guard stood outside it. "Hi. I'm just here to see Thomas."

"Sorry, but you cannot go in. Karina has ordered he be left rest for the next hour undisturbed."

"Okay. Thanks." *Guess I'll get something to eat and come back later.*

In the banquet hall thirty minutes later, Henry had almost finished the bowl of porridge. Tracey sat beside him. This time Tracey ate her breakfast, but Henry noted that she still ate with a little reluctance, taking small mouthfuls in between long bouts of just stirring her food.

"It doesn't taste as bad as it looks, huh?" Henry said.

"I guess not but I'd kill for some waffles and toast instead."

"Yeah, I'd love to be able to eat bacon and eggs but hey, I guess this has got to do."

"I don't know what you guys are complaining about," Jasper said. He licked his left paw and then his tail before continuing. "I'm getting better food here than back home. These guys could teach Mr. Anderson a thing or two on spoiling your cat. Beats nuts and milk any day."

Edward and Conor walked in, sitting down to eat their breakfast.

"Good morning, Mister Simmons and Miss Maxwell," Edward said merrily. "Oh, and Jasper too." The Englishman winked at the cat. "I heard you went hunting earlier, Henry."

"Yeah," Henry said, not wanting to elaborate.

"Aye, we also heard you ran into a wee bit of trouble."

Miralda – the girl who brought Henry's clothes to him when he first arrived - served the airmen porridge. "Here you go, sir."

"Thanks," Conor said.

"Word gets around here fast, huh? I got scared and almost got us and a boy killed," Henry replied to Edward's question.

"Fear in battle is a natural thing," Edward said. "I remember my first time in aerial combat at fifteen thousand feet. We were fighting the Germans and I was scared stiff. Luckily, everything turned out all right, even if we did lose some men."

"Like my father used to say when I was a wee lad," Conor added, "a little fear is a good thing."

"Yeah," Tracey joined in, "don't be so hard on yourself, Henry."

"Sure." Henry replied, his words not fully convincing.

A soldier entered and announced, "Stand for His Majesty King Argoth and Her Majesty Queen Cyren."

Henry wiped his face with a napkin and stood. So did Edward, Conor and Tracey.

King Argoth entered after Queen Cyren. He had short black hair, gray in places and a beard. Argoth wore a purple tunic with a gold rimmed neck hidden under a weighty gold chain. The king looked pallid and shivered despite wearing a heavy bearskin coat. Henry guessed the man was in his mid-50s.

"Be seated," King Argoth said in a weak voice. "So you are the new arrivals my wife has told me about?"

"Yes, Your Majesty," Edward answered on their behalf.

Argoth studied each of them.

Henry saw Cyren whisper something into Argoth's ear.

"Young man, come to my side, please," Argoth said.

Henry moved back his chair and came to the king's side.

"You are a handsome boy. He reminds me of our son."

"Thank you, Your Majesty."

"Do the people know about them?" he asked Cyren.

"Not yet. Zymbion will let us know when the time is right to tell them." He returned his gaze to Henry again, briefly glancing at his breakfast. "Please be seated. Your breakfast will grow cold."

* * *

An hour later, Henry decided to check up on Thomas. The guard who was posted outside the rescued boy's room allowed Henry to enter.

Thomas was sitting on the bed sinking his teeth into a juicy red apple. He placed the apple down, standing to attention when Henry opened the door and came in.

"Good morning, sir," Thomas said.

"Relax, man, sit down. I'm not royalty or anything."

"Certainly, sir. Thank you for saving me yesterday."

"Hey, it's no prob. I just wish I didn't freeze when throwing the spear. Sorry about that." Henry looked at the bruises and wounds on Thomas's right thigh. "How's your leg?"

"The pain is almost gone."

"That's great. Maybe later we can do something together."

"I would like that, Sir Henry."

"Just call me Henry. I'm not a knight."

"All right, Henry, I would love to join you later when I feel better."

"Okay. So, do you mind if I ask what you were doing in that forest?"

"Me and my parents always collected apples and other fruit there. That is the only part of the forest that has food like that. My father told me Zymbion blessed that area with lots of fruit years ago."

"Did anybody else go with you, like brothers or sisters?"

"I have no sisters or brothers. Just me."

"So what do you do for fun?"

"I would go hunting with my father and our dog, Teya." Thomas lowered his head. "But both are gone now." His words were laced with sadness.

"I'm so sorry, man." Henry looked around the room, trying to think of something to break the awkward silence. "Okay, Thomas, I better let you rest some more. I'll see you later, okay?"

"All right, Henry. See you soon."

Henry returned to spear practice with Xongrelan and tried to rebuild his confidence. Henry had been training for only ten minutes when Karina paid him a visit.

"Master Henry, may I speak with you a moment, please?"

Henry passed the spear to Xongrelan and walked with Karina to the sorceress's room. From a bronze chest, Karina removed the coin.

"After what happened yesterday in the forest, I think it is best you have this." She placed the coin in Henry's palm.

"Are you sure? I mean, I don't know about keeping it on me. It's a pretty big responsibility."

"This coin was meant for you. I think it will protect you when you are in danger."

Once again Henry could feel the pulsing from it. "Whenever I hold it, I get this feeling of power. Is it supposed to do that?"

"I presume so, but tell nobody about the coin or that you have it."

"Don't worry, I won't." Henry slid it into a pocket in his tunic. "I'd better get back to my training."

"I will meet you at the training area tomorrow morning to show you how to use it."

"Okay, looking forward to it."

* * *

Henry woke up with the first rays of sunshine breaking through the butter yellow curtains in his room.

"Morning, sunshine," Jasper greeted, sitting up, tapping his tail on the ground.

"Hey, Jas', good morning."

"If they give me a juicy steak it will be," he joked.

"You don't ask for much, do you?" Henry returned with a grin.

"I can't help it if I have good taste."

"Yeah, sure." Henry rolled his eyes heavenwards while wondering how Mr. Anderson kept such a fussy cat satisfied back home. The boy whistled as he put on a cream-colored tunic which he stuffed inside his maroon-colored trousers.

"Somebody's happy this morning," Jasper said.

"Well that's because Karina's gonna show me how to use the coin."

"Oh, that's great. Then you'll be able to make yourself useful 'round here."

Henry shot Jasper a look, trying to figure out if the cat was being sarcastic or not.

"Well it's gonna be cool. You can come and watch me if you want."

"May as well. Got nothing better to do. Not interested in chasing mice here. Can we eat first?"

"Sure."

After a hearty breakfast of porridge and freshly baked bread for Henry and thick chunks of chicken meat for Jasper, both met Karina in the training area. She stood leaning against the fence, reading a bulky tome. Henry thought she looked attractive for a woman her age in her white shirt and black leather trousers. A violet jerkin was over her shirt. She raised her head when she heard Henry and Jasper approaching.

"Ah, you came. Good. Did you bring the coin?"

"Yeah, it's here." He took it out from a pocket in his trousers, holding it in his palm.

"Good man. Now to make sure nobody sees what we are doing here." With a wave of her right arm, a black, shimmering wall surrounded the training area. Henry thought that this might raise suspicions but did not question the sorceress's motives.

"First thing you need to do is relax." Karina placed a hand on his left shoulder. "I know you are nervous so breathe."

Henry sucked in two deep breaths, exhaling each slowly.

"Good. Do that again."

Henry repeated his inhalations and exhalations, his nerves calmed and mind became more focused.

"Excellent. Breathing is a huge part of magic. You have to have a clear, calm mind before using the coin." Karina returned to leaning up against the fence which surrounded the training area. She picked up the book. "Do you see this? I want you to make one like it using the coin's power."

Henry shut his eyes, holding an image of the book in his mind. He felt a tingling sensation in his fingers as the coin pulsed harder. He heard Jasper gasp and opened his eyes. The book appeared for a few seconds hovering over his hands before disappearing.

"Focus, Master Henry. Focus is key. I want you to make the book appear beside your friend there."

"You can't make it appear beside her, Henry, can ya?" Jasper said with a nervous chuckle. "I don't want something falling down on me."

"He will not let that happen," Karina said.

"No, Jas', I won't."

"Close your eyes again and concentrate." Karina said. "Focus on your breathing; once you have mastered that, everything will fall into place."

"Got it." Sucking in another mouthful of air, with his eyes shut he exhaled. Feeling the coin pulse faster once more, Henry kept his mind centered on the book appearing beside Jasper. That familiar tingling sensation returned to his fingertips but Henry remained focused. A few seconds later, there was a *thud* close to where Jasper sat.

"Whoa, you did it, Henry!"

"Yes, congratulations, Master Henry. You have mastered concentration. Well done. Now for something a little harder." She pointed to an archery target opposite where the boy stood. "I want you to hit the bullseye with a fireball using the coin."

"A fireball?" Henry said, his voice raised in concern. "Wouldn't that be dangerous?"

"No. I placed a spell on the target so it will not catch fire. Go on." Karina gave him a confident smile. "I know you can do it."

Henry shut his eyes, letting the coin's pulse guide his senses. His fingers tingled once more but this time each fingertip became hot, almost as if each were burning. Next he heard a spark. A great heat now came from above his palm. This caused him to open his eyes. Henry's mouth was agape as hovering above the right palm was a bright orange fireball.

Cool, Henry thought.

"Excellent. Now throw it at the target," Karina said.

Henry focused on the target in front of him, zeroing in on the gold circle at its center. Casting his arm back, he launched the fireball hitting its mark. It left a scorch mark but did not do any further damage.

"I did it!" Henry punched the air.

"Nice shot, Henry," Jasper said.

Karina walked towards the boy and stood in front of him. "I want you to think of something you fear."

"Why?"

"Just do it, please."

"Um… okay." He thought for a moment until the image of a fearsome animal entered his mind.

Karina smiled. "Thank you." She took a few steps back. With another wave of her right arm, a tiger appeared on the opposite side of the training area.

"Oh crap." He looked at Karina in dread. "K-K- Karina, wha- what are you doing?"

"This is what you feared most," she said.

"You tricked me! Are you trying to get us killed?" Henry asked.

"You will face dangerous situations while you are here so you will have to learn how to defend yourself."

The tiger growled, licking his lips, revealing large teeth. Its yellow eyes honed in on Henry and Jasper while ignoring Karina. After a brief intense stare, it moved towards them, now focusing on Jasper.

"What the hell? Karina, you gotta do something," Henry barked.

"You have the coin. Time to use it," she advised.

"But I don't know what to do," he snapped back.

"You do, just breathe."

"That's easy for you to say, lady. You're not about to be eaten alive!" Jasper retorted.

Okay, focus, Henry thought. I can do this.

The tiger roared again, making both Henry and Jasper jump. It walked closer, now halfway between its two intended victims.

Karina just leaned against the fence, keeping her concentration on the boy. "Remember what I said: focus is key."

Yeah, if I can live long enough to do it, Henry thought. Come on, get yourself together. Shutting his eyes and holding out his right hand again, he inhaled a long deep breath. Drowning out Jasper's cries along with the tiger's growls as it drew closer, Henry thought of an image of a fireball in his mind. His fingers tingled once more, growing hotter with each passing second. His palm was almost burning now when he heard a spark. This was followed by the crackling of a flame. Henry opened his eyes; hovering above his palm again was another lethal fireball.

Henry gasped as the tiger was only mere inches away, its tongue again licking its lips.

"Henry, throw that damn thing now!" Jasper cried, hiding behind the teen.

God, I hope this works, Henry thought.

Unleashing one last fearsome roar, the tiger launched itself at Henry and Jasper. The boy threw the fireball, hitting the tiger's stomach. The animal disappeared into a dark cloud of mist, just as its teeth were about to pierce the flesh on Henry's face.

Jasper cowered, still looking away as Henry said, "It's okay, Jas', it's gone."

"Phew, I thought we were dead there."

Henry wiped sweat from his forehead as Karina clapped.

"You did it, Master Henry. You managed to use the coin in the face of danger. I knew you could do it. Now you are ready to face anything that comes your way. But still practice your breathing." She waved her right hand; the black shimmering wall surrounding them receded. "That is it for today. You did well. Go back to your room and relax."

"Thanks Karina." *I need a rest after that. That was close, too close!*

* * *

In the months that followed, Henry and Thomas developed a great camaraderie. They played and went hunting together. Sometimes when they were alone, Thomas would talk about how he still missed his parents and dog, Teya.

Henry and the airmen were learning to master the sword along with other weapons but Henry had the upper hand with the coin. It gave him the natural ability to handle weapons such as swords and bows. Every time he'd hold it, Henry would stop, take a few deep breaths as Karina showed him. The coin's pulse would grow stronger, thumping against his palm, its power creeping up his arm, spilling out into every fiber of his body. Now he and the weapon were one and he swung it with grace and skill, becoming ever adept with each practice session.

One day Henry and Thomas were at weapons training, deep in the midst of a swordfight. Jasper, Tracey and Hannorah watched the two boys fighting. A scorching hot sun bearing down on both combatants and spectators. Back and forth the bout went, each of Thomas's thrust and swipes met with deft counters by Henry.

After twenty minutes, both boys stopped, the heat sapping their energy. Henry held up a hand. "Wait… hold up. No more… okay?" he said, taking in a gulp full of air while wiping sweat from his soaking forehead. "Let's take a break."

"Yes, let's."

Henry and Thomas sat down on the sandy ground inside the wooden fence where the soldiers also trained, and joined the three other spectators. Henry's tunic clung to his back. He took a drink from a metal canister.

"You guys did great," Tracey remarked.

"Thanks," Henry said.

"Keep it up and the Sadarkians will not stand a chance," Hannorah said.

"I hope so." Henry took another swig from the canister.

"Hey, go easy on that, Henry. Last time you drank too much water you were peeing all night and kept me awake," Jasper scolded him.

"Thanks Jas'." Henry's cheeks went scarlet. "I'm sure that's just what these guys needed to hear." He cleared his throat. "It sure is hot."

"Yeah, hotter than it usually is back home," Tracey replied.

"Too warm for practicing," Thomas added before accepting the canister from Henry and drank some water. "This reminds me of a time me, father and mother went for a ride through Harma Woods."

"Where's that?" Henry asked.

"About two hours ride from here," Thomas replied. "We used to go there on hot days like this. It would take you to a lake. We would eat there and pray afterwards." Thomas's voice trailed off, his gray eyes focusing on the ground. Henry could see his friend attempting to hold back the tears.

"You really miss them, huh?" Tracey asked.

"Every day." Thomas cleared his throat and focused on the tower looming over the training area. "What is in that tower over there?"

"There's a diamond there given to these people by their god or something," Henry answered. "It's supposed to protect this place from Sadarkians."

"Have you ever seen it?" Thomas asked.

"Nobody is allowed to go near it except guards on duty," Hannorah said.

"I would love to see the diamond sometime," Thomas said.

"It would be cool to see," Henry added, then he thought about his coin. *Maybe we could sneak in using the coin's magic.* "What if we try and take a quick look at it."

"This is a bad idea," Hannorah warned. "You know the rules."

"Hannorah is right, Henry. I do not want you to get into trouble," Thomas said.

"Yeah, I know the rules but we won't get caught. I promise." Henry countered with a confident grin.

"Well, if you want to, Henry, then I am in," Thomas replied.

"Then, I will not be taking part in this," Hannorah told the two boys and got up to leave.

"I'm with Hannorah on this one," Tracey said standing too. "I think you guys are crazy doing it. Come on, Hannorah, let's go." Tracey and Hannorah made their way back to their rooms.

Thomas stood up. "I guess it is just me, you and your furry friend there. Lead the way, Henry."

"I don't know about this, Henry," Jasper said. "If we get caught, we're screwed."

"I know but we have to have some fun too. And anyway, we're only having a quick look."

The entrance to the tower was easy to find since anyone could go into it, but anything above the fourth floor was restricted to guards and royalty. The hallways were richly decorated with sometimes blue or magenta carpets and its walls were painted with what looked like gold paint. There was a long spiraling stairway in the corner of the first floor that opened up onto the entrance of each floor.

Henry, Jasper and Thomas had at last reached the sixth floor. Henry tapped the coin hidden in his pocket, secretly wishing for all three to be invisible. He held his breath as they reached the fourth floor, guards with spears and oval steel shields standing two feet away from the entrance. More guards were positioned Henry guessed about 100 feet away further down the hallway. This was more than what was seen on previous floors. Henry, Jasper and Thomas stopped, each waiting a second to see if the guards would notice them. When they hadn't, Thomas asked:

"Why are they not looking at us?" he whispered.

Henry had to think fast of a way to avoid telling Thomas about using the coin. "Oh...it's a trick Karina thought me."

"Nice trick."

"Can you guys shut up and get moving?" Jasper whispered firmly. "I wanna stay alive."

Slowly they continued to creep up to the sixth floor, peeping around the corner when they got there. They stood still as a guard walked past them. A further soldier stood in front of a door with a diamond symbol carved on it.

"Well I am done for the evening," said the soldier who just passed them.

He looked to be in his 40s, battle-weary with a scar on his left cheek.

"Lucky you. I still got a few more hours left," the guard by the door replied.

"See you tomorrow, Matthew."

"Bye."

"That must be where the diamond is kept but I guess this is the end of the line," Henry admitted. Then inspiration struck him. "Jasper, you run on down the hallway and go around the corner. When you're a good bit away from the guard, meow or say something to make him come to you. He won't see you so don't worry."

"I am not gonna lose my life on this."

"You won't. All you have to do is distract the guard," Henry said. "He won't see you so you won't get caught. Just do it long enough for us to get in."

"I don't know, Henry..." Jasper answered.

"Come on, Jas'. Please?"

Jasper sighed. "Oh all right. But I'm sleeping on the bed next time and you're on the floor."

"You got it."

"Here goes nothin'." Jasper walked passed the guard slowly and wandered around the corner to the right, walking out of sight. Henry heard a "meow" and so too did the guard.

"What was that?" Matthew said before investigating.

Seizing their chance, the boys half sprinted to the door, making sure it didn't creak when they opened and closed it.

The floorboards, lime in color, were thick and heavy. The room had a long dusty wooden table to the right and an empty cupboard. A chair was beside it. In the center on a platform was a glass case with the multi-colored diamond.

As Henry stepped closer, a ray of sunshine shone through the stained-glass window, illuminating Zymbion's diamond. Both boys went slack-jawed by its splendor.

"That's awesome," Henry said.

"It is more beautiful than anything I have ever seen. Do you think we could hold it?"

"I don't know." Henry knew there wouldn't be any alarms like in museums back home, but he was still wary of touching it. Henry examined where the diamond was contained, his eyes roving over every inch of the glass case and its surroundings. There did not appear to be anything that would trigger an alarm.

"Do you want to touch it?" Henry asked, now confident that no alarms would be tripped.

"Yes, as long as it will not get you into trouble."

"It won't. Come on."

Henry knew the platform was a bit too high for him to reach the diamond. He noticed the chair in the far corner but it didn't look sturdy enough to hold his weight.

"I need your help. Do you think you could give me a hand getting up to it?"

"Sure. Climb on my shoulders. But wait, do you think there is some spell on it to stop us touching it?"

"I don't know. Guess we're gonna find out."

Henry climbed onto Thomas's shoulders and sat on them.

"Whoa-" Henry said as the boys stumbled back and tried to find their balance. When Thomas had settled under Henry's weight, he walked to the glass case. Henry lifted the glass lid while taking the diamond from an indigo-colored cushion on which it rested.

Stepping back from the platform, Thomas let Henry climb down. Both boys looked at the diamond. Little streaks of refracted light flashed across their faces.

Thomas stood back for a moment.

"Wow, it's really beautiful," Henry remarked.

"It is."

"We'd better put it back now before someone catches us. Help me up again, will ya?"

"No. Instead," Thomas's voice altered to that of a deep, menacing tone. "I will take that."

Before Henry's eyes, his former friend grew in size, transforming into a Sadarkian.

Oh crap, what've I done? Henry thought.

Thomas snatched the diamond and struck Henry with a hard right hand, which felt like he was hit by a boulder. It knocked him out.

*　*　*

CONTZAK'S HOUSE

In a valley north west of Little Zargothia where Slyvanon and other troops waited to meet with the spy, Slyvanon thought about when he was young. Of course, he wasn't always called that name. His real name was Sylvam. He did not have many happy memories as a child but had a bad one that haunted him at night. It was many years before the Great War began. One day, while walking home, he was beat up by four human adult male bullies, resulting in a permanently crippled back. They knocked him down, kicking and punching him. Their jeering still rung in his ears while he slept.

    This brutal beating did not engender any sympathy from his father, Porok.

"Look at him. He is useless to us now," Porok often said. "I wanted a son that could go hunting with me and provide for us, not a cripple like him!"

After putting up with this verbal abuse for three years, Sylvam could take no more and ran away from home. An old mage named Contzak took him in, giving him shelter and food in exchange for helping him around the house. Contzak showed young Sylvam basic magic but when the old mage left to go to town, Sylvam read books on the dark arts, practicing them when Contzak was not around.

Sylvam knew if he were to be successful in using dark magic in getting his revenge on humans, Contzak would have to be killed because he was the only one who could stop him because they were his spells. One day Sylvam made some stew, collecting poisonous berries from the forest. Once the stew was almost done, he put the berries into it. He sat, watching Contzak eat the broth, waiting for the berries to do their job. Soon, Contzak began choking and fell off his chair, gasping for breath.

Sylvam knelt down beside him. "Sorry, master," he said before covering Contzak's mouth, hurrying the old mage's death. Sylvam left the house and made his way to Prince Gronach's town. Many mocked him because of his appearance calling him, "Slyvanon" meaning, "Sly cripple". At first it made him grit his teeth in anger but he used that to fuel his determination to prove them all wrong and gain his revenge. Slyvanon prayed one night to Hernacious to help him in his plan of ridding Zargothia forever of any human presence. Hernacious answered his call. Together they formed a deadly pact with the god granting an extra seventy years onto Slyvanon's life.

Slyvanon easily won over the young prince with his magic spells. Soon Prince Gronach brought him into the inner circle, making him a personal advisor. As soon as Gronach became king, Slyvanon poisoned the king's mind and made him do his bidding, which began the war against the humans.

So far all of Slyvanon's plans had worked. He would rather have had Zakarius killed Argoth when he had the chance, but he knew other opportunities to end Argoth's life would present themselves. For now, the destruction of the town's defenses was enough. Once the shield was down, he could kill Henry and Argoth, and then he would finally have the revenge he sought for so long.

Snapping out of his reverie, Slyvanon used a puddle of water for a scrying spell. It showed him the events that had unfolded in Argoth's hidden haven. The diamond's magic prevented him from learning its location, only allowing Slyvanon to see the spy. He had received word from 'Thomas' the night before by a raven with a note tied to its leg. The message said that the spy planned to steal the diamond today.

Slyvanon erased the puddle's images and grinned in triumph. His plan had worked. He knew that Argoth or Cyren would never leave an abandoned human boy to wander the woods alone and without food, so Slyvanon used this to his advantage. Using one of his spells, he transformed two of his guards into human form. All that needed to be done now was to ask Hernacious to break the diamond's magic, revealing Argoth's secret location. Then it would be taken to Zakarius.

* * *

Henry awakened with a thumping pain in the rear of his skull.

Cyren was at his bedside, dabbing his forehead with a wet sponge. Jasper sat at the end of the bed beside Henry's feet. Henry's head was lowered, too ashamed to look at those around him.

He tried to sit up but Cyren's firm hand placed on his chest prevented him.

"Try not to move too much. You took quite a blow," Cyren said, dabbing the sponge yet again.

Edward and Conor were each sitting on a seat, Karina was staring into a sacred scroll. Hannorah along with Tracey, looked at Henry, worry etched on both girls' faces.

Argoth on the other hand was standing at the end of the bed, sour-faced. Henry knew he was furious. He had a right to be.

Cyren stopped dabbing Henry's forehead and dried it with a towel. "Tell me, young man, how the diamond got into Sadarkian hands?" she asked in a calm voice.

"Thomas tricked me into looking at the diamond. We just wanted to see it. I didn't know he was going to take it. What happened after he knocked me out?"

Cyren filled him in. "He jumped out the window and stole a horse. He used some explosive powder to make a hole in the wall to escape."

"I'm so sorry, Your Majesties. We were only trying to have a bit of fun in seeing the diamond." Henry still could not make eye contact as he apologized.

"Fun?" Argoth scoffed. He took a deep breath before continuing. "How did you get past the guards from the fourth floor onwards?"

Henry swallowed hard. "I used some of the coin's magic and then used Jasper to distract the guard outside the diamond room."

"So you were a part of this too?" Argoth asked Jasper.

"Yup… I'm the idiot who went along with it," Jasper replied, also too afraid to meet Argoth's fearsome gaze.

"So this was all part of some childish game?" Argoth barked.

"How was I supposed to know Thomas was Sadarkian?" Henry said.

"I do not expect you to know that; I did expect you to follow the rules. Nobody but guards and royalty are allowed above the fourth floor. Because of you, I have had to increase the number of guards on the fourth, fifth and sixth floor as well as send men out into the forest to warn us if Sadarkians approach. The people out there, the very people you were brought here to save, could now be in serious danger!"

Karina intervened. "This may not be the boy's fault."

"Are you taking his side, Karina?"

"No, Your Majesty. I think he was meant to do it."

"What are you babbling on about?" Argoth said.

"It says here that the stealing of the diamond is a test to prove who is the most special amongst the Foretold Ones."

"Give me that." Argoth swiped it away from Karina's hand. The king read aloud: "In a moment of deception, the Diamond of Zymbion will be stolen. The one chosen by the Elders will be tasked with going to retrieve it, thus testing if he is worthy of fulfilling his role." Argoth let the scroll slip from his fingers and it fell onto the floor. "Have we not been tested enough?"

"I can understand why you are angry, sire, but it is Zymbion's will, not ours," Karina reminded him.

"I know I screwed up big time, Your Majesty, and I'm really sorry." Henry said. "But if this is some test I gotta do to save the people here, then I'll do it. I don't know how I'm gonna do it but I will. I wanna make it up to them and you."

Argoth swiveled his rings and exhaled a lengthy frustrated breath. "Sorry for being hard on you but we have been safe here since we came and now we are all in danger." He paused again, taking a deep breath before continuing in a calm voice. "I keep forgetting you are young. It must be difficult for you being so far away from home and having to cope with all of…this. But I must warn you, Henry, getting the diamond back will be difficult."

"I know, but if that scroll is anything to go by, it's what I'm here to do."

"Henry's right, sir. He must do it but I suggest we give him some men to help him," Karina advised.

The king considered this for a moment. "Xongrelan, I want you to go to the stables and prepare horses and dracorns. Then round up ten men. You will be Henry's escort and protection."

"Wait, my head still feels dizzy. Is there anything you can give me?" Henry asked.

Karina looked at her apprentice and said, "Hannorah, if you will?"

"Yes, mistress." She sat down beside Henry and put her soft palm on his forehead. "You are going to feel a little dizzy for a few seconds after this but then you will be fine. I promise." Hannorah's gentle smile put Henry at ease. He almost recoiled when the whites of her eyes turned sky blue and her fingertips began to warm up. The heat penetrated Henry's skin, for a second the thumping pain increased, but soon passed.

Hannorah's eyes returned to normal as she removed her hand. Just as she had warned him, Henry felt nauseous, the room swaying a little but in a few heartbeats this passed too.

"Are you all right, Master Henry?" Karina asked.

"Yeah, I'm good."

"Then let's get moving and get that diamond back before it is too late," Argoth said.

"I will send one of my servants to help you with the armor," Cyren told Henry.

"Okay. Thank you, Your Majesty."

"Be careful, okay? Come back safe and sound," Tracey said, placing a hand on his arm. He could feel more behind the touch of her fingers on his arm. He saw in her eyes a genuine concern for him. *Does she like me?*

"I will," he replied.

When everyone left, Henry got out of bed and began to get dressed.

* * *

Daniel waited until everyone had left before opening the door, shutting it behind him once he was in the room. Henry paused as he was getting dressed and groaned upon seeing him enter.

"What do you want, Daniel?"

"Oh, not much, really… just to say I was right all along. If you are supposed to save us, then we are all in trouble. I mean, you put all of my family and friends out there in danger."

"You don't have to rub it in, okay? I feel bad enough as it is."

"Now if it were me on the other hand-"

"Well it's not so get over it," Henry said while putting on his shirt.

A knock came to the door.

"Come in," Henry said and a tall male Volark with long, baby pink hair, wearing a golden-bronze colored tunic with matching trousers, entered. "My name is Vyma. Her Majesty sent me to help you with your armor."

"As I was saying before I was interrupted," Daniel continued. "If it were me, then I would not have put us in this position. I would have behaved like a true hero is supposed to."

"Yeah well, you're not in this position. I'm going to make things right."

"I doubt it," Daniel scoffed.

"Just get out. I'm kind of in a hurry here."

Daniel threw Henry one last demeaning glance before leaving.

Thank God he's gone. I don't need this right now, Henry thought. With Vyma's help he was soon armored up properly.

Tracey wanted to come but Argoth forbid it as she wasn't fully trained yet.

Henry found the mail shirt and armor were heavy and warm, the open-faced helmet with the nasal guard made him sweat. Still, he understood they would protect him if he came under attack. He dreaded the task of recovering the diamond as he left his room.

* * *

Tracey sat in the banquet hall, stirring the porridge which was big lumps of grain bobbing up and down in a sea of creamy goo. Her mind drifted towards home. She wondered what her father was doing now. Did he worry about her or even noticed that she was missing?

Heavy footsteps entering the banquet hall snapped Tracey out of her momentary homesickness.

"Good mornin', Tracey," greeted Conor.

"Is it?" she answered, flatly.

"Is what?"

"Is it a good morning?"

"Oh," He sat down beside her, casting a sympathetic gaze. "Something the matter, love?"

Miralda arrived with a wooden bowl of hot piping porridge for Conor. "There you go, sir," she said, smiling as she placed it in front of him.

"Thank you," he replied with a nod of gratitude. Conor waited until Miralda left to continue his discussion. "Well?"

Tracey kept staring at her bowl. "Well what?"

"Is something the matter?"

"No… yes… I don't know. This place is screwing with my head."

"I know the look of homesickness when I see it."

"That obvious?"

"Very." He blew on a spoonful of porridge. "So who're ya missin'?"

"My dad, friends, everyone."

"Aye, know how you feel, lass. I miss my girlfriend and friends too." Conor took another spoonful, swallowing it.

In her peripheral vision she saw him watching her as she just concentrated on her bowl.

"What are you doing today?" he asked.

"Got more sparring training soon. You?"

"I'm free this afternoon. Why don't I spar with you?"

Tracey shifted uncomfortably in her chair. "Uh, I don't know…"

"It'll give us a wee chance to get to know one another better."

"Oh okay," she said with false enthusiasm.

"Great, see you in an hour." Conor continued eating. "Oh, and I'd eat that too if I were you. You'll need it." He winked with a mischievous grin.

An hour later, Tracey sat on a fence waiting for Conor. Bored, Tracey tapped the tip of her wooden sword on the top of her sandal.

"Sorry for keeping you waitin'," Conor said.

"It's okay. Wasn't waiting long anyway," Tracey replied, still staring at her feet.

"Are you ready?"

"Sure." Tracey got down off the fence and looked puzzled as she saw Conor with his fists raised. "Where's your sword?"

"Won't be needing that today."

"Why?"

"Cos I'm gonna show you how to defend yourself if you lose your weapon. Hit me."

"What?" Tracey said, her voice raised in disbelief.

"Hit me." This time he beckoned her with his right hand.

"You serious?"

"Very. What you waitin' for?"

Tracey swiped her wooden sword to the right. Conor caught her arm and with both hands, threw her over his shoulder.

"Ow," she yelled, rubbing her back to ease the pain after hitting the ground hard.

Conor kicked her weapon away out of reach. "Now let's see you fight without it."

Tracey wiped some sand from her forehead before looking at Conor with determination in her eyes. She stood up, now riding her clothes of sand. She shook her limbs, adopting a karate stance, her right foot in front of the left.

Conor eyed the girl's movements closely, taking a quick jab to the right. Tracey bobbed her head to avoid it.

"So, are you used to hitting girls?" she joked.

"Nah, but you're going to need all the training you can get. Those ugly bastards aren't going to go easy on you."

"So I take that as a yes then." Tracey off-loaded a quick succession of jabs. Conor avoided them all except the last one which caught him unaware on his jaw. He stumbled back a few steps.

"Nice one," he said, rubbing his jaw. "But you're not gonna do that again."

"Wanna bet?" Tracey lunged in again with another hard right hook but Conor sidestepped it, delivering a slap of his own.

Tracey rubbed her stinging cheek.

"You don't lunge in like an oaf. You watch every step, girlie, not unless you want to meet a quick death."

"I'll remember that." She did not have time to get comfortable as Conor delivered another punch to the stomach. Tracey was equal to it, however, catching his hand, wrenching it to the right, following up with a quick karate kick to his stomach.

Conor hit the ground with an expression of surprise. Panting, he got up. "Nice move. Where did you learn that?"

"My dad knows karate so he taught me. Said it'd keep me safe from jerks." They began circling each other again, each paying close attention to the other's stance. "Where did you learn how to fight?"

"I was picked on as a wee lad. My father taught me as well. He was a boxer. Did well for himself; won a few belts in his time. When I joined the air force, they showed us some moves too in case we went down in enemy territory."

"I see. How long were you in the air force before coming here?"

Conor stood still for a few seconds, expressionless, and then feigned another right hook causing Tracey to jump. "Always be ready. Don't let your concentration slip." Again they circled one another. "To answer your question, about four years. I always wanted to be a soldier. My granddad was a general in the Scottish army and I wanted to be a soldier too. I love planes so that was a way in for me."

"So being in the army is a kind of a family tradition?"

"You could say that. Anyway, enough talkin'. Let's do what I came here to do, prepare you to fight. Cos you haven't shown me anything so far that says you'll survive out there. " Conor shifted his weight behind another stinging punch, connecting with the girl's soft cheek but Tracey was ready for its follow up as she ducked, delivering an eye-watering uppercut into the Scot's midsection.

Conor doubled over, clutching his crotch.

"Guess my fighting skills don't suck now, huh?" Tracey said with arms folded. A proud grin spread across the girl's face. She waited a few moments for Conor to catch his breath before asking, "Want to continue?"

Red-faced and with spit drooling from a corner of his mouth, Conor waved her away. "No… I think that's all… for today."

"You sure?" Conor gave a thumbs up. "Cool. See you around." Tracey walked away smiling, proud that her deceptively innocent appearance fooled another man into thinking that she was weak.

* * *

Xongrelan and ten infantry soldiers with long swords and spears awaited Henry at the gate.

"Henry, we are ready to ride out when you are," Xongrelan said.

"I'm ready but we don't know where exactly 'Thomas' is."

"We have this to guide us." He held in his palm a black semi-oval gemstone that tapered to a point. Xongrelan gave it to Henry.

"How will this take us to him?"

"Karina gave me that to give to you. She said Zymbion gave that to her a while back. It will point us in the right direction as we get closer. Say these magic words to activate it." He removed from inside his belt a scroll which was rolled up and tied with a piece of chord.

Henry removed the chord, opening the scroll. "What do these words say?"

"Hermanicas triana tootalan."

"And that means…?"

"Show us the way," Xongrelan replied.

Henry gave the scroll back to Xongrelan. He closed his eyes, tightening his fingers around the stone. He shut his eyes while saying, "Hermanicas triana tootalan."

Without delay, Henry felt the stone vibrate from within his grasp. He opened his fingers and it floated in the air, acting as a compass, pointing to his right. Henry caught the make-shift compass and put it in a pouch attached to his belt.

"Cool. Okay. Let's go then."

"You will ride Madrin the dracorn," Xongrelan said to Henry.

The boy looked at the brown beast and saw its wings appear. "Um, do we have to take the dracorn? I'm afraid of heights," Henry admitted.

"I understand but you must take Madrin. It will be faster than riding normal horseback and right now, every second counts."

"Okay, I'll do it," Henry agreed. He got up on Madrin. Removing the stone from the pouch, it floated a few inches in front of him, again pointing to the right. The stone stayed hovering in front of him. He shook the reins and Madrin took flight.

Just as Xongrelan had said, the stone changed direction every few minutes until twenty minutes later they arrived at their destination. Henry put the magical make-shift compass into its pouch.

Henry and the soldiers were on a cliff top overlooking Slyvanon and his party below in a rocky U-shaped valley. He estimated that there were over 100 soldiers. Henry saw an old Sadarkian standing on a rock, both hands raised while holding the diamond.

"Who's that?" he asked Xongrelan.

"That is Slyvanon."

The soldiers were lined in several rows, kneeling in veneration. There were five black dragons sitting down near where Slyvanon stood. Scores of horses were also there. To Henry, it looked like some ritual was being carried out.

"This test will be harder than I thought," Xongrelan said.

"There's no way we can take on those guys. What do you think we should do, Xongrelan?" Henry asked.

"I think we have to sneak in. Do you think you could do some invisibility trick?"

"I can try but it's gonna be hard when I'm up high."

"With the power in that coin, it should not be too hard. Just concentrate. When you are low enough, you could maybe use the coin's magic to snatch it from him."

Henry took a shaky breath before replying, "Well, I guess it's worth a try. Here goes nothing. Wish me luck."

"You will do well, Henry. I believe in you," the Jenorme said, smiling and patting Henry's armor twice. Putting his right foot in the stirrup, Henry pulled himself up onto Madrin, swinging his other leg over.

"If you are caught, then we will provide cover for you from here but only for a few minutes," Xongrelan said.

"Got it." Henry stared at the distance from their position to the edge of the mountain and inhaled another long breath.

"Men, get into position," Xongrelan ordered. They cleared the way.

Henry shook the reins and Madrin galloped. Henry closed his eyes, wishing to become invisible. A gust of wind circled around them for a few seconds after Henry made his wish. Madrin jumped off, swooping down below.

* * *

Slyvanon held up the diamond and shouted, "Hernacious, behold the diamond of Zymbion. Break its magic."

It floated in the air. A bolt of thunder struck it. A ball of light quickly enveloped the diamond. Little streaks of lightning crashed within the ball that was surrounding the sacred object. The lightning stopped and the diamond drifted into Slyvanon's hands.

* * *

Malcolm, an archer in the watchtower was startled when the bubble appeared without warning leaving Little Zargothia exposed. He called to Sir Dreyfus.

"Sir, the veil has been lifted. We are visible now."

"I will tell the king at once." Sir Dreyfus ran to the throne room. "Your Majesty, the town is unprotected."

"When did this happen?" Argoth asked.

"Just now, sire."

Argoth's face was awash with panic. "Ring the town's bell. Get the men into formations. Tell all civilians to stay inside their homes. We must be ready for an attack."

* * *

Slyvanon cackled when the diamond floated back into his hands again when its magic had been broken. "It is done. Argoth's kind are now at our mercy!"

The soldiers cheered, grabbed their weapons and then got on their dragons while others got on horses.

Slyvanon gasped when the diamond was snatched from his grip. "We have been tricked again." Slyvanon closed his eyes, trying to remember a spell that would help him reveal the location of the thief. Finally he thought of one after about ten seconds of running many others through his mind.

"Tyenan amaz truini param," he said. This meant, 'show what I cannot see'. To his right, he could see wavering in and out of sight, Henry on a dracorn, flying to the east.

"Fire your arrows to the east, men. That boy has taken the diamond."

The soldiers trained their bows in the direction Slyvanon pointed to and unleashed their arrows.

***

Henry had willed his coin to take the diamond from Slyvanon. It had poofed into his hands in a cloud of dark smoke. He put the diamond into a pouch but was instantly filled with consternation when he saw the soldiers pointing their bows at him.

"Crap. How did they see me?" he muttered. "Madrin, take us back to Xongrelan and the soldiers quickly," Henry commanded.

The dracorn weaved in and out of the rainfall of arrows.

Henry battled to regain control of Madrin as an arrow struck his armpit where there was a gap in his armor.

"Arrgh," he cried. He wheezed, his breathing becoming labored. His eyes widened as he coughed up blood. Henry's invisibility spell had been broken. They were now open to archers' attack.

Henry realized something peculiar was happening. The arrow was somehow ejected from his armpit. The wound healed itself within seconds. He took slow, deep breaths, calming himself. When he had recovered from being hit by the arrow, he snapped back into action.

"Are you all right, master?" Madrin asked.

"Yeah… I am now," Henry replied.

The dragons now took flight after Henry and Madrin, bombarding them with flames.

"Hold on. This is gonna be bumpy," Henry warned. He ducked the blasts of scorching flame.

Madrin had almost reached Xongrelan and the others on the cliff. Henry cast out his hand, splaying his fingers.

"I wish for them to be taken home." Just as Henry had finished making his wish, a golden star whooshed around Xongrelan and his men. They vanished.

"Can you do the same for us, master?" Madrin asked.

"I can't. It would take too much concentration."

"I may be able to help you, sir," said Madrin.

"How?"

"If you use your magic when I blow my fire, we might be able to strike them all at once."

"Let's try it."

Madrin changed direction, facing the dragons. With Madrin's breath of fire and with a wave of Henry's hand, the single line of flames stretched into several lines, having a wider, stronger impact. The dragons' wings and their riders were charred, forcing some soldiers to fall, buying Henry and Madrin valuable time.

The dracorn resumed its course to Little Zargothia, flying as fast as he could.

* * *

Slyvanon cursed Henry as he flew out of sight. Zakarius would be furious when he found out that Argoth's men had taken back the diamond. Slyvanon knew that all was not lost, however. Their town was now exposed and with the spy who had posed as Thomas, they would have little difficulty in locating and destroying it.

A soldier, almost out of breath and whose armor was covered in blood, ran to Slyvanon. "I bring bad news, Lord Slyvanon. Our spy has been killed while riding one of the dragons."

"Blast that boy. His Majesty will be angry when he hears this." Slyvanon looked to the skies. With outstretched arms he cried, "Hernacious, listen to my prayers. Please help me!"

Just then, Slyvanon's whole body shook and jerked as something overcame him. It stopped without warning, a monochrome red hue falling over his eyes. His jaw dropped and head jerked back as it felt as if his spirit was being ripped out of him. He felt himself zipping through the air at a phenomenal speed over many forests and meadows to where Argoth's safe haven lay. Slyvanon stumbled back, nauseous as he returned to his body once more.

"All right, my Lord?" a guard standing nearby asked, holding the confused wizard.

"Yes," Slyvanon answered, straining to recover his strength. He rubbed his eyes, the monochrome red hue now disappeared. "I have seen where Argoth's lair is. Fire the cannon to notify King Zakarius."

"But, my Lord, what about the diamond?"

"We do not need it. Hernacious has shown me where the humans hide. Fire the cannon at once."

* * *

With a soldier on either side of him, Zakarius stood on the battlements of his castle awaiting the signal to advance. He thought about when he was captured. The journey was still vivid in his mind. Upon arriving at Mordoch's castle, he was thrown into a dark dungeon.

"I know Karina will save me," he kept telling himself, over and over.

As the days turned into weeks and weeks to months, it became a less convincing mantra. Soon, he abandoned any hope.

Nemus did not like Slyvanon when they first met. He hated Slyvanon for separating him from Karina. The old wizard had tried to convince him to join his own kind, saying that Argoth and his people didn't care for him. If they did, they would have come to save him.

"She will come. Just you wait. She will bring a whole army to destroy you," Nemus shouted while Slyvanon laughed at his words. Nemus retreated into his dark corner again, cheeks wet from crying.

Karina did not come, however. Slyvanon was right all along. She had abandoned him. Zakarius remembered the devastation of realizing Karina had tricked him into thinking she actually loved the boy.

When Zakarius realized that he would never be rescued, he surrendered to Slyvanon and joined the Sadarkians. Soon the wizard showed him magic that Karina never taught him. Over time a great rapport formed between them. Slyvanon gave him a new name, which derived from the Sadarkian word "zakar" meaning, "great one" or "brave leader". Zakarius had more freedom to do what he wished in Mordoch's kingdom, even being allowed to join Mordoch's army. He thought it strange though, that Mordoch never really acknowledged him, almost as if he did not know that Zakarius existed or walked in his castle.

More and more, he had learned to hate Argoth, Karina and all mankind for their betrayal. Slyvanon had often said that great things lay ahead for the lad. He said once that someday Zakarius might even be king. The very thought would fill him with excitement. He strove to show leadership qualities in all his actions.

When he learned of the plan to kill Mordoch so that he might take the throne, Zakarius was initially shocked, but then began to realize the possibilities of having his revenge on Argoth if he were king himself. This would be done once he was crowned, and so it was.

From beyond the sea of trees shot a cannon ball that exploded in the air.

"Saddle the horses and dragons immediately. We leave within the next fifteen minutes," Zakarius ordered.

* * *

Henry saw the palisade up ahead. Flapping his wings, Madrin landed near the well.

Argoth and Sir Dreyfus waited for Henry to return. Henry dismounted and then took the diamond out of the pouch.

"Hurry, boy. Come with me," Argoth said.

"Henry, wait," Tracey called out.

Henry stopped as he saw the girl running to him, an amalgamation of worry and confusion spread across her face.

"What's happening?" she asked.

"No time to talk, Henry. We must hurry," urged Argoth.

"Sorry," Henry said to her as he ran on with Argoth and Sir Dreyfus.

Along with Sir Dreyfus and Henry, they dashed to the tower. Argoth ordered his men to open the doors as they raced up the stairs.

Once inside the diamond room, Argoth took the diamond, placing it back in the glass case…but nothing happened. The town was still exposed.

"Why did it fail?" Argoth muttered to himself.

Karina, who had just walked in, offered an explanation. "The first part of the test is finished but there is a second part."

Baffled, Henry asked, "What do you mean? I got the diamond from Slyvanon."

"Yes, Master Henry, but the most important part of this test is now supposed to be carried out." Karina took the scroll from inside her jerkin, rolling it out for all to see. "It says that now the Foretold One must go above the clouds where the magic will be restored only through the powers of the Elders."

"Do I take Madrin to get there?"

"You must contact Zymbion through the coin," Karina replied.

Henry took the coin from under his armor and held it before the sorceress.

"Rub it and say you wish to speak to Zymbion," Karina advised.

Henry did as he was told. Soon a great light projected from it, filling the room. Henry was overawed by Zymbion's presence and was brimming with trepidation.

"You have done well so far, child," the god said, "but now comes the true test. I have sent for Laya, the fastest unicorn from my realm. She will take you to the room where the diamond's powers might be restored by a device created by the Elders. Even I do not know if it will work. All these events were created by those greater than I. If you are *the* Foretold One, then the moment the diamond is returned, Argoth's town will become invisible again."

"The unicorn is here," Argoth said, as it descended from the clouds, flapping its wings, hovering outside the window. The unicorn was bigger than a horse but also possessed a bright radiance.

Henry's mouth opened in amazement at Laya's beauty.

Zymbion continued, "From Little Zargothia, you will be taken to the Mount of Lilies and from there, it will transport you to my realm. Karina, you shall accompany him and be a witness in the final phase of this test."

"My god, if it pleases you," Karina replied, "I would rather send my apprentice, Hannorah, on this mission."

"You may."

"I do have one question," Karina said. "Will it not take them days to travel there?"

"The unicorn will travel faster than anything in this land."

"What happens if Henry is not *the* Foretold One?" Argoth wanted to know.

"Then use every soldier at your disposal. I am forbidden from attacking any of Zakarius's soldiers. Please hurry to the Mount of Lilies." When Zymbion finished, the holographic image projected from the coin, faded and the bright light slammed out, returning the room to its normal state.

"Your Majesty, can I take this off?" Henry pointed to the helmet. "It's uncomfortable."

"Yes. You should not meet any trouble along the way."

Henry took it off and sighed with relief while rubbing his head. It ached a little from the tightness of the helmet.

"Sir Dreyfus, fetch Hannorah," Karina said. The soldier nodded and left. Shortly after, Sir Dreyfus arrived with Hannorah.

"You wanted to see me, mistress?" the girl said.

"Yes. I am sending you on your first mission. This will help me decide if you are ready to move onto the next stage of your apprenticeship."

"What is the mission, mistress?"

"You must ride with Henry to the Mount of Lilies and go to Zymbion's domain to restore the diamond's powers."

"Zymbion's domain?" she said, bewildered.

"Yes. Do not be afraid. I think you are ready for this."

"I- I am. Just a little scared, that is all." Hannorah looked at the large unicorn. "Are we to go on *that*?"

"You are. But first, let's get you changed." Karina placed a hand on Hannorah's left shoulder. In an instant, she wore a suit of armor. A sword was in a silver scabbard by her side.

"Now you are ready," she said with a smile.

"Thank you. I will not let you down, mistress."

"I know. Now hurry. Be careful climbing out that window," Karina said.

Henry regretted not having time to change his armor. Once the window was opened, Laya moved closer. Up close, her appearance was more intimidating. Henry guessed that Laya was twice the size of a horse, with her skin being snow white, her eyes as black as a night's sky. Her silky white mane billowed as a light breeze whipped around her. A large brown leather saddle made for two riders was on Laya's back.

Henry looked at the gap between where the window was and where Laya hovered. "Can you come closer?" he asked her. Laya flapped her wings, inching closer to the window, dropping just underneath it so that Henry would not have any difficulty in getting on the unicorn.

Mounting the unicorn, he waved Hannorah on to do the same.

"It's okay, it's safe," he assured her. She climbed onto the window ledge, with Henry lending her his right hand. Hannorah put her left leg on the stirrup still holding onto Henry's hand, and swung her other leg over the saddle. She then wrapped both arms around Henry's waist, holding on tight.

The unicorn's horn on its forehead was unusual. Henry could not resist touching it. Stroking the protruding luminous horn, he could feel every spiraling ring. It felt glassy. Henry caught Hannorah secretly admiring the unicorn's astonishing beauty. Her eyes were opened wide in amazement as she studied every inch of the magnificent creature.

"There is no time for admiring the animal. Go," Karina said, slapping its back.

Spreading its feathery wings, Laya soared high above the clouds.

They traveled so fast the wind tugged at their hair so fiercely it almost felt it would scalp the pair of them.

After traveling for what felt like an hour to Henry, he saw the famous mountain nearby. The lilies Henry had expected to be white and beautiful looked brown, withered and decayed. Its peak was further up and as the unicorn flew higher, the temperature became colder.

Landing on the flowery ground, the unicorn's hooves gently went from a mild gallop to a trotting stride, a walk and finally the animal stopped. Henry was about to dismount but Hannorah put a hand on his shoulder. "I think we must stay on the unicorn."

"What makes you think that?" he asked.

"Not too sure... I just get the feeling we should stay on it."

Tucking the wings by its side, one by one the spirals on the unicorn's horn glowed from the bottom up. Both teens shielded their eyes from the blinding glow projecting from the horn's tip. The mountain was instantly cocooned in a white light, restored to its beautiful former self almost immediately.

Without warning, every lily began to illuminate. When it looked like they would explode with light, when Henry was squinting and in need of looking away, each flower shot out a snow white beam. The beams combined into a large column that began to spin.

Henry and Hannorah covered their eyes but found themselves and the unicorn rising from the ground without the animal flying. As the rotation of the column sped up, a strong gale blew. They were drawn into the light and while they were steady, the world around them was a blur of motion.

Once they stopped moving, the funnel of light retracted. Hannorah and Henry looked around them. They were in a room where the walls and floor were made of glass. Behind to their left, a rainbow-colored waterfall flowed over crystal fragments. Unicorns grazed to their right.

Henry was speechless. He knew Hannorah was overawed by this place from the look of wonderment in her eyes. At the end of the beautiful hallway were steps leading up to a shining white door.

"Wow, this place is the bomb," Henry said when he dismounted and touched one of the glass walls, gazing at the waterfall.

"The bomb?"

"I meant this place is really beautiful."

"It is."

"PLEASE," a voice spoke, making both teenagers jump, "MAKE YOUR WAY TO THE DOOR." The order echoed through the hallway.

Henry and Hannorah walked to the steps.

Upon reaching the top, the door opened. Both teens' mouths opened in further awe as they walked farther into the room. A little pond was to their left as they entered. Neon-style blue lights glowed deep beneath the pond. Six oak trees, three on each side, stood like columns in the room. Little sparrows flew between each one.

They continued walking as they saw a pale-skinned, white-bearded man who wore a long, shiny himation which fell down to his toes, standing on the opposite side of this mysterious room. A leafed crown was on his head. To the man's right was a glass door with a small channel underneath it. Hannorah and Henry knew that this was Zymbion, and both prostrated before him.

"Arise, Henry, Hannorah."

Henry was surprised to learn that this man was the voice he heard from within the portal outside his school. His voice was softer now but still brimmed with a slight tone of authority. Zymbion held a jagged fragment of crystal towards Henry.

"Child, make your way to the door and slit your hand with this. Let the blood flow into the channel. If you are the true Foretold One, then the door will open."

Henry rose, studied the fragment and with a shaky hand, he took it. Grimacing, he slit his right palm, drops of blood dripped into the channel.

Almost instantly, the door illuminated; beams fell around it before the structure vanished.

"I did it!"

He could now see inside another room. In it was another pond in the center.

"Congratulations, Henry. You may place that diamond in the marble hand in the next room," Zymbion instructed.

As Henry stepped on a stone, a marble hand rose up from the water. He placed Zymbion's diamond in it.

Marble fingers closed around the diamond. From the tiny spaces between the fingers, a pale pink light was visible. It reminded Henry of the effect of shining a torch through his own hand. The diamond was held for a moment, then was released. Henry knew that its magic was restored. As an act of caution, he waited for permission to take it.

"It is safe to touch, child," Zymbion told him.

Henry took the diamond. As he walked out of the fountain room, the door reappeared. Henry looked at his own palm.

"My hand hasn't healed. Strange. Can you heal it, sir?"

"No I cannot. It is part of your mission in Zargothia. You will understand later. For now put that back to where it belongs in the glass cabinet so that Little Zargothia can be hidden again."

"Yes, sir, I will." Henry bowed as he replied.

Zymbion raised his left hand. In the water of the pond to his left, it showed Sadarkians on dragons flying towards Little Zargothia.

"Go quickly. Zakarius has met up with Slyvanon and they are now on their way," Zymbion said.

With that, both teens mounted the unicorn and left Zymbion's home.

The landscape was nothing but a mere blur as they raced towards Little Zargothia. The unicorn soared over another mountain. Argoth's town lay just ahead.

"Come on, hurry up!" Henry said to Laya. "I can see Sadarkians not far from here."

A guard in the watchtower saw Laya approaching. Henry heard as they were closer, the guard giving orders to open the tower's door. The town's bell was rung warning citizens to take cover.

Both riders got down from Laya and ran up the stairs.

Tracey was there amongst a large crowd that had gathered. Henry had caught sight of her. For a couple of seconds, their eyes had locked onto one another. Henry could see relief and joy in hers, along with a smile that said she was glad he got back okay.

"Hurry, Henry. Come on," Argoth yelled, snapping the boy back into action.

* * *

"We are almost there, Your Majesty," Slyvanon said. "On my signal, give the command to attack."

Zakarius drew his sword and raised it in the air. He awaited the word from Slyvanon. At the king's command, all hell would be unleashed on Argoth's town.

* * *

Henry and Hannorah reached the fifth floor. Argoth snatched the diamond from Henry's hand before racing to the sixth floor.

Argoth dashed into the room. From a window, he could see Zakarius's dragons preparing to bellow a storm of fire on them. The king removed the glass case and was about to place the diamond on the cushion when it slipped from his grasp.

"Blast you!" Argoth cursed as it rolled under a chair. He kicked the chair out of the way, swiping the magical object from the ground. He placed the diamond on the cushion and covered it with the case.

* * *

Slyvanon gripped the king's right arm. "Att-" Slyvanon stopped abruptly. His eyes were no longer covered in the monochrome red hue. Little Zargothia had vanished. "No!" he cried as they flew over it.

"Where has the town gone?" Zakarius questioned while looking around him in frenzy.

"I have no idea, sire. Zymbion must have helped them," Slyvanon answered, sounding defeated.

"This could be a trap." Zakarius turned his attention to the soldiers. "Retreat, fall back! We have been tricked."

* * *

Argoth saw the bubble envelope Little Zargothia as Zakarius, along with his soldiers, flew overhead. Argoth and his people's haven were hidden again. Argoth saw his men below raising their swords in the air, cheering and hugging one another once Zakarius was out of sight.

Through the efforts in training and co-operation that Henry had shown, Argoth had been impressed by the boy, but not totally convinced. Now at last he looked at him and knew without a shadow of a doubt that Henry was indeed *the* Foretold One

ZYMBION'S DIAMOND

Chapter Four

A Glimpse Into the Past

Darkness had fallen as the people of Little Zargothia celebrated. A blazing bonfire lit up the town's center. Puppet shows were held for children.

Some men drank ale with their comrades. Women and children danced around the bonfire.

Henry sat with Conor, Edward, Jasper, Tracey and Hannorah, watching the festivities.

Karina joined them. "Hello everyone," she said with a beaming smile.

"Hi Karina," Henry replied as the others acknowledged her presence with a 'hello' or nod.

"Master Henry, do you remember when I told you some of Zargothia's history?"

"Sure I do."

"I could not tell you everything because it was not the right time, now it is. Would you, Conor and Edward come to my room? I will explain everything now."

Henry and the others exchanged puzzled looks as they got up to follow the sorceress.

"You must stay here," Karina told Tracey.

"Oh, okay," she replied with a slight frown. Hannorah stayed with her.

"Only Henry and the other two can see this. I am sure he will tell you everything afterwards," Karina said.

"Yeah, I'll catch you later, okay?" Henry said. Tracey nodded but he could see from her folded arms and tight features that she resented being excluded.

When all three Foretold Ones were in the room, Karina shut the door. She pulled a bulky book from a bookshelf. It slid the whole bookshelf to the right, revealing another room with a long table. On that was a large chest.

"Before you came here, Zymbion appeared one night to me and gave me this chest." Karina unlocked it. Inside was rose-colored foam with a square box containing a coin shaped hole. "He said when the moment was right after the test was passed, then you were to put that coin in this hole. By putting your hand on it, all would be revealed. The Elders gave this to Zymbion. That wound on your hand can reveal the truth about the Foretold Ones and this world's history. Remove the bandage around your wound and put your hand on the coin."

Henry unwound the cloth around his palm, put the coin in the hole and placed his right hand on it. The coin glowed; its golden hues sneaking out between his fingers.

Before Henry and his friends' eyes, three beams projected from the coin, each hitting the foreheads of all three. In Henry's mind, a movie played with the opening shot of a cluster of stars in space.

A male voice spoke. "Many centuries ago when the universe was being created, twelve celestial Elders each made their own world. They decided to come together and called themselves 'The Assembly of the Elite.'"

An image of people in what Henry could describe as caveman clothing, congregated before a huge stone altar, kneeling and bowing.

"Together they created worlds and appointed a god to each. Each god was given the power to create homes for their worshippers or protect them from harm, but not the power to create life. The Elders feared that this power would be abused. Hernacious was the original god in this world, the Sadarkians the first humans. The Elders were not pleased by the original humans' cruel behavior and how Hernacious tolerated it. The Elders warned Hernacious that if his people did not change their ways, they would be punished. They did not listen."

The next image to be projected into Henry's mind was that of what were once humans now being zapped with a lilac-colored beam, transforming from their human state into Sadarkians.

"Eventually the Elders grew tired of their behavior. As punishment, Hernacious's people were cursed and changed into the creatures they are today. Another god was created and named Zymbion. Under the new god, a new race of humans were made. They were kinder to animals and nature. Volarks, Jenormes and other beings were also made and put into their own worlds.

"Hernacious hated the new humans and plotted his revenge. He hatched a plan to rule the world. Without people to worship Zymbion, the god would become completely powerless because it was the power of the people's prayer and belief that gave the gods their dominance. For many years, Hernacious wondered how he would destroy the humans. He knew that Zymbion would prevent a direct strike at them."

Next Henry was shown Slyvanon in a room lit only with candle-light, kneeling, deep in prayer. Without warning, Hernacious appeared in the form of a dark sphere of light with two purple eyes glaring at Slyvanon. The wizard retreated into the corner of his room and cowered.

"Hernacious hatched a plan. Striking a deal with Slyvanon, they worked together to bring about the downfall of the humans with Slyvanon becoming supreme ruler by killing the king when he was no longer useful.

"Slyvanon learned of Turnaz and Nemus's friendship with Karina. He decided to use this against Argoth. He had Turnaz killed and later in Nemus's life, using the knowledge that Nemus would gain from the castle, Hernacious ordered Slyvanon to turn King Mordoch's soldiers against their king and capture Nemus, convincing the young boy that his human friends had abandoned him."

Now a clip of a Sadarkian army of what looked like thousands of soldiers clad in black armor, charging at Argoth's castle. Their cannon firing, breaching Argoth's walls.

"Using his knowledge of Argoth's castle, Zakarius would launch a surprise attack. The Elders learned of his intentions and decided to intervene. Taking pity on Zymbion, the Elders gave him a sacred scroll outlining certain events. You now have this scroll. One of those events mentioned was your birth, Henry. They knew that if you were born in this world then your life would be at risk because they foresaw the attack that drove Argoth's people from their lands."

Now Henry saw himself as a baby inside an orphanage. His mother, Suzanne, and father, Jack, stood over his cot. He could see a close-up image of his mother's eyes filling with delight upon seeing little Henry, cooing and laughing while waving his arms about.

"For your own safety, they sent you to another world to live until you were seventeen. The Elders gave you a uniqueness that would bring the right people into adopting and raising you with a good heart. You were a creation of the Elders and not the people who you thought were your parents."

As he clutched Suzanne's right index finger, a look of delight spread across her face. The scene changed to when Suzanne and Jack brought Henry home. He was put in a cot beside their bed.

Henry was speechless; his face a picture of confusion. "You mean I'm not their son?"

The voice didn't respond, continuing on with the story instead. "But the intervention of the Elders came at a cost. Hernacious took his revenge, seeking out each Elder and killed them. In order to do this, he learned of a sword that was crafted with a blade made of steel called tyrin."

Next, Henry saw a group of men in white monks' clothing, standing around a large rectangular stone slab, their hands outstretched. A green jagged beam shot forth from each of their palms into the center of the slab. A sword of some kind was crafted.

"This sword was made by all of them in case one Elder used their power for evil purposes. It is the only weapon that can wound or kill an Elder. Hernacious learned of this by torturing one of their servants. While their guard was lowered, he killed six and the other six fled to a secret location. If he had slaughtered one more, then he would have gained the power to create life. He also learned this from torturing the sixth Elder before killing him. Hamorin, leader of the Elders, cast a spell so that it would take killing seven of them to take their power of creation."

A tall, muscular being of what Henry guessed must have been nearly ten foot and who he thought was Hernacious, towered over a cut and bruised

Elder who was on his knees, shielding himself with both arms raised over his head. A blood-red beam shot out from his chest into Hernacious's.

"Hernacious did gain some of their powers. Though he could not make any being or creature, Hernacious can prolong life using the Elders' powers and he prolonged Slyvanon's by seventy years. He granted Slyvanon a mind that would always be sharp.

"Now fearing for your life even more, The Assembly of the Elite then made the coin to protect you. Only a member of their bloodline can use its powers. That is how you came into this world through your blood. Its inscriptions from the ancient language of the Elders read, 'Ell Kcantar Marckian Krakgome La Battoolus – Only the Worthy Shall Survive the Final Battle.' The symbol in the center of the coin represents the two warriors who will meet in the battle: you, Henry, and Zakarius. Use it sparingly, Henry. If you use too much magic in a short space of time, it can weaken you."

The next clip from this 'movie' he was shown was of Edward and Conor, plummeting towards the portal in their plane. Then he was shown Jasper being sucked into a similar portal outside Mr. Anderson's home.

"The coin also sought out others from your world to help you. All these events were predicted in the scroll. Hernacious managed to learn of the contents of the sacred scroll as he read an Elder's mind before killing him. He now knows every event and tries to stop them in some way. To safeguard you, Henry, the Assembly did not mention one last event that is to take place during the battle. They also warned that in the final war, no god could interfere. It is to be fought simply between the Sadarkians and whatever allies Argoth gains. Good luck in your fight, child, and to all humankind."

The beams retracted to the coin and feeling a little nauseous, each shook their head. Judging by the overwhelmed expression on their faces, Henry guessed that the others must have seen the same thing he did.

The wound had healed on Henry's right palm. He was dumbstruck. An expression of hurt laced with a hint of surprise was now on his face as he tried to let the newfound information about the true identity of his parents sink in.

"I gotta get some fresh air," Henry said and left.

* * *

Zakarius returned to his quarters. He ripped the scabbard from his belt, throwing it at the stone wall.

"I want spriniys here on the double," he barked. Spriniys were paiges who helped a king remove his armor.

Three male spriniys came running to his room, helping him take off his armor.

When they were finished, he dismissed them with a snarl. Enraged, he overturned the table in front of him. Drawing his sword, he sliced all the paintings on his wall. The deaths of Argoth's people were tangibly close but were swiped from his grasp at the last second.

I should have taken the spy's advice and had him kill the boy. If I had killed him then Argoth's people would be destroyed. I think it is time I asked Hernacious for help.

Zakarius focused on the small flame devouring the wick on the thin beeswax candle. Closing his eyes and calming his breathing, he meditated.

A biting chill accompanied by a low-gust wind that bore a terrifying growl, invaded the room. All other flames on the candles were quenched except the one that was in front of him. Zakarius jumped as the flame turned from orange to an eerie black and increased in size, curving outwards. In its core now appeared two turquoise eyes. It was Hernacious.

"I hear your prayers, Zakarius," the god said, his words dripping with malevolence. "Zymbion interfered in our affairs yet again. That child will not defeat you because I know of a weapon that even the Elders do not know about."

"Where is it, Great God?"

"Many miles from here on an island. Hidden in a cave, protected by a savage beast. This sword is the only thing that can kill the boy."

"How is this sword different from others?"

"It contains magic from the Elders: I got some of their powers, stored some in this weapon. It is only their magic that can kill the boy."

"Tell me how to go to this land and I will get the sword."

"A two-day journey east from your location is a sea of oil not water. At the shore is a galley with a boatman waiting for you. Only you can travel to the island and take the sword. This place is called the 'Island of No Return'. The beast who has been charged to protect the sword you must be most careful of."

"Is there anything you can give to help me?"

"Yes."

A small chain with a locket on it materialized in Zakarius's palm.

"Wear this at all times and you will not be seen. Once the monster that guards the sword is defeated, the weapon is yours."

"Thank you, Great God." Zakarius bowed his head.

"Do not fail me. This will prove once and for all if you are worthy of being king."

The flame shrank to its original size. Zakarius examined the silver locket. Opening it revealed a small round ruby embedded inside.

Tomorrow I will begin the journey to the island, Zakarius thought, *and take the sword. Then I will kill Henry Simmons.*

* * *

The next morning while sitting alone on the grass and with her eyes shut, Tracey concentrated on all the tranquil sounds around her, from the chirping of birds to rustling of leaves in trees close to where she meditated. A gentle breeze kissed her cheeks. A cacophony of scents from a myriad of roses blooming in overgrown bushes swirled around her.

She took a deep breath once the meditation was over. Tracey picked up the sword once she got to her feet. Inhaling another long breath, she swung her sword right and left, hacking and thrusting before falling back into a defensive stance, repeating the maneuvers again before it became as natural to her as walking. She thought Sir Dreyfus would be proud if he could see her now.

"Impressive," a voice said from behind.

Tracey turned around to see Daniel standing there, admiring her moves. She hoped that was all he was admiring. It was the first time since arriving here that she saw how muscular his arms were underneath his custard-yellow tunic. Daniel's legs were also well toned as straps from his sandals went just above his calf.

"Thanks."

"Care to spar with me?"

"If you want."

Daniel drew his sword. "Before we start, can I give you a little advice?"

"Sure."

"You are standing too rigid. You have to allow yourself enough space to move. Make yourself flexible."

"Got it."

"Now attack me. Do not hold back."

"Are you sure?"

"Yes."

Tracey charged at him, swinging left and right, Daniel avoiding her every attack.

"Is that the best you got? I thought you would not fight like a girl."

"Remember what I said about being cocky?"

"Sorry."

"That's more like it." She ran at him again, her sword held above her head, aimed at him.

Daniel sidestepped the girl in an effortless, fluid move, putting his sword at her stomach.

"Again, too rigid. Never give into your anger. Like my father says, channel it into your attack without giving into it." He took the sword away from her waist. "Come on, try again."

Tracey took her position once more. She watched Daniel as he juggled his sword from left hand to right, shifting his weight from leg to leg like a boxer.

"This time I won't take it easy on you," she said.

"I would not want it any other way," he replied with a smirk.

Tracey held her sword up again, running at him. As she was a few steps away from where he stood, she tripped on a small hole in the ground. Daniel dropped his sword and caught her. As he caught Tracey, his head was less than two inches away from hers, both their lips uncomfortably close. She stared into his eyes, for the first time seeing something in them that made her stomach flutter. Daniel returned Tracey's stare with one of his own. She could sense a longing in his.

Clearing her throat, Daniel straightened up and helped the girl to her feet.

"Thanks for the catch," she said smoothing down her pink shirt and black trousers, her cheeks scarlet with embarrassment.

"I could not let you fall."

"Yeah, like I said, thanks."

"You see, I am not that bad after all."

"No, I guess you're not." In his eyes she could see that he wanted to flirt even more. "I got to go. Thanks for the lesson."

"You are welcome," he answered with a slight bow.

* * *

Henry wandered around the little town, with both hands in his pockets and his head lowered in sorrowful contemplation.

How could they lie to me all this time? Why didn't Mom and Dad tell me the truth? The images Henry had seen in Karina's room ran through his mind like a mini-slideshow. *Did they ever love me?*

"Henry?" Tracey called out. "Henry, wait."

"I'm not in the mood for talking, Tracey. I just want to be on my own."

"I get that. I bumped into Captain Johnson after training and he told me about what you saw."

"Yeah…I kind of wish I hadn't seen it."

"Look, I get it if you don't wanna talk but I know what it's like to be adopted."

This stopped Henry in his tracks. "Wait…are you saying you're…?"

"Adopted? Yeah. Not too many people know that, okay, so don't tell anyone."

"Well, look where we are. I hardly know anyone here so your secret is safe."

Tracey grinned at his remark.

"So... how long have you been adopted?" he asked.

"Since I was six. My dad left my mom when I was born and she died of cancer and I was put into care."

"Sorry to hear that. It must've been really hard for you."

"It was at first, then I got used to it. My other dad's really cool. I guess sometimes I put on a brave face at school and enter Fortnite tournaments just to fit in. Deep down though, I just feel sad I've lost both my parents. Can't believe I'm telling you all this."

"Yeah... we've more in common than we thought. Um...look, sorry but I gotta ask, why did you go out with Sid Connors? He's a dick."

"I didn't see that when we first started going out but after a few dates, I saw what he's really like so I broke it off."

"Okay. Good call," Henry joked. They shared a brief laugh. Then an uncomfortable silence hung between them for what seemed like a few minutes as they continued to walk on.

"Thanks for telling me, Tracey. I know it wasn't easy. And I know what it feels like being alone and sad. I go through that every day."

"Yeah but you got this god for a dad, right? How cool is that?"

"I guess it's cool all right," Henry replied, both laughing again. As they laughed, Henry looked into her eyes. They were warm and inviting. He wanted to kiss her, but wasn't sure if she wanted him to or not. That awkwardness crept in again, filling him with unease.

"I got to go. I'm beat after today. There's a lot to take in."

"Okay, I understand."

"See you later."

On the way to his room, he thought about the spell he had put on her using the coin.

I feel really bad about that now. She's had it tough just like me. Henry then remembered something that his adopted father, Jack, had said about politicians and their abuse of power, "Just because you have power doesn't mean you abuse it."

"I guess you're right, Dad. Maybe it's time to break the spell." Henry held the golden coin in his hand, concentrating on its shiny exterior. "Coin, I want to break the spell I put on Tracey." The magical object shone brighter than before. It pulsated for five seconds before returning to normal.

I think it's broken. I guess now she mightn't like me as much. We'll have to wait and see.

* * *

As the galley anchored on the Island of No Return's shore, Zakarius stood up, looking beyond the beach to a jungle. Further on, nestled inside a high mountain, was a hole, or as Zakarius guessed, the entrance to the cave.

"Lower the gang plank," Zakarius commanded.

Two crewmen wearing cyan robes, opened the hatch and lowered the long and wide piece of wood which appeared to be sturdy enough to walk on.

Picking up the quiver of arrows Slyvanon had given him, he slid the quiver's strap over his shoulder. He gripped the bow in his right hand. Zakarius walked down the gang plank.

Hacking his way through tall, overgrown blades of grass, the grasses hemmed him in, crowded around him like enemy soldiers, pressed in on all sides. With boiling breath and sweaty rigidity, they tried to rob him of the air he needed to breathe. Little insects crawled up and down the tree barks. Creepers hung from various branches. The dense, humid air made Zakarius's back drenched with sweat.

The farther Zakarius ventured, the more on edge he felt, always keeping a hand on his sword's hilt. Overflowing leaves drifted on swampy waters to his right. Reptiles with light brown scaly skin, small in height ran around in a widelegged stance, chasing other creatures.

As he walked farther into the jungle, night began to fall but Zakarius's eyes adjusted to darkness. The cave was near and Zakarius managed to drink some water that was in a nearby lake. From the opening, he could see a strong flare of firelight. He estimated it would take another hour to reach the cave.

The whole jungle was now in darkness as the two moons shone. Before entering, Zakarius sharpened the edge of his sword on a whetstone, then sheathed the weapon.

Entering the cave mouth, the air changed; it was no longer hot but chilly. Further in, its walls were craggy and dripping wet. A long sloping passageway greeted Zakarius, taking him deeper inside.

Coming to the end of the slope, it led to a long walkway, which turned to the right, where a strong fire was burning. He heard flames crackling and smelt food being cooked on what he guessed was a spit. The sound of someone, or something, chomping on a piece of food, made Zakarius's hairs stand on end, his heart thump faster. What made him even tenser was the shadow he could see upon approaching its lair. Joined at its waist were three bodies with three heads and six arms. Their upper bodies were human; their arms were muscular. Each had a weapon of some sort. From the rumblings and shouting, Zakarius learned that they each had a name: Erander, Gergon and Jamos. Erander possessed a sword like a claymore, Gergon had a flail and Jamos was armed with a halberd axe. All three had curly black hair.

If I kill one of them at a time, Zakarius thought, then it would make it harder for that thing to attack me because of its brothers' dead weight.

Picking up a rock, he threw it as far he could. It rattled off the wall.

"What was that?" Jamos asked.

"There could be an intruder," Gergon said.

"Let's investigate," Erander replied. "I think the sound came from over there."

All three held their weapons. Zakarius ran to the fire. Using water from a large jug, he poured it onto the fire. There was a loud hiss from the inevitable steam.

Jamos gasped. Erander and Gergon looked around frantically. All the brothers' grips on their weapons tightened.

"The intruder can move fast," Jamos remarked.

"There might be more than one, Jamos," Erander said.

"How can we fight what we cannot see?" Gergon asked.

"I can solve that," Jamos bellowed a flaming breath and ignited a new fire.

Zakarius recoiled from the flames.

"We still cannot see anyone in here except us," Gergon said.

Zakarius watched Gergon searching for a shadow, a footprint or any trace of a thief. Zakarius was out of ideas. The only option now was a direct assault.

"If we cannot fight an invisible thief running about, then maybe we can fight them when they are still." A breath of ice came from Erander as he blew a wall of crystal, shimmering ice to the far left of the fire. It missed Zakarius by a mere inch.

As he dived out of the way to avoid the icy wall, he struck the back of his neck against a jagged rock. This snapped the chain of his locket, leaving him exposed.

"Aha! We have found our intruder," Erander said with a broad, sadistic grin.

"Let's kill him. Make it a slow, agonizing death," Gergon suggested.

"I agree, Gergon. I love my food nice and crispy," Jamos said, blowing a little ring of smoke from his mouth.

"Let me show him what I can do." Gergon puffed. A strong breeze hurled Zakarius against the wall.

In the impact his sword slipped from his grasp. Gergon sucked in air to bring the sword to his mouth. He munched on the weapon as if it were an apple.

"We will see how you fight without your weapon," Erander said as the three brothers approached.

Zakarius now had only his bow and arrows. Then he noticed something shiny and metallic in the corner. It was a shield of some sort. Firing his arrows, Zakarius made a dash for it, leaping over the semi-circular blade on Jamos' halberd and ducking the spikes of Gergon's flail.

"Do not let him reach that!" Erander swung his sword low. Zakarius somersaulted over it and performed a diving roll to reach the shield.

Jamos' cheeks ballooned as he blew another fiery breath. This time it bounced off the shield, ricocheted off the wall and hit Jamos' face. Clutching his scorched cheeks, he dropped his halberd.

Using a magic trick that Slyvanon had taught him, Zakarius levitated the weapon. With all the strength in his right arm, forced it towards the head of Jamos, killing him.

"Jamos," Erander roared, as his brother's upper body was now a lifeless weight. "You will pay for killing our brother!" With a combination of their weapons and powers, the remaining brothers attacked Zakarius.

Dodging the blade and fire, Zakarius was almost out of breath and knew that something had to be done soon or he would die. Running onto a wall, he jumped off it and performed a back flip. But while in the air, Erander discharged bolts of ice against him. Zakarius, using a deflection spell, sent the bolts straight back. One struck Gergon's neck and froze it. Zakarius reached his quiver and took a few arrows. He peppered Gergon's frozen neck with a number of them. After a few had become lodged in it, the ice broke. Gergon's head fell off.

Erander watched in dismay. "Die, you little bastard," he cried while firing lightning bolts of ice from both hands. Zakarius ducked and rolled out of their way. Erander, dragging the weight of the other two, approached a stalactite.

As he retreated, Zakarius found himself backing into a dead end.

"I have you now. I will enjoy watching you die." Saliva oozed from Erander's mouth. He licked his tongue along his yellow-fanged teeth. Erander picked up Gergon's weapons as a measure of caution.

Zakarius kept a watchful eye on the stalactite, waiting for the right moment. He knew from the strain on Erander's face that the remaining brother was finding it hard to move, dragging the dead weight of the other two.

"I will make this long and painful." Erander was now under the hanging sharp object.

"Not today, my friend," the king said. Using magic to transform an arrow into an axe, he threw it with all his might. Erander realized the king's plan too late. Zakarius's arrow hit the stalactite's root.

Erander screamed as it separated from the ceiling, going straight down his throat. The final brother gurgled blood and collapsed.

Putting a hand up to the wall, Zakarius took a moment's respite. A face of rock shuddered, dust falling from the ceiling, Zakarius was suddenly alert again, would the whole cave collapse upon him? The moving rock slid to the right revealing a chamber and an impressive looking sword.

Zakarius walked forward, lining up another arrow on his bow, his eyes scanning the darkness for anyone waiting to attack.

When he stepped inside the chamber, it was nothing but a cold mist on the floor. There was also a swirling cloud of smoke around the weapon. Something invisible held it up.

Putting his arrow back into the quiver, Zakarius stretched out his arm to reach for the magical weapon. Its hilt was jet black. A flame was skillfully crafted on the blade to make it look like a snake slithering along it. His arms and hands tingled as a feeling of infinite power surged through his whole body while both hands gripped the hilt.

"Now I will finish you once and for all Henry Simmons with this," Zakarius muttered, his eyes gleaming in almost delirious glee.

Swaddling the special weapon with a cloth he had found, Zakarius abandoned his old sword while sheathing the new one into the scabbard. Realizing that he had not that many arrows remaining, Zakarius took the flail and claymore.

Hmm, this might be useful too, he thought while looking at the shield. Zakarius put it into his sack.

One problem still remained and that was his chain. It was broken. He had to fix it somehow.

Maybe if I use my magic to solder the links and let it cool, I might be able to wear it again, he thought.

While the red-hot links were cooling, Zakarius ate some bread and pieces of meat the brothers had stored. It banished the hunger and gave him enough energy to press on.

Several hours had elapsed. Zakarius touched the links that were broken. They were cool and the chain was safe to put on. Putting the locket over his head, he then tested its power. Facing the silver shield towards him, he stared into it unable to see his reflection. Zakarius was invisible once more. He was now ready to return to the galley. He stopped at a lake near the cave to refill his retainer with some water.

Journeying into the jungle, he could hear crickets adding to the night's noises. As he trudged through muddy ground, the heavy sack was slowing him down and began to hurt his back. Placing it down on a patch that was not muddy, Zakarius stretched his arms and yawned before carrying on.

After walking for three hours, Zakarius smiled with relief when he saw the galley.

Thank Hernacious I made it, Zakarius thought, as he stepped onto the boat and sat down. When the anchor was raised, the galley set off towards Zakarius's home.

With a venomous smile, he glanced at the sword that could mortally wound Henry. He looked forward to inflicting further pain on Argoth and his kind.

KING ARGOTH ON HIS THRONE

Chapter Five

Preparing for War

Henry was to Argoth's left, as the king took the head of the long war room table. Jasper was with the others around the table, Karina opposite Henry, Cyren, Sir Dreyfus, Damone and Xongrelan, Edward and Conor. Argoth stood up and addressed everyone while pacing the floor.

"You all know why we are here this evening. We have to come up with some plan to beat the Sadarkians. I am open to suggestions."

"Aye, Your Majesty. I have a wee one. We could use the turret gun we collected from the plane wreckage. It'll be useful against Zakarius's army."

"And is it in working order? I thought everything was destroyed when your…plane went down."

"There's a bit of tinkering to be done to it but maybe with a wee bit of Henry's magic it can be fixed."

"I am sure Henry will not have any objection in looking at it," Cyren said while staring at the boy.

"No, Your Majesty. I'll use the coin to fix whatever is wrong with it."

"Sorry to interrupt but we would need something bigger than a unicorn or horse to carry this," Conor added.

"I may be able to help you there, Sergeant," Karina said, "but you and Captain Edward would have to come with me on a little trip."

"Aye, we'll do that. Where are going?"

"A two day's ride from here. We are going to use a large bird called a Hudson Hawk. I believe this beast will be big enough to carry this weapon of yours," Karina said confidently.

"Is this Hawk friendly?" Conor asked nervously.

"I have used her before on a previous mission so she will recognize me." Henry guessed Karina noticed the fear in Conor's voice when she added with a smile, "You need not worry, Sergeant, she does not bite."

"Aye, that's… reassuring," Conor replied with an unconvincing grin.

"Good, now that is sorted," Argoth interjected, "next, comes the issue of numbers, more men. Our army will not be enough to take on Zakarius's. We need to recruit soldiers from the other realms."

"I can travel to my home and ask my brother to loan us some of his men," Cyren said. Cyren's brother, Etherus, succeeded his father, King Devreenus, to the throne ten years ago.

"I cannot allow that, my love. It would be too great a risk. Damone will carry out that task. With a dozen men to go with you, will you travel to Eviranna tomorrow and ask your king for assistance?"

"Yes, sir," Damone replied.

"Xongrelan, I will ask you to do the same. Ask for as many as your king will lend us."

"I will, Your Majesty."

"Letters will be written for you to present to your kings." The two nodded their understanding and Argoth turned to the sorceress. "Karina, I want you to develop potions that we can use at long range, something that will at least slow them down if not stop them in their tracks."

"Certainly, sir, there are potions that can temporarily blind Zakarius's men, but I will need to pick some flowers from the royal garden to make them."

"Permission granted. Sir Dreyfus, come up with an attack plan. We need to innovate if we are to beat Zakarius's army. Bear in mind, our resources and men are very limited."

"I have been thinking about that for quite a while now, sire, and what about the mercenaries at Ludongorg?" Sir Dreyfus asked.

"They will not join my army."

"They might if they think they will be free of Sadarkians."

"Yes, but they never joined us all this time so why now?"

"Because until now, we did not have Henry."

Argoth mulled over what Sir Dreyfus had just said. "True. I will have a messenger sent to them later today under armed guard."

"If they join us, sire, I believe we could use them in an ambush. It is part of a plan I have but it is dangerous."

"War always is, what specifically do you mean?" the king asked.

Using the maps on the table, Dreyfus explained in great detail, pointing to the routes that would be taken using various different formations of Argoth's soldiers on the battlefield.

Argoth spoke when Dreyfus was finished. "It is dangerous indeed…but it just might work. Timing is everything. Also for a plan like that, I would need the men to construct siege towers right away. I will lead the campaign -" various objections were raised, but Argoth accepted none of them. "I want to make one thing clear: if anything happens to me on the battlefield, then all command will be transferred over to Queen Cyren."

"Thank you, my Love, but let's hope that will not happen," Cyren said.

"I will see to those siege towers right away." Dreyfus was about to leave but Argoth stayed his move, then placed a hand on Henry's right shoulder.

"Henry's training will also need to be increased. If he is to take on Zakarius then he must practice all day, every day. He must be ready for this." Henry groaned in disappointment.

"I can arrange that, sire."

As Dreyfus was leaving, Queen Cyren shared an idea with the others. "I believe we can recruit another ally you may have forgotten about, my king."

"Oh? Who?" Argoth asked.

"The unicorns."

"The unicorns?" he replied with an incredulous laugh. "They will not take part in any battle since they were cursed by Hernacious."

"I may be able to persuade them."

"But that would mean you traveling to the forest of Aandour. I cannot allow that. You could be attacked. Besides, Queen Eusaba would never agree to go to war."

"Yes, she would never agree if she saw you coming with armed men, but if Eusaba saw me, then she might be more willing to talk."

"I agree with Her Majesty," Karina said. "Unicorn magic could sway the battle in our favor."

Argoth glared at Karina before contemplating on the suggestion. "All right then, you may travel but with armed guard. No argument."

"Not too armed though," she replied. "That may frighten her instead of gaining her trust."

"They will be instructed to wear light armor and carry only a sword each. So they appear to be only a ceremonial, honor guard."

"If it pleases you, I will leave in the morning."

"Very well." He returned to his seat. "I believe that is all. For all our sakes, I hope these plans work."

* * *

It has been a while since I was here, Cyren thought as she made her way on horseback through a roadway with a line of multi-colored trees on each side. At the end of the road was a large rock where Queen Eusaba lived. It was believed by many humans that the rock led to a vast network of underground chambers. Cyren and her men could hear rustling in the treetops. She knew it was the unicorns retreating into hiding. Colorful hues from their tails were like little spheres of light hovering between the branches. Cyren had read in an old book that unicorns in Zargothia were different from those in Eviranna. Here, over three hundred years ago, they had evolved from just being beautiful white horses with a horn on their head to now also having wings. In her world, unicorns had no wings. As far as she knew, they could always make themselves invisible both in Eviranna and here.

In an instant, a unicorn that transformed into a man with a horn on his head, appeared before them. They halted. He was holding a spear and wore a loin cloth. His dark hair flowed down to his shoulders; his skin was glittering white.

"Halt. What is your business here?"

"We come in peace. I am Queen Cyren."

"I know who you are, Your Majesty, I want to know why you are here."

"I wish to speak to Queen Eusaba."

The guard studied each of Cyren's soldiers. "If you want to proceed, then please leave your swords here. No weapons of any kind are allowed beyond this point. You can collect them when you leave."

"We will do as you ask," Cyren said.

Her soldiers removed the scabbards from their belts, placing them neatly in groups of four, the hilts positioned against one another in order for them to remain standing.

"You may proceed." Floating to the side, he allowed them to pass.

Cyren and her men rode to the rock where she dismounted.

A slight echo of a woman's voice spoke from the rock. "Why are you here?"

"We come in peace and ask for your help."

"Our help in what?"

"In fighting the Sadarkians."

"You should know, Queen Cyren, that we are peaceful beings."

"I am aware of that, Your Majesty, but with your help we can be rid of Zakarius's army forever."

A black door appeared in the rock and Queen Eusaba emerged through it. Two guards, who had transformed themselves into human-like males, and who Cyren thought were Eusaba's own personal bodyguards, flew down from the trees. The unicorn queen also appeared in human form. Her entire body shone as if a hundred candles glowed beneath her skin. Eusaba's face was porcelain white; her pupils as black as night. When she spoke, her voice had a lyrical tone.

"You know what Hernacious did to us after the Great War, even though we had no part in it. If we take part in this battle, he could hurt us even more."

"No. The Elders themselves said that anyone who takes part in the final battle will not be touched by the gods."

"Do you have proof of this?"

"Yes." Cyren was given the sacred scroll by a soldier. She in turn handed it to the queen. Eusaba's eyes scanned over the scroll. She gave it back when finished. Turning her back to the humans and the Volark queen. With hands on her hips, she stared at the skies, undecided in what action to take.

"I will need to consult my council," she said and went inside her rock, with its black door sliding shut after her. For a while Eusaba and her men deliberated inside the large rock. Eventually she emerged with her bodyguards.

"We have made our decision," Eusaba said.

* * *

After eating one of their daily bowlfuls of porridge and hard wholemeal bread that they had become accustomed to since arriving in Zargothia, Conor and Edward went for a walk around the town.

"Fancy a pint?" Conor asked.

Edward looked at him with an arched eyebrow. "This early?"

"Aye, why not, sir? I've got nothing on today and if what they say is true about what's ahead of us, I'd need something to settle my nerves."

"I'm sure Henry wouldn't mind making you some coffee with the coin. You need a clear head, MacCall, now more than ever."

"Maybe but one wee drink is not gonna bother me too much, is it?" Conor replied, momentarily forgetting his friend's rank.

Both men turned around as they heard stones being crunched behind them. Sir Dreyfus approached. "Gentlemen, now that you are aware of the battle plan, you will need some training."

"What kind of training?" Conor asked.

"You will have to know how to fly a dracorn."

"You mean one of those flying horse thingies?" Conor replied.

"Yes," Sir Dreyfus answered with a half-smile.

"No way. It's bad enough I have to ride a damn horse but not one while it's airborne."

"Airborne?" the knight said baffled.

"He means while it's flying," Edward explained.

"But if you are to take part in the battle, then you have to prepare for it," Sir Dreyfus insisted firmly. "Meet with me at the stables in an hour and do not be late."

"Of course," Edward said before Conor could object.

Sir Dreyfus nodded before leaving.

"There is no bloody way I'm getting on one of those things, sir."

"MacCall, you have to. If we're to beat the Sadarkians, we have to do everything possible, even if that means going outside our comfort zone."

"That's easy for you to say, sir. You won't be pissing yourself while on that dracorn thing. Christ, why out of all the pilots in the world were *we* chosen for this?"

"Fate chose us for a reason. See you there in an hour."

Conor sighed, "Righto, sir. But I don't care what you say, I'm going for that drink afterwards. I'll need it."

As Conor entered the stables, he saw Edward petting down a fully saddled dracorn's mane. The beast seemed at ease around the captain.

"You ready, sir?" Conor asked.

"Yes, you?"

"Need you ask?" Conor replied, his answer lacking confidence. His own dracorn stood only a few inches away, munching on some straw scattered on the floor. Conor looked at the armor pads protecting his arms and kneecaps. "These things are a little heavy. Why do you think we need them?"

"That is to get used to them for the battle," Sir Dreyfus said as he walked in. He, too, wore armor.

"Aye, I understand that but could we not just do without them today, since it's our first time on a dracorn an' all?"

"No." His answer sounding final. "Before we take off, you must bond with your dracorn. Ask it its name."

Conor stared at him in surprise. "You want me to talk to it?"

"Yes, you have to. This will help you ride easier with each other."

"All right," Conor replied. He swallowed the feeling of humiliation as he said, "Hello. My name's Conor. What's yours?"

"Corbus. Do not be afraid, master."

"Easy for you to say."

Edward learned from talking to his dracorn that its name was Terramin.

"All done? Good, let's go." Sir Dreyfus wandered over to his own which stood alone opposite the pilots'.

Conor took a deep breath as he put his left foot on the stirrup, swinging his other leg over, heaving himself onto the saddle. Looking over, he saw Edward get onto Terramin with ease.

"Let's go, Cimball," Sir Dreyfus said, shaking the reins. Cimball pivoted towards the pilots, his nostrils flaring, excitement lurking in his oily black eyes.

"Here we go, gentlemen." Sir Dreyfus cast a determined eye towards the horizon, once again jerking the reins. "Yarr!"

Cimball stood on his hind legs, kicking and neighing wildly. Biting his mouth-piece, he galloped out of the stables, his wings appearing after a puff of brown mist dissipated. Cimball took to the skies.

"Come on, MacCall," Edward encouraged as his dracorn too galloped out of the stables.

"God help us," Conor mumbled as he spurred his.

"Not so hard, master," Corbus barked.

"Oh, sorry," Conor replied, red-faced. Corbus's hooves pounded the ground like thunder before spreading its wings. "Woah." Conor held onto the reins with all his might as Corbus soared higher. The belly-gunner closed his eyes, afraid to look down.

Wind and feathery substance from clouds hit them as their dracorns flew higher before steadying off. For the first time in a long while, Conor gained a new appreciation and perspective in being airborne, as the horizon looked beautiful, painted in bronze and pink hues. Conor gazed at Edward again, his captain unflinching, seeming unfazed by the dizzying height they flew at. Of course heights were nothing to these men as they flew all the time but this was different. They were no longer within the safety of a plane.

Sir Dreyfus drew his sword, aiming its tip at a ruin of an old castle, only a stony archway now standing. Banking right, Cimball flew towards the ruin.

Edward and Conor's dracorns swooped down.

Cimball leveled off without touching the overgrown grass which soon threatened to hide the archway. It then zipped under the dilapidated structure before soaring again, flying over a forest that lay ahead.

Conor felt wind whipping at his face while descending. The archway's shadow shrouded him in momentary darkness as he passed through. After he pulled the reins, Terramin re-joined Sir Dreyfus and Edward.

Once they cleared the forest, Conor's eyebrows raised both in confusion and dread.

"What the hell," he gasped.

Standing below were a column of Argoth's archers, aiming their bows at them.

"Get ready. Arrows incoming!" Sir Dreyfus warned.

A loud sound similar to a whip being cracked, erupted as arrows were released, heading straight for the three riders.

"Christ!" Conor cursed as Corbus weaved to avoid the missiles. Conor saw more arrows being taken from their quivers. Their tips glinted as they were aimed again.

"There's more incoming," Conor shouted to his friends.

The skies darkened behind them for a brief second before arrows rained on them. Again Conor held on for his dear life as Corbus banked to the left, weaving in and out between each arrow fall.

Once it seemed like five minutes had passed, the longest five minutes in Conor's life, he looked back, sighing in relief as they were out of shooting distance. Sir Dreyfus pointed with his left arm to an open meadow on a mountain top. Cimball swooped down towards it.

"Thank God we're going down," Conor muttered as Corbus followed Cimball and Terramin.

As Terramin's hooves touched down, he came to a halt after a quick trot. Conor dismounted.

"What the hell d'ya think you're playing at?" Conor barked at Sir Dreyfus.

"What do you mean?" he replied while getting down from Cimball.

Edward dismounted Terramin too.

"What do I mean?" Conor said, exasperated. "I mean what the hell were those archers firing at us for?"

"That was to prepare you for the battle. That is what this whole exercise is about," Sir Dreyfus answered.

"We could've been bloody killed," Conor yelled back.

"I had faith in your dracorns to keep you safe."

"Oh, really? Well, I'm glad one of us had faith in 'em. A warning would've been nice," Conor shot back.

Sir Dreyfus folded his arms, staring at the Scot. "I would have thought by now, Sergeant, you would know to expect the unexpected in war."

"Aye, on a plane maybe, but not on a blasted dracorn!"

"I think what my friend is trying to say," Edward interjected, "this is all new to us so we don't really know what to expect here."

Sir Dreyfus unfolded his arms, presenting both men with a more understanding gaze.

"Out in the battlefield there will be no warnings. *Anything* can happen at *any* time. If you are not prepared for that, then you will be dead before you know it."

Conor and Edward exchanged a look of concern before lowering their eyes to the grass in short contemplation.

Sir Dreyfus opened a pouch on his saddle, taking out a short axe.

"What are you going doin' with that?" Conor asked.

"It's time to go hunting," Sir Dreyfus replied, sliding the axe into his belt. "Come."

Later that evening, the three men sat in front of a small campfire, a hare roasting over a spit they had constructed. Corbus, Cimball and Terramin grazed as their riders talked. Aromas of burning wood accompanied by scorched flesh assaulted everyone's noses. The fire's glow illuminated the area.

"Can you tell me how Argoth's men got here before us?" Conor asked.

"On dracorns like we did."

"Oh, I see." Conor stayed quiet before unloading the next question that had been on his mind for a while. "So how long have you been a knight?"

"About thirty years," Sir Dreyfus answered while stoking the fire with a stick.

"You must have seen your fair share of battles," Edward said.

"That I did."

"Do you have any children?" Edward shot Conor a glance of surprise when the Scot asked this.

"One son, Daniel." Sir Dreyfus looked directly at Conor with an expression that knew what the next question would be. "And no, he has no mother." He stoked the fire once more, his words laced with sadness. "She died giving birth."

"Sorry to hear that," Conor replied. "Mustn't have been easy raisin' a young 'un on yer own."

"No, no it was not. He is stubborn like his mother and refuses to listen to me sometimes." Sir Dreyfus cleared his throat before asking, "Anyway, what about you, gentlemen? Have you any children?"

"I do," Edward answered. "Two of them. One boy and girl. My son wants to be an architect and-"

"An architect?" Sir Dreyfus said, puzzled.

"Yes, he wants to build stuff like houses."

"Oh, I see. And the girl?"

"She wants to go into medicine like her mother."

"A noble ideal. Daniel just wants to be a knight like me. I would rather he be something else. I cannot stand the thought of losing him on the battlefield. I train him to defend himself but that is as far as it goes. I told Argoth I do not want him joining the army."

"What did the king say?" Conor asked.

"It's the boy's choice at the end of the day when he turns 18. He will not stop him joining."

"But surely he'll make an exception for you?" Edward said.

"No. The law is the law, no exceptions for anyone."

"Bet that doesn't sit well with you?" Conor said.

"No."

"Yes, I'd hate the thought of my son joining the army too," Edward said.

A silence fell onto them as Sir Dreyfus continued to roast the hare. An hour later after eating, all three rode back to Argoth's castle.

* * *

Tracey browsed through various clothes in the store, even though she did not like any of them. She was trying to clear her mind, she felt confused.

What the hell am I doing here? the girl thought. Everybody seems to have a purpose but what am I supposed to do? I'm always kept out of meetings.

Karina interrupted her thinking. "Hello, Tracey."

"Hi. Is everything okay?"

"Yes, fine," she replied, "well with me, at least. Something bothers you, though. I sense confusion."

"Gosh, you really are a mind reader, aren't you?" she said, sarcastically.

Karina chuckled at her response. "I do not need to read minds to know when someone is confused like you are."

"Yeah, I guess I am. I mean, we all know what Henry's supposed to do and those air force guys too. But why am I here?"

"Everything happens for a reason, Tracey; you have a purpose here too. I think you are here to give Henry strength."

"Me? Give Henry strength?"

"Yes, I see the way he looks at you. Sometimes a woman can give a man strength in ways his male friends cannot."

"What do you mean?"

"I was married for many years and every morning I woke up, I used to look across the bed at the man I loved. It used to make me so happy it gave me a reason to come home every day."

"Wait, are you saying I should marry Henry cos I'm telling you now, that's not gonna happen."

Karina laughed and shook her head. "No, no, I am not saying that at all. I meant that sometimes gentle words from a woman can give a man great encouragement."

"Oh, okay. I think I know what you mean." Tracey approached her next question tenderly. "What happened to your husband?"

"He was killed by Sadarkians in the war."

Tracey felt like kicking herself after hearing this. "Oh, I'm very sorry." *I knew it was a dumb idea to ask that.*

"I best be going. You know where I am if you need to talk. I am sure Hannorah would be happy to talk to you too."

"Thanks. And yeah, she's kind of cool to talk to."

"How is your training with Sir Dreyfus coming along?"

"It was hard at first but I'm used to it now."

"Good. For a change tomorrow I will have Hannorah train you. She might go easier on you" She winked before leaving.

"Thanks. That'll be cool."

Thoughts of meeting death on the battlefield sent a cold chill through her. It was one thing to die in a match in Fortnite or Call of Duty, rebooted Doom even, but this was real life.

Oh, Henry, what have you gotten me into? she sighed, raising her head in defiance, suppressing doubts. *It doesn't matter, I'll have your back out there.*

* * *

Karina sat in her room in the lotus position, letting the sound of a gentle breeze coming in an open window be her point of focus. It kept her mind from wandering while she tried to concentrate, remaining focused at all times on one thing: being one with everything around her.

Today was different for it marked the anniversary of when she first learned she had magic. Even the wind couldn't stop Karina from hearing screams of her younger self, crying out for her mother whose face was buried in her father's shoulder. The woman was crying while keeping her eyes shut. Her mother couldn't bear to watch as Karina was dragged away by the Order of Onosis – monks who lived deep in a valley, half a mile from her home.

Her first use of magic happened when she was only sixteen. Karina was walking home from school with her friend Patria, a girl with ash-blonde hair and two inches smaller than Karina. They talked about the usual things: school work, their shared hatred for the horrid teacher, boys they liked. Their discussions were cut short when a twig from a fallen branch, snapped in a bush just a few inches away from where they stood.

"What was that?" Patria asked.

"Not too sure."

A young fawn popped its head out from behind the bushes. It looked left and right before taking a further two steps. Soon it fully emerged from behind the bush. Karina sensed that it was just as wary as they were.

As the fawn stopped in the middle of the road, its eyes locked with Karina's. A sharp pain throbbed in her forehead just between her two eyebrows.

"My... head..." Karina massaged her forehead but heard a young male voice repeating the same line. At first it was faint but grew louder with each time it was uttered.

"Please... do not hurt me. I am... lost," the voice said. When she looked up, it seemed to be coming from the fawn. The timid creature blinked its eyes, twitching its ears twice before bolting across to the other side of the road when he was spooked by a small flock of birds taking flight from a tree.

Karina was shaken from her reverie by Patria whose shouts filled the shocked girl's ears.

"Karina... Karina! Are you all right?" Patria shouted. "Karina, answer me!"

"Yes... yes, I am fine." Her headache had subsided leaving her to feel normal again...but how could anyone be normal after hearing that? she asked herself.

"Is something wrong? You turned white there for a second."

"I am fine now. I... felt ill." She didn't want to tell Patria about hearing the young animal.

Karina was afraid the girl would think she had turned insane. "Let's just go home."

Later that night in bed, her thoughts still centered on hearing the voice. If it spoke now, it would reverberate around her room. A chair was near her door where some of her clothes lay across and a small wardrobe was opposite it.

How is this even possible? she thought. How can I hear an animal speak? Am I going mad?

A week passed by without any incident until one evening she walked through the woods with her mother, carrying baskets of fruit from the marketplace back to their home. Karina stopped in her tracks, putting a hand up to her belly. A sickening feeling was suddenly in her stomach. It was a warning sign to turn around. She couldn't be sure of this but her senses said otherwise.

"Mother, I think we should go home a different way," Karina advised.

Her mother, Adia, a tall woman in her late 30s with long blonde hair and piercing hazel eyes, turned to face her daughter with a look of skepticism.

"What is wrong now? Afraid an ogre is going to come charging out?" Adia smiled after saying this. But she should have listened to her daughter.

Stepping out from behind a cluster of trees were three mercenaries. Karina knew them by their uniforms, which were purple tunics (bearing an emblem of a black rose) over chainmail. She heard her father speak of them a few days ago. They were dissatisfied soldiers who broke away from Argothos' army only to serve the highest bidder. Two of them carried swords while the third who had dark scraggy-hair and was unkempt, carried a bow. A quiver of arrows was slung over his right shoulder. He now aimed one at Karina. The shortest of the three, a bald man in his late 20s with a well-toned physique, took a step forward.

Adia moved out in front of Karina to protect her. The second man also took a step towards Karina and Adia. Karina could see from his dark brown eyes that he had a sinister intent which betrayed his clean-shaven, benevolent appearance.

"Please do not hurt us. We have nothing." Adia put down the food basket and motioned for Karina to do the same, which she did. "Here, take our food. Just let us pass."

The bald man leered at Karina, a perverse hunger lingering in his eyes as if he were staring at a tasty piece of chicken. "I have no interest in your food, lovie… but your daughter on the other hand..."

"No… you cannot have her." Adia, still standing in front of Karina, began backing away slowly, forcing her daughter to do the same.

"You are not exactly in a position to defend her…" chuckled the man aiming his bow at Karina.

"Just give us the girl and we will let ya go free," Baldy warned with his right hand now moving to his sword's hilt.

"No, she is not yours to take!" Adia cried.

"Wrong choice, missus," replied the archer, letting loose the arrow.

Time seemed to slow down for Karina as the arrow was fired. Something tingled in her veins, as if some static energy surged through her body. Karina's vision became fogged over in a bright white hue. She reached out her hand and the arrow changed direction, turning and hitting the clean-shaven man in the neck. He grabbed where the missile became embedded, coughing up some blood before keeling over. Her vision returned to normal.

The other mercenaries looked on in dismay, which soon turned to anger.

"You little bitch," Baldy snarled, his sword unsheathed. Sunlight glinted on its blade, as well as the arrow tip now facing her as the archer now lined another one on his bow.

"Get away from us," Karina screamed. She stepped aside. Both eyes were once again fogged over. Karina thrust her hands forward. A shockwave knocked both men back at least ten feet from where they stood. Adia gasped, putting a hand to her mouth.

What happened? Did I just do that? Dumbfounded, the girl stared at her hands. The eerie hue over her eyes now disappeared.

"We have to go." Adia picked up the basket of fruit while keeping a close eye on the thugs who lay unconscious. She looked back at Karina who still looked at her hands in amazement. "Come on, Karina, we have to go before they wake up!"

Karina picked up her own basket and they ran.

* * *

That night Karina lay in her bed, her eyes red from crying as she listened to her parents argue as they were in the kitchen. Dreyfus, aged four, slept in his parents' room.

"This cannot be happening. First my aunt and now Karina," her father Detrok said. She imagined him saying that with his hands raised in despair.

"Karina is not like your aunt. She is good. She protected me."

"But she still has magic. That means there is still a chance she could be evil."

"Not everyone who has magic is evil," Adia protested.

"No…but I am not taking any chances."

"What does that mean?" There was no answer. Adia waited a moment for a response but none came. "Well? What do you mean by that?" Karina could hear Detrok walking to her parents' room. Karina jumped when he slammed the door.

Every day it weighed heavy on her mind what her father meant by that he was not taking any chances. What had he planned? Even in school she found it difficult to pay attention to what the teacher said with various scenarios running through her head, none of them good.

Why did I have to have this power? Karina thought two weeks later at school while totting up some figures they were asked to add.

Later that day as she walked into her yard, she saw a tall man with a shaved head, a primrose monk robe with a green sash over his right shoulder, standing outside her house. He looked at Karina as she walked closer to the door.

"Hello," he greeted in a soft voice.

"H-hello," she stuttered, sizing the stranger up, afraid to approach him.

"You have nothing to fear." His words were now soothing, almost hypnotic in nature. Her guard was lowered, any doubts about this man melted away. Karina felt as if her body was no longer under her control, something willing her forward.

"Karina... no!" Adia screamed as she flung open the door. Detrok held her back as the woman kicked and lashed out, trying to break free.

Karina wanted to look at Adia but something or someone willed her not to. The girl had guessed it was this man who now controlled her mind.

The stranger whistled. Two other men dressed the same as him, emerged from behind the house. Her heart thundered as the first man stepped forward, touching her forehead with his right index finger. Karina wanted to run but was rooted to the ground. His finger touched the space between the two eyebrows. Everything went dark as she collapsed.

When she regained consciousness she was alone in the monastery belonging to the Order of Onosis. Karina later learned that the man who made her faint would become her master. His name was Orkinad. He showed Karina how to hone her powers for healing but also striking a balance when using magic to defend herself but not to venture too far into dark magic with the intent of killing someone unless necessary.

After spending five years in this monastery, Karina was given the option of returning home to Adia and Detrok or staying on. She chose to stay on but visited her parents once every month. In her fifth year there, she met a young Prince Argoth at a party held in the castle and they became close friends.

Now that Karina had managed to quell any noise in her mind and was fully back in the present, she heard a new voice, one that almost made her jump.

"Be still, my child," a male said. "No need to be afraid. It is me, Zymbion."

"Sorry, My God. It has been a while since we last spoke."

"It has. I come bearing a message… a warning about the battle."

What Zymbion told Karina made her lips quiver. A tear wandered down her cheek.

Letting out a long exhalation, she got up and changed into ceremonial clothes for the Remembrance Bonfire. But what Zymbion told Karina weighed heavy on her mind…especially the sacrifice that had to be made when the time came.

* * *

With a damp tunic moist from sweat after over two hours of exercises and sword training, Henry found it difficult to carry on or remain focused with aching arms and legs. Taking a deep breath, he charged towards Dreyfus with his wooden sword in the air. Their swords clashed as they battled, with each move countered by the other. Dreyfus took a swipe at Henry, but the teen ducked. The blade grazed the hairs on his head. Henry, however, lost his footing, falling back.

Dreyfus held the tip of his blade to Henry's Adam's apple. "What have I told you before about charging in without watching your footing? If this were a real fight, you would be dead! Always keep your balance. Never rush in."

"Yes, sir."

"On your feet and we will try again." He caught Henry's hand, pulled him up. He gave him back his sword. "This time, no charging in."

Henry brushed the dirt from his clothes and took his position. He found it difficult to focus as the sound of engineers working on siege towers distracted him.

"Do the sounds from over there bother you?"

"Yeah. I kind of find it hard to concentrate."

"The sounds you hear now will be nothing compared to those on the battlefield. You must block them out or you will die. Just focus on killing those around you."

Dreyfus attacked again without warning, this time with a little more intensity. He struck high and hard with Henry holding the sword horizontally to the left, the knight's blade crashing down on it. Henry stumbled back a step or two and arched his neck back as Dreyfus took another swing, the sword missing his jaw by a hair's breadth. Dreyfus juggled the sword from his right hand to the left and performed a straight thrust to Henry's abdomen. The boy dodged it by spinning around and performed a leg sweep, taking Dreyfus off his feet.

With Dreyfus flat on his back, Henry kicked the knight's weapon away. He pointed his own sword at his tutor's throat.

"Give up or die."

"Good, Henry. You have mastered defense techniques." Henry then fell back as Dreyfus swept his right leg under Henry's. Clamping his knee on the boy's weapon and forcing the other on his chest. He stared into the teen's eyes.

"Just because the enemy is down, it does not mean he is defeated. They are only defeated when they are dead. Understand?"

"Yes, sir."

"When you have the chance to kill, do it."

Henry nodded again, but he wasn't sure he could.

Dreyfus stood up. "That is enough for today. You are doing well but there is room for improvement." Sir Dreyfus gathered up the swords, rolling them up in an ox skin cloth. "I will see you tonight at the Remembrance Bonfire."

"Remembrance Bonfire? Oh wait, that's something you guys do to remember the soldiers who died fighting the Sadarkians."

"Yes."

"Yeah… I heard some people talking about that. It sounds like fun."

"It is. You will be there?"

Henry nodded. "You betcha."

"Good. See you then." Sir Dreyfus left with the swords underneath his right arm.

Henry massaged his chest as it hurt a little from the weight of Dreyfus's knee. Just when he thought things couldn't get any worse, he heard Daniel's voice.

"Well, not only do you look like a peasant, you fight like one, too."

"Just go away, Daniel!"

"Oooh, did I upset you?" he sniggered.

"If you're so good, why weren't you chosen?"

"Obviously Elders and gods make poor choices too."

Henry stared intensely at Daniel who had his arms folded and an eyebrow arched. "Well, if you're better than me with a sword, why not prove it?" Henry watched on with delight as Daniel's over-confidence diminished. "I do not have to prove myself to you."

"Likewise," Henry shot back.

"Anyway, I do not have time to stand around chatting. I am meeting my aunt in a few minutes." Daniel strutted off, his head cocked high, his arms swinging by his side, marching more so than walking.

"It is fun when he talks to you like that?" Hannorah said sarcastically, approaching Henry from behind.

"Not really. I just wish he'd get lost and get over whatever problem he has with me."

"Daniel does not get over things easily." Hannorah looked at Henry's chest as he rubbed it. "Are you hurt?"

"Kinda. I was practicing with Sir Dreyfus and he pinned me down with his knee on my chest. It's not so bad now though."

"Here," Hannorah placed her hand in the area he was rubbing, "let me help." The gentle heat Henry experienced before returned as her fingers pressed against his sternum. Her fingertips became hotter as the heat intensified around his heart until the nagging pain was gone. While she was healing him, Henry noticed that she held him in an amorous gaze. He sensed a wanting in her, to do more than just heal him. He sensed she wanted to take this further, much further.

Does she have the hots for me? he thought before pulling away. "My chest feels fine now, thanks."

"Good. So, do you care to try some of your sword skills on me?"

"Nah, I gotta go. I've had enough for today."

"Scared of being beaten by a girl?"

"No, of course not."

"Then face me."

"Err. No, I really gotta go."

"Oh, all right," she replied, her response laced with disappointment. "Maybe later then?"

"Yeah, sure." Henry waved and left. Hannorah was pretty and he knew that, but Tracey was the one he wanted. His heart belonged to her but the question that always loomed in his mind was, would she want him now that the spell was broken?

* * *

Tracey watched from her room window as Henry trained with Sir Dreyfus.

"Yes," she shouted when Henry took down his tutor. She groaned in disappointment when the boy was a victim of a well-timed counter-attack.

I hope he's okay, she thought when he rubbed his chest. She'd liked Henry in school; he was okay, if a bit of a wuss.

Tracey always knew he was smart and that they liked a lot of the same things. Her hesitation was always he was too readily beat up by the other boys and after all she'd been through as a kid, losing her parents, the insecurity she still felt about being adopted, she wanted someone who could take care of her, be there for her. It was only here, seeing just how hard Henry was prepared to work to save these people, that she was starting to see that Henry was the kind of man she wanted. She only had to see him for what he was, not what she thought he'd been.

Her eyes zoned in on Hannorah's hand as the other girl touched Henry's chest. Tracey felt a pang of jealousy and confusion shoot through her.

Whoa, where did that come from? It became clear to her that since they came here, she had gotten to know Henry better and it was seeing Hannorah do this that made her want him even more.

* * *

That night, Henry sat and watched as the bonfire blazed. Jasper sat beside him. Food was being distributed. Henry saw men slobbering on pieces of meat. Guards patrolled the area to keep order. Women danced with their female friends and husbands while children ran and played games. Henry wished he could be one of the children, running carefree, not having the burden that he had. A few months ago, all that he had to worry about were exams, now there were much more important matters on his shoulders - like saving people. There was also the fact that his parents were not his real parents. He was still struggling to process that. Henry hadn't a good night's sleep since he found out that he was chosen by the Elders to save Zargothia. This began to show a little with dark circles sometimes under his eyes and ratty mood swings.

A shadow of a tall woman loomed over him. He turned around to see who it was.

"Oh hi, Karina."

"Hello, Master Henry. Mind if I sit with you for a while?"

"Yeah, sure. Take a seat."

Karina sat on the hard ground.

Henry was silent gazing into the bonfire.

"Is there something wrong? You are very quiet," Karina said.

"I guess I'm just tired from all the training." Henry's posture was rigid and tense. "Do you think -" Henry paused, unsure whether or not to continue.

"Do I think what?"

"Do you think...we'll win this battle?"

"Well... the odds do seem to be against us. Zakarius has more soldiers than we do. Our only hope is you. Is that what troubles you: the battle?"

"Yeah. I'm afraid that if I fail, then all the people here will be killed. You, Argoth and the others believe in me... but I can't believe in myself."

Karina put her right arm around Henry and rubbed the boy's arm. "What you are feeling is only natural, Master Henry. All soldiers are afraid of dying."

"But that's the thing, Karina, I'm not a soldier. I'm chosen by these super gods or whatever you call them, to protect everyone here."

"It is at times like these I would like to use my magic and make everything better. Unfortunately, I cannot, but you can talk to me any time you feel the need to."

"Thanks, Karina. I appreciate that."

"As for the battle, every man, Jenorme and Volark can make a difference on that day. You will not be alone on the battlefield."

"Do you think I can beat him?"

"Zakarius?"

"Yeah."

"Oh certainly, but it will not be easy. But with practice, perseverance and self-belief, you will be evenly matched when you two meet."

A thought struck Henry. "You know how I have this coin that can do amazing things?"

"Yes."

"Well why can't I just wish that Zakarius and his army were dead?"

"Magic is never that easy, Henry. A wish that big would require great strength."

"But I'm the son of an Elder-thingy, aren't I? I should be able to do that."

"I cannot speak for the coin but when I was your age, there was a wizard named Maki in our village. He was very powerful. When our village came under attack from a group of mercenaries and they killed some people, Maki swore vengeance. He read over every spell book he had. He put a death curse on all of the men who attacked us."

"How many of them were there?"

"Over one hundred. It worked too but he was left crippled. The poor man could not walk for the rest of his life. The strength and power of that spell was so great that it took a lot out of him. So can you imagine what it will do to you if you made the same wish he did?"

Henry nodded his head. Being an invalid for the rest of his life was not a welcome prospect. He also remembered the warning the Elder gave when he saw Zargothia's history.

Then Henry laughed as he thought of something. "Just say I did survive the battle and was returned to my home, what then? The people I thought were my real folks, aren't. There's so much of that life that I've missed. Exams, the normal sort of things. Rites of passage, ya' know? How can I just go back? How can I feel the same way about them as I did before coming here? What can I do to make it right for Tracey? She didn't deserve to be ripped away from her life either."

"Those are hard questions and I do not have all the answers. I lost many friends, including my husband during the war. I would love to have someone to return home to that loves me with all their heart. But I do not and that is why I envy you, Henry. These people, the ones you call 'Mom' and 'Dad', they do love you, right?"

"Yeah, of course, but I'm not their son."

"Does it matter? They chose you. Whether you are their child or not, if you give them happiness and they make you happy, is that not reason enough to go on loving them?"

Henry sighed. "I guess you're right. I just wish I could meet my real folks."

"Life is not easy, my friend, and will get harder when you get older." Karina looked away as she continued. "Sometimes sacrifices have to be made for those you care for most."

"That's okay if you know you're going to grow old but I don't know if I'll live long enough to turn eighteen." Henry paused for a moment and then asked another question that had been pressing on his mind for a few days. "A few days ago, when the coin was in that box and it showed that I was *the* Foretold One, how come you didn't recognize me when we arrived?"

"I did not see what you did. I only heard the voice but could not see anything. I think it might have been a precaution taken by the Elders in case the chest was stolen, like the diamond was from the tower."

"How do you know we saw a sort of movie about this place?"

"A movie?" Karina replied.

"Yeah, you know the thing we saw in your room."

"Oh, well Zymbion told me you would see something in your mind."

"Oh right." Henry yawned, stood up and stretched his arms. "Thanks for the chat, Karina, but I'm gonna get some sleep. Sir Dreyfus wants me up early in the morning for more training."

"Good night, Master Henry."

Henry waved back at Karina as he continued to his quarters.

* * *

Henry tossed and turned, unable to lie still while nightmares plagued his sleep.

He wore golden armor as he stood alone on the battlefield with smoke all around him. Many bodies surrounded him, some whole, limbs separated from torsos, swords, axes and other weapons embedded in some. Blood covered faces and uniforms. He walked around to see if anybody had survived. All that was before him were his comrades: Argoth, Karina and the two airmen, all slain. He knelt down beside Argoth and wept.

"I'm sorry, Your Majesty. I tried, I really tried."

Argoth opened his eyes and grabbed Henry's arm. The king's chestnut eyes looked menacing. "You failed us, boy. You have let my people down!"

"I didn't mean to. Let me go." Henry freed his arm from Argoth's grasp and ran.

While Henry fled, he saw someone emerging from the smoke that shrouded the battlefield. It was Karina; her throat was slit. Blood cascaded onto the white shirt. She walked in an ethereal manner while pointing a finger of blame at him.

"Why did you fail us? I wish you had never come here. The Elders should never have chosen you."

"Not you too, Karina. It's not my fault." Henry ran from the woman.

"You cannot run from your mistakes forever," Karina yelled as Henry ran deeper into the smoke.

Henry noticed Cyren sobbing as she stood over her son's grave. Dressed in black, she patted her eyes with a handkerchief. But there was another grave beside her son's - it was Henry's. He retreated slowly from her.

"You did your best but it was all too much for you," she said. Cyren offered a hand of sympathy. "You could not save my people. Do not worry, I forgive you."

He turned and fled into the smoky abyss again until she was out of sight. Henry wondered where he could run to escape this horror.

In the dense fog, Henry tripped over a log. He fell onto damp grass that was bathed in blood. Not far from where he fell, he heard footsteps crunching the grass. From behind the smoke, a faint outline of a person could be seen, running the blade of a sword along the ground.

Riddled with anxiety, Henry tried to get to his feet but hands shot up from the moist earth and held him down.

Zakarius was in full view now.

Henry wriggled to break hold of the undead hands that pinned him.

Zakarius placed a foot on Henry's chest.

"What a pathetic excuse for a hero you are. I will enjoy hacking you limb from limb." With both hands wrapped around the hilt of his sword, Zakarius raised it.

"No. No please," Henry pleaded while struggling to break free.

Zakarius's baleful laughter rang into the skies.

Henry screamed as the sword came crashing down.

Henry sat up in his bed as he gasped. The night's darkness was all that surrounded him now. He got up and walked to a nearby window, opening it for some fresh air. Henry stared at the ground.

"I really hope I don't let you guys down," Henry said as he then stared out into the sky littered with bright stars.

* * *

The next morning, Argoth stood in his chambers, looking out his window. He sighed as he recalled his first taste of what one can lose because of war.

He remembered the day well. He was a boy, no more than ten years of age. He stood beside his mother, Alexandria, in her room as they stared at the street. Three bodies in carts, made their way up to the castle. Everyone stopped and stared in disbelief as their princes, killed while fighting in battle, passed them. Some threw roses, daisies and other flowers into the carts, each a mark of respect. There had been a civil war between Argothos' soldiers and disillusioned ex-soldiers hell bent on overthrowing the king. It lasted two years until a truce was made. But not before Argoth lost his brothers.

Argoth cried. It became too much to hold back his tears.

"Your three brothers: Alexander, Eric and Harlow are dead. Now you know the cost of war, my son." Alexandria held a shaky breath before continuing. "There is no greater loss than that of your children. I hope it is something you never experience, my child."

Years later, while fighting in a battle, he too would feel the loss his mother felt. Argoth was in the thick of combat, surrounded by his own men clashing with Mordoch's forces. He was fighting a soldier when he heard someone scream,

"Argoth, look out!"

Argoth saw a guard sneak up behind him just in time to block his attack. The young man that warned him was not so fortunate. Because he warned the king, he dropped his own guard and was killed from behind. That young man was Aranok – Argoth's only son. He was eighteen years old when he died.

Argoth took out a blood-red cloak from a wardrobe. He wiped away a tear as he held the folded cloak. Argoth jumped as Cyren spoke.

"You have to let him go."

"You gave me a fright there. Never heard you walking in." He looked at the cloak again. "I know, letting go is so hard though."

"I know, my love. I miss him too but living in the past never helps."

"If only he did not have to warn me, then he might still be-"

"Shh," she said with a finger to his lips. "Blaming yourself will not help either."

"But-"

"No buts." Cyren offered him an understanding, sympathetic smile and said, "It is all right to think of him, I do every day but we cannot continue to blame ourselves. He would not want that."

Argoth lifted his eyes from the cloak and met hers. "You remind me of my mother sometimes; she was always right too." He tapped the cloak twice as he continued, "It *is* time to let go and I think I know how."

* * *

Henry spread out his arms as he was being helped into his armor by a servant named Jarold.

Can't wait to make this gold like the color of the coin, Henry thought.

Jarold stopped when Argoth walked in carrying a red cloak.

"I want a word with Henry in private," Argoth told Jarold. The servant left.

Henry eyed the blood-red cloak Argoth was holding. It was edged in gold, something about it demanded his attention but Henry could not define what.

"The battle is almost upon us, Henry. I feel your armor would not be complete without this." Argoth handed Henry the red cloak.

"Thank you, Your Majesty. I will take good care of it."

"Please do. It was my son's."

Henry stared at Aranok's cloak in amazement. "I... I don't know what to say."

"No need to say anything. Just wear it well." Argoth's usual serious countenance lapsed. He gave Henry a rare broad, heartfelt smile under his thick beard.

"I won't let you down, sir."

"I know." Argoth patted Henry on the right shoulder twice before leaving.

* * *

Sunlight filtered through scrawny branches while birds chirped. The sound of water running beyond the trees surrounded Henry, Hannorah and Tracey as they walked through Egorthinia.

Tracey asked Hannorah, "Do you mind if I ask you a personal question?"

"How personal is personal?" Hannorah replied warily.

"Nothing too personal."

"All right. Go ahead."

"Were you ever tempted to use your powers for something bad?"

"Like what, revenge?"

"Yeah, something like that."

She thought about her answer for a few moments and said, "Yes, a few times when Daniel annoyed me but Karina made me take an oath. If I break it, my powers are gone."

"Guess she's very strict on that rule, huh?" Henry said.

"You have no idea."

"Oh, I think I'm beginning to," Henry replied, knowing that he would not want to dare challenge the sorceress.

"Of course, I am not as powerful as you, Henry. I bet many are jealous of you."

"I don't know about being jealous. Having all these powers is pretty cool an' all but sometimes I'd give anything just to go back to being normal... whatever that is." A bee buzzed around Henry's head. He swatted it away.

"But look at all the good you can do like healing people, *saving* people, giving them hope. These are all the things Karina says what makes a person with powers, special. You want to give up something like that?"

"She has a point," Tracey chimed in.

"Well… since you put it that way," Henry said in agreement. "So, how long have you known Karina? How did she become so powerful?"

"She does not talk much about how she got her powers. Once she told me she was trained by a monk far away from here but that is all. I do know her husband died during the war and this made her an even fiercer warrior. Her powers grew too."

"Did you ever see her use her powers when she was pissed?" Henry asked.

"*Pissed?*" Hannorah's voice was riddled with confusion.

"Yeah, you know, pissed off, angry."

"Yes, about a year ago. We were traveling through here when we were attacked by two thieves-"

Henry shot her a worried look, *Now she tells us there's thieves here!*

Hannorah continued oblivious to his concerns, "She warned them about who she was and one of them threatened to kill her if she didn't give them money. She used her magic to pick him up and pin him against a tree. The other ran away afraid she would do the same to him."

"Did she hurt the other guy?" Henry said.

"No, but she warned him if he ever crossed her path, it would be the sorriest day of his life. It scared me."

Henry ducked as he heard the buzzing of the bee hovering over his head. As he crouched, the coin, which was tucked inside a pouch attached to his belt, fell from its confines onto the ground.

"Ow!" Henry said, wincing. The bee had shot straight down, stinging Henry's neck.

"What's wrong?' Tracey asked.

"Damn bee stung me,' Henry answered, rubbing the area he was stung.

"Let me see.' Hannorah removed his hand. There, forming on the nape of his neck was a little red mound. "Stay still." The girl placed her hand over it. Henry felt a warm sensation surging down his spine, shooting back up again. When the warm sensation shot back up, he felt what he thought was the bee's stinger being pushed out through his skin.

But that wasn't the only sensation he felt. Hannorah's touch was a lot gentler than before. When he looked into her eyes, he saw something lurking within them that was more than a friendly glance. He saw in them a look of love.

"I have to go. Sorry," Tracey said abruptly, spinning on her heels, stomping back to the castle. Henry had thought about calling after her but he felt trapped in this awkward moment.

*What would I say? Sorry? I mean, we're not officially going out or anything, right? Yeah, she was my prom date but still...*Henry knew this attempt at making himself feel better or trying to reason his way out of this predicament was failing miserably.

Got to thank Hannorah at least. "Uh... thanks for healing me but I'm sure the coin would've done it anyway.'

"Maybe, but it is my instinct to heal people. Especially warriors like you." She winked at him and revealed some of her front teeth with a mischievous grin.

Can this get any more awkward? "Uh... thanks, Hannorah." He picked up the coin. "We better catch up to Tracey. I don't want her to get lost."

"Come on, then. Will race you." Hannorah had just finished her sentence when she ran.

"Hey, not fair!" Henry closed the pouch and ran after her, avoiding the temptation to use the coin's power to gain on her.

* * *

Two hours later, Tracey walked towards the sandy training area, groaning when she saw Hannorah leaning up against a fence with her arms folded, looking content. Something wrapped up in a flour sack was at her feet. Hannorah smiled when she saw her.

"Hello, Tracey. I was not sure if you would come."

"Oh I wouldn't miss this for the world," she replied with a false smile. *Careful, she could read my mind or something. Think happy thoughts.*

Hannorah unfurled the flour sack revealing a number of wooden swords. "I got these from Sir Dreyfus. He said we can borrow them for a while."

"Cool." Each sword was crafted differently, some with a longer blade than others. Some cross guards were wider. One sword in particular attracted Tracey's eye. Its blade was of medium length and the pommel was in the shape of a love heart.

"Do you mind if I have first choice?" Hannorah asked.

"Sure."

As Hannorah ran her fingers over each hilt, Tracey's heart sank when Hannorah took the sword she wanted. Hannorah hewed the air two times testing it before settling for that one.

"I think I will take this one."

"Wouldn't be the first time you took something I like." *Shoot! Did I really just say that?*

Hannorah put down the sword and presented her with a stare of concern. "What do you mean?"

Tracey gave a little nervous laugh while replying, "Nothing. I'm just kidding around, you know, joking."

Hannorah's voice grew stern. "You were *not* joking. What is wrong?"

"Nothing, okay? Just chill. Forget I said anything." *Nice going. Now she must think I'm a total bitch.*

"I would like to think since we are friends; you can talk to me about anything. Did I do something to upset you?"

"No, okay? Can we just get on with the sparring or something?"

"No sparring until you tell me what is wrong. I know something is bothering you."

Tracey sighed, giving in. "All right, fine. I think I'm falling for Henry."

"Falling for Henry?" Hannorah said, confused but then a wave of realization washed over her face. "Oh, you mean you love him?"

"Well, love is a strong word… but yeah, I'm getting there."

"And that is why you stormed off when we were in the woods?"

"Bingo. So now that we've got that out of the way, can I ask you an awkward question?"

"If it helps you feel better, then yes."

"Do you like Henry?"

"Am I attracted to him?" There was a short but uncomfortable pause. "Yes, I am."

An air of awkwardness hung between both girls as they were silent for a minute which seemed like an hour to Tracey.

"So, are you… going to ask him out?" Tracey asked.

"If you mean am I going to pursue him, then no. I would not do that to you."

"I don't know if I'll ask him out. I mean, okay he has cute eyes and the whole power-of-a-god thing going for him but other than that…" *Wait, am I trying to talk myself out of being with him or what? Geez, can't believe I am thinking these things…especially about Henry.*

"So, when are you going to tell him?" Hannorah asked.

"Don't know. I wouldn't know what to say."

"You better think fast because he is coming."

Tracey turned around to see him walking towards them. He waved at them as he drew near. She waved back with a smile of consternation.

"Okay. This is going to be super awkward so I'm leaving now," Tracey whispered to Hannorah.

"What about sparring?"

"We'll do it tomorrow." Henry walked passed her.

Before he could speak, she said, "Hi, Henry. Bye, Henry," and walked rapidly back to her room.

Henry stared at her, befuddled, with a hand on his hip. "What's up with her?"

"I think it is best you talk to her yourself."

"Why? What's wrong?"

"It would be better coming from her. Trust me," Hannorah said while rolling up the flour sack.

"Is it serious?"

"Kind of."

"So you're going to keep me in suspense, huh?"

"If you want my advice, leave her alone until tomorrow. You will like what she has to say." Hannorah winked before leaving, letting Henry mull over what Tracey could possibly want to tell him.

What could it be? he thought while his heart leaped with joy. Guess we'll find out tomorrow. Henry walked back to his own room, whistling "The Real Slim Shady" he used to listen to from one of his dad's CDs. He loved to whistle that song when it seemed like his luck began to change. Unlike the other times, however, he hoped disappointment would not be around the corner.

* * *

Tracey sat in the banquet hall alone, chewing the last piece of hard bread thoroughly to make it easier to swallow.

They really got to fire their baker, she thought while brushing some breadcrumbs off the table onto her plate.

Karina walked in with a broad, warm smile. Tracey noted from the sorceress's indigo dress, that Karina would have fit right in with the people back home in the 1960s. Her coffee brown hair with traces of gray flowed as she walked towards her.

"Good morning," Karina greeted cheerily. "You look like you slept well."

"Thanks. I didn't sleep too badly, I guess."

Karina pulled out a chair, sitting beside the girl. "So, what have you got planned for today? Does Sir Dreyfus have more training for you?"

"No." *Thank God.* "Why?"

"If you are not busy I have a chore for you. It will help you build up your strength."

Oh, great. Just when I thought I had the day off. Tracey hid her disappointment behind a smile. "Oh, really? That sounds great. What do you want me to do?" she replied, feigning enthusiasm.

"When you are finished here, I want you to go collect some logs from the woodcutters' yard. They will give you a sack to take them home in. Bring them to me. It will help build up your strength carrying them."

"Okay. I am nearly finished here so I should be able to go over there soon."

"Good. You can take that furry animal Jasper to keep you company. I sense he is bored here anyway."

"Okay, will do."

"Good girl." Karina stood up and pushed her chair back under the table. "I know all this is tiresome for a young girl like yourself, but you need to be prepared physically and mentally for the battle. Never let the men around you think you are weak."

Tracey looked at Karina with a sense of newfound respect. "Thanks for the tip. I won't let you down."

"Oh I know." Karina with her left hand squeezed Tracey's left shoulder a little in affection.

Gee, I didn't know she thought so highly of me. Tracey stood up too, pushing her own chair in. She left her mind heavy with thoughts of the upcoming battle. *Karina's right. I gotta take every chance I get to train. I wanna be able to go back to Harleyville and see my dad again. Henry needs all the help he can get too.*

Tracey along with Jasper arrived at the woodcutters' yard. Rows of logs were stacked neatly on top of one another. The house there was a much larger version of a log cabin she'd seen in movies of people living in a snowy, remote mountaintop. Except this looked big enough to house four or five people. She imagined a warm blazing fire lighting inside. One of the woodcutters greeted her with a scowl. His arms were muscular and hands quite large, twice the size of hers. His once cream tunic was a dirty gray from greasy patches, which she guessed were from him eating like a slob. He held a rusty axe in his right hand.

"Friendly looking guy, huh?" Jasper whispered.

"Quit it, Jasper. He'll hear you," Tracey shot back in a low voice.

"You that girl the witch sent?" the woodcutter asked in a semi-growl.

"You mean Karina the sorceress?" Tracey corrected him. "Then yeah, I am."

He eyed her up and down. She could tell he was wondering if a skinny girl could carry a sack full of logs.

"My name is Nicholas. Wait here," Nicholas snapped. He slammed his axe into a tree stump used for placing logs on it to cut.

"I wonder what crawled up his ass?" Jasper remarked.

"Shh… he'll hear you."

"I ain't afraid of him."

Nicholas returned with a sack stuffed with logs. It proved little difficulty for him to carry with bulging muscles threatening to burst through the material in his dirty tunic. "You sure you can carry that?"

Tracey eyed the sack in doubt for a few seconds before pretending to sound confident. "Just watch me." She managed to lift the sack two inches off the ground before dropping it again.

This is going to be a long walk home. "Yeah, I'll be fine."

"All right," Nicholas said, unconvinced, with his arms folded and a smug smile broadening with each second as Tracey dragged the sack along. "Have fun, girlie," he added with a sneer.

"I bet he's a real hit with the ladies 'round here," Jasper quipped.

"Shut up, Jasper."

"Hey, just cos you can't carry that doesn't mean you have to take it out on me."

"Remind me again why I brought you along?"

"Because you like my charming company."

"Yeah… you keep tellin' yourself that." Tracey grunted as she managed to lift the heavy load over her shoulder.

Thirty minutes had passed when she decided to take a break. The back of her shirt bore a broad circular sweat patch.

"Why didn't I bring some water?" she asked herself.

She stood up in alert as some twigs snapped to her far right. Tracey drew her short knife from a scabbard hidden underneath her shirt. Her blue eyes darted from tree to tree, scanning for any danger.

"Looks like we got company," Jasper said.

"Shh… it could be Sadarkians."

"No it's not."

"How do you know?"

"Because I can smell a pain in the ass a mile away in this world," Jasper finished. As soon as Jasper replied, Daniel stepped out from behind a tree. He came armed with a long sword sheathed in an orange-red leather scabbard.

Tracey groaned as Daniel saw them and walked over.

"Hello there, Tracey."

"Hey, don't mind me. I'm not here at all," Jasper said.

Daniel continued ignoring the cat. "Here, let me take some of those logs for you." He opened the sack, taking five logs.

"Thanks for lightening the load," she replied.

He looked up to the sky as dusk began creeping in. "We better move. There is only two hours of daylight left. You do not want to be around here in the dark."

With aching arms and back, Tracey picked up the sack that was a little lighter now that Daniel carried some of the load.

"So how come you are getting the logs and not Henry?"

"Karina thinks it will build up my strength by getting them."

"Hmm. I guess she is right. Well, kind of."

"So you think I couldn't handle this by myself?"

"No. I meant I am surprised she did not ask Henry. He probably would have used a dracorn to get them."

Dammit, why didn't I think of that! "Yeah, well, I can manage just fine."

"Yet here I am helping you," Daniel replied with a devilish smirk.

"There's no need to rub it in." Tracey continued to walk and not return his stare, wanting to hide the strain on her face from heaving the flour sack.

"I am not trying to." Daniel's voice had softened, no longer bearing any element of snobbery. "This job is hard for anyone, no matter who it is."

"Do you do chores like this all the time?"

"No, I do much worse. I have to clean out the dracorn's stables. You think horse dung is bad, nothing compared to a dracorn's."

Tracey chuckled imagining Daniel with a scarf over his nose while shoveling dracorn crap into whatever it is he shoveled it into.

"It is not funny," he replied, his own answer laced with a tinge of laughter.

"Sorry, I just can't imagine you cleaning stables."

"Well I do. My father insists on it. He says it teaches me humility... or something like that."

"Your dad is hard on you too?"

"He always is. No matter what I do, it is never enough. I know he loves me but still…"

"Yeah, my dad pushes me hard too."

"What does your father do in your world?"

"He's a teacher."

"What does he teach?"

Tracey had thought about telling Daniel the truth but she knew he would not understand the subjects her father taught. "Lots of things."

"What do you want to do once you leave here? Assuming you will leave here."

Thanks for the vote of confidence. "I'd like to design clothes."

"Well I am sure you will do well whatever you choose to do in life."

"Um, thanks, Daniel. That's sweet of you."

All three walked on in silence for a while. She could see in her peripheral vision that Daniel was trying to think of something else to say. Words didn't come easy to her either for once.

Oh my God, please don't let him do what I think he's going to.

* * *

Henry sat in his room, enjoying a frothy hot chocolate he conjured up with the coin. While bringing the warm delicious drink to his lips, Henry wondered where Tracey was. Earlier when he passed her room she wasn't there.

Through the tiny slit in his ajar door, he saw Hannorah walk past. She wore a flowy black dress. It seemed to blend in with her hair.

Hey, maybe she knows where Tracey is. "Hannorah, hold up." He carried the hot chocolate with him while running out the door.

"Yes, Henry," she said while turning around.

"Do you know where Tracey is?"

"I think Karina asked her to get some logs. She should be back soon."

"Where would she get those?"

"At the woodcutters, about an hour's walk from here."

"This time of the evening? Damn, I better find her. Thanks Hannorah." He guzzled down the rest of his hot chocolate, wiping his mouth after drinking the last drop. He put the cup back in his room. Taking a dark green hooded cloak that laid across his bed, he ran out of the room and down the stairs.

* * *

Tracey's back ached even more as did her arms but still she continued on without complaining. Deep down, she knew the battle would be worse than this so dealing with pain in her arms and back would be nothing compared to what was to come on the battlefield.

"Do you know how much longer we have?"

"We should be there in about ten minutes," Daniel replied.

"Oh, thank God," Tracey sighed in relief.

The girl looked at Daniel in puzzlement as he put down his logs. "Why are you stopping? We're almost there."

"Tracey, before we go on, there… there is something I want to say." His eyes met hers. She noticed that he looked at her differently, his usual confident stare now being replaced with what she called puppy-dog eyes.

Oh God, it's not what I think it is, is it? I gotta stop this right now. "Like you said, Daniel, it's getting late so we better keep going."

"Please… this is hard for me to say. For a while now I have felt… something for you and-"

"Daniel, I really got-"

"Let me finish, please. I… like you… a lot, Tracey. I have never said that to a girl before so this is why it is hard for me to say it now."

He moved in closer, touching her right arm with his coarse left hand. "I know I have no powers like Henry but I am just as brave… if you only give me a chance to prove it." Daniel moved his lips closer to hers. The girl took two steps back.

"Daniel, I'm sorry. I know it took a lot for you to say that… but I can't do this. Sorry."

"You would rather Henry."

"Right now… I don't know what I want."

"I think we both know that is a lie." Daniel dropped the logs and brushed passed her as he walked away.

"Seriously? You're leaving me bring the logs back on my own?" Daniel walked on without answering. "Yeah, that's real classy. Thanks!" Then she mumbled, "Jerk."

* * *

Henry had come upon Daniel walking with Tracey, carrying some logs for her. He hid behind a tree, watching with interest. For a moment the boy held his breath as he thought Tracey and Daniel were about to kiss but smiled as she pulled away. Henry felt some satisfaction as Daniel stormed off after being rejected.

Henry stepped out from where he hid, making his way towards Tracey. "Need some help with that?"

"Sure, if you're going that way." She waited until Henry had picked up the logs. "So how much of that did you see?"

"See what?"

"Don't play dumb with me, Henry. You know what I'm talking about."

"Okay, all of it."

"Then you know I don't wanna talk about it."

"Sure, whatever. Let's get these back."

Ten minutes later, Karina met the two teens in a storage shed beside the dracorn's stables. After giving a quick glance in, Henry wondered if there would be any room to put the logs they brought. He guessed Karina could use her magic to make more room. After the sorceress congratulated Tracey on a job well done, Tracey and Henry headed to their rooms.

As Tracey stopped at her door, Henry could feel her looking at him as he passed. He too stopped, his eyes staring at the ground before turning around.

"Can I ask you something?" he said.

"Let me guess, it's about earlier, right?"

"Uh-huh." His answer made her blush and avoid eye contact. "Why didn't you kiss Daniel?"

"Look I don't really wanna talk about this now, 'kay?" Tracey pulled down the door handle and paused as Henry said,

"Was it because of me?" Her silence confirmed it. "So you like me?"

"I can't do this now." Henry caught her hand as she pushed open the door.

"Wait… please, just answer me." Tracey slowly pulled her gaze away from the door handle back to him.

"Yeah… it was," she said in a meek voice.

"Really?"

"Are you seriously going to make me-"

He pulled her towards him, giving her a slow kiss. At first he sensed her surprise when their lips met but then she became comfortable with it. Even though it was only but a moment, it seemed to last much longer. Henry wished he could do this every day.

Gathering himself, he pulled away. "Sorry. I… couldn't help myself." Embarrassed, Henry ran a hand through his brown hair. "I probably shouldn't have done that. Sorry. I, uh, gotta go. Good night."

He had half opened his door when he heard Tracey clearing her throat. "Ahem."

She stood with her arms folded, presenting him with a bemused stare. "Didn't your mom ever teach you it's rude to leave a girl like that?" Before allowing him to answer, she grabbed his tunic pulling him in, now passionately kissing him, wrapping her arms around his neck. It lasted for what seemed like half a minute and then they broke their embrace.

"Good night. See you tomorrow." Tracey gave him a wink with a mischievous grin before entering her room and closed the door.

"Wow." Henry's head reeled from what just happened. He had to steady himself, resisting the temptation to pinch his left arm to see if what had occurred was real. "Guess this means we're now boyfriend and girlfriend." Henry punched the air while smiling with glee as the girl he had been after for three years finally wanted him, and it had nothing to do with magic, just pure emotion.

* * *

Soon Henry and Tracey's romance blossomed as they jogged and sparred together whenever they got the chance. Henry saw Tracey as more than just a girlfriend, he now saw her as a confidant, someone that truly understood him. He noticed that she opened up more to him too. Especially when they sat alone at night, arms around each other and she resting her head on his shoulders, looking up at the stars, telling him things that he guessed she never told anyone else. Now that they were close, Henry never felt alone anymore.

One day three weeks after they officially became a couple, Henry and Tracey were sparring in the training area. Tracey blocked Henry's attack meeting her sword with his as he struck high. Seeing an opening, she gave a quick kick into his abdomen, sending the boy staggering back a few steps before he fell backwards.

"You shouldn't rush in," she replied with a half grin, imitating Sir Dreyfus's voice.

Henry groaned while sitting up. "Is that so?" Catching her unaware, he performed a quick leg sweep, knocking her down. He climbed on top of her, pinning the girl's arms and legs down before she got a chance to scramble for the sword that fell out of her right hand.

It was now Henry's turn to imitate their tutor when he said, "Always expect the unexpected." Both teens laughed and Henry rolled off her. They lay on the ground just staring up at the sky, each catching their breath.

"Never thought I'd say it but I'll miss this if we get back home," Henry said.

"What, me kicking your ass?"

"Ha, you wish."

"And that's *when* we get back home," Tracey corrected him. "No ifs. You gotta believe in yourself."

"I do."

"No you don't."

"Yes, I do."

"Are we really gonna do this back and forth for the next few minutes. Just agree with me. You know I'm right."

Henry stared at her after she said this. Despite her best attempts at keeping a serious expression, it melted away after a few seconds when she erupted in laughter. Henry laughed again.

"You're like my mom. She always has to be right."

"That's because girls usually are right… and they're smarter than boys."

"Don't know about that," Henry scoffed.

"Hey!" Tracey gave Henry a gentle nudge into his ribs with her elbow.

"Trying to break my ribs now?" he said, rubbing them.

"Don't be a wuss," she joked. "But seriously, Henry, you really have to start believing in yourself. Now that everyone here knows who you are and why you're here, you can't go around talking like that. You have to believe you're going to win."

"No, you're right. It's just so hard having everyone relying on me to beat Zakarius. The guy's older than me and has more experience with magic. He could beat me."

"But if you believe deep down that you're going to beat him and train harder, then you will."

"Easy for you to say, you won't have to go up against him."

"You forget this is all new to me too. I've never fought in a battle before. Hell, I've never even held a sword before!"

"Makes two of us, except in Middle-Earth videogames but that doesn't count."

They both chuckled again and Tracey got up. She brushed the sand off her trousers and helped Henry up. She held onto his hand, moving closer into him until their eyes were just a few inches away from one another.

"I believe in you, Henry. I know you can do this. Just come back safe; make it through. I-" Her voice broke and with watery eyes, she continued, "I can't lose you not when I… I… well you know…"

"You mean the L word?"

"Yeah… that," she replied wiping away tears that sauntered down her cheek.

"I… feel the same way. It's hard for me to say it too…but you know I do."

"Never doubted it for a second since you kissed me outside your room." She caressed his cheek with her sandy fingers. "The last few weeks have been the best in my life. You've made me so happy. I don't want to lose that."

"You won't… I promise." Henry leaned in and kissed her. They both held each other tight for a few minutes until Henry broke the embrace.

"I better change my clothes and freshen up before the sand sticks to my hair permanently," Tracey said.

"All right. Catch you later."

After picking up her wooden sword, she waved goodbye while walking to her room. Henry knew that that was a tall promise to keep but he was going to do everything he could to make sure he would. Tracey was the best thing that happened him in a long time and he wasn't going to let anything stop him from being with her.

* * *

The next day, Argoth, Xongrelan, Damone and a garrison of 100 soldiers, rode to Hallow's Point. They met with the soldiers sent from Nevarom and Eviranna. For two weeks, Argoth, Dreyfus, Karina, Xongrelan, Henry and the other Foretold Ones, discussed the attack plan many times and strategic alterations were made.

Finally after many hours of planning and preparing their armies, for Argoth and his allies, it was time to go to war.

QUEEN CYREN

Chapter Six

No Turning Back

A sentry marching on the wall, noticed two Sadarkians holding a human prisoner wearing a lemon tunic, approach the drawbridge. He shouted to Lieutenant Emar below.

"Two soldiers approaching, sir, with a prisoner."

"Let them in," Lieutenant Emar said.

They entered when the portcullis was raised. Emar greeted them.

"Where did you apprehend this man?"

"I am Veran, sir. We caught him wandering in the woods near the castle. He was stealing our food and hid in the woods, waiting to kill us. He almost got me but my friend, Wernach, was around to pull him off. What will we do with him?"

"Take him to the dungeon. His Majesty will decide his fate when he is ready."

Veran saluted and with Wernach, took the prisoner to the dungeons.

A day later, Wernach and Veran went to the dragon keep. They entered a tunnel with an oval bricked ceiling. Wernack held a torch as the tunnel was dark and gloomy. Up ahead, they could hear the loud flapping of wings and ferocious growling interlaced with the clanging of chains.

"Are you certain everything is in order with their meal?" Wernach asked.

"Yes. I have followed the instructions very carefully." Veran was about to draw his sword.

"No. It will only provoke them," Wernach warned.

"What if they attack us?"

"The dragons were put under some spell by Lord Slyvanon so they will not attack us."

The guards stood at the entrance to the dragon keep. Each beast regarded them with a threatening glare as their volcanic orange eyes glowed. Wernach and Veran swallowed hard upon seeing the giant black beasts up close. Wernach counted sixteen in total. There was a gutter built especially for each dragon. The food would be dropped at the base of the gutter and slide down a little channel to where the dragons were shackled.

Veran fed the dragons on the right side and Wernach fed the ones on the left. They approached each one with great care, keeping their distance.

Veran jumped as two shook their heads aggressively but did not attack him. Another blew smoke through its nostrils.

"That is the last one," Wernach said, watching the hungry beast devouring the tiger. "Our job is done. Let's leave and let them eat."

"Yes, let's leave before we become their next meal."

"Like I said, they are under-"

"Some spell, yes I know but I am not taking any chances."

* * *

Cyren and Damone walked around the town. She wanted to speak to him about her family back in Eviranna.

"Thank you for meeting me. I know you are busy making preparations for the battle," Cyren said.

"My pleasure, Your Majesty." Damone shook his head in incredulity. "I still find it hard to believe you are a queen when it seems like only yesterday you were a princess back in Eviranna."

"I know. The years have flown by. And stop with all this 'Your Majesty' nonsense while we are alone. Call me Cyren. You knew me long before I was a queen."

"But I have to. Protocol and all that."

"Yes, when around other people but not when we are alone."

"All right. So what did you want to see me about?"

"I just wanted to talk about my family back home. Did you learn anything from any of the soldiers?"

"Yes. They are safe and well."

"What of my sisters, Acacia and Harmonia?"

Damone did not answer straight away; he hesitated, as if he were withholding something from her.

"Well? Is there something wrong?" Cyren asked, seeing his hesitation.

"Acacia has left Lord Trem. He has been thrown out of where they are hiding."

"Why?"

"He hit her," Damone answered.

Cyren cursed under her breath. "Poor Acacia. I hope she is all right. I never liked him from the moment we met. And Harmonia, what about her?"

"Still has no suitor."

"I am not surprised," Cyren scoffed. "She was always hard to please."

Damone laughed. Cyren looked at him, baffled. He noticed her looking at him and said, "I am not laughing at what you said, Your Maj- sorry, Cyren. I remembered the time we went out hunting, me, you and Harmonia and we got lost."

"Oh yes," she said with a gentle guffaw. "We nearly wandered into, 'The Forbidden Dales', as my father called them. He said there were wolves there. Poor father was worried sick and we each got a tanning when we came back."

"My backside was sore for days afterwards."

This made Cyren laugh again. "Sorry," she said. "I was not laughing at your beating. It is just we were wandering around for ages and the next thing I know Harmonia goes missing. When you looked for her, she jumped out and frightened you."

"How could I forget?" His cheeks were scarlet. "Good times, eh?"

Cyren's laughter abated. After a mournful sigh, she replied, "Yes, they were. I miss them."

"Me too."

Cyren knew that they were good times but a year after that incident, Damone lost both parents to a plague that killed half of Eviranna. He was the only member of his family to survive.

"I hope this war will be over soon so I can see my family again," Cyren said.

"We all do."

Cyren and Damone continued to walk on, sharing childhood memories. This made the queen want to see her sisters and brother even more. Silently she prayed that when the time came for her to fight alongside Argoth and Henry, that they'd win the battle, to end all this misery.

* * *

Edward sat on a chair in his room as he stared at the black and white photograph of his family. In it, he and Sandra stood behind their two children: Sarah and Mark then 14 and 12. Everyone was smiling. Edward smiled at the goofy grins on his children's faces. Edward always kept this picture inside his flight suit.

Conor had returned from taking a walk in the garden. He saw his friend looking at the photo. "Thinking about them again, sir?"

"I always am. You know every day before we'd go on another raid, I'd always look at them and wonder if I'd get home safely. Now it's different."

"Aye, I know what you mean. At least during the war, we kind of knew what to expect. But here, God knows what's going to hit us."

Edward never took his eyes off the picture. "I thought I'd grow old and see my kids go to college. See Sarah become a nurse and Mark an architect. He loved drawing houses and building things with his little wooden blocks. Now I might miss all that 'cause I don't know if I'll ever see them again."

Conor sat beside Edward. "Do you remember what you used to tell me before we'd go on a mission?"

Edward smiled before answering, "Yes. What we do today will make a difference in the grand scheme of things."

"And we did. The way I see it, we were chosen for a reason. I know together we can make a difference."

"Look at me, you'd think by now I'd be used to war."

"Aye, but this one's different. Still, I know we'll make it through."

"I hope so, MacCall. I really do."

* * *

The cock crowed as the first rays of daylight graced the skies. Cyren stood at her window in a pink gown that flowed to her feet. Her arms were folded and her mind was set on one thing: Argoth going into battle.

Argoth entered their room and slowly walked up behind her. She moaned with pleasure as he began to massage her shoulders. "I know you are worried but this battle must be fought."

"I know, but I wish I could go with you," she said.

"We discussed this. It is too dangerous for you to come with me."

Cyren turned to face him. "Then I will stare danger in the face with you. I am just as good with a sword as any knight you have."

Argoth removed his hands from her shoulders. "You know I cannot allow that. I would be too worried about you. If they managed to kill the woman I love and I survive, then my life would not be worth living."

"I cannot stand here and be so helpless! Why can *you not* see that?" Cyren returned.

"Please, let's not argue. This could be our last moment together. I do not want to spend it fighting with you. I would love for you to come but it is far too dangerous." He turned her to face him and cupped her face in his hands. "My heart was ripped out the day Aranok was killed. What do you think it will do to me if *you* were killed?"

"And how do you think I would feel if you died out there and I not being able to do anything about it?" She moved away from him and stood over by her wardrobe, staring into the mirror fitted on it. "No, Argoth, I am not taking that risk. My place is out there beside you, not here like some… cowering maid."

"Please, Cyren, you are more precious to me than anything in Zargothia. Please stay here, stay where Damone and the guards can protect you. It will be safer."

"Sorry, my love, but I *am* going with you."

Argoth smoothened down his clothes and fixed her a stern stare. "Then I am no longer asking you as your husband but as your king, I command you to stay here with Damone and the other guards."

She straightened her posture, returning an equally determined glare. "Do not dare do this to me, Argoth. I have stood by you since we got married. I fought with you when Zakarius attacked us all those years ago and I will again. You know as well as anyone you would do well to not argue with me when my mind is made up."

"But I am your king and I say-"

"I know who you are and despite what you say," she cut in. "I am your wife and I will fight with you on the battlefield. In case you have forgotten, my kind will be out there too. What example will I set by not being there?"

"But-"

"No buts. I am going and that is it. Is that all?"

Argoth looked at her with a stony expression. She saw in his eyes a combination of anger and frustration, but also one of defeat.

"Yes, that is all," he replied flatly, his eyes not meeting hers as she left.

* * *

Karina sat in the Royal gardens. She let the vast array of aromas from each flower invade her nostrils. This helped calm her breathing. Karina liked to meditate often in the gardens before archery. When her meditation was finished, she made her way to the training ground.

Removing the claymore from her scabbard, Karina struck left and right, sometimes slicing the air diagonally. As she did this, memories of when Zakarius was Nemus flooded her mind. The image of an innocent smile on his ten year old face was first to cross it. She stopped for a moment, remembering the first time she saw him by the river with his father, a boy full of hope and love. Not being able to have children with her own husband gnawed away at her every day. When Turnaz wrote to her to take him, she felt it was as if Zymbion himself had finally answered all her prayers.

Karina cared for him like no other, sometimes forgetting that Nemus wasn't her own son. When he first arrived at Zargothia, he found it hard to fit in, always being teased and bullied by the older boys in his school. A number of days he would come home with bruises over his eye or lip. With a gentle stroke of her hand, the bruise and pain would disappear. He would hug her in gratitude and she held him close to her chest, smoothing down his scraggy black hair. Karina closed her eyes and could almost smell the coconut oil she'd give him to wash his hair with. Then another memory of when he was fifteen played of how they would go for rides on their horses near the River Balonia where she first found him with his father. He would often talk about Turnaz and all the times they'd go fishing together whenever his father had time. Karina smiled as she could almost hear his laughter when recounting a funny tale he'd tell about the games of hide and seek his mother and Turnaz used to play with him as a child.

Karina inhaled a shaky breath as the horrid memory of the day of what she thought was Nemus's head was sent to her in a box. To Karina, it felt as if she had lost her husband all over again, another loved one lost to the blasted Sadarkians.

Karina's mood turned dark as she gripped the claymore's hilt tighter, her knuckles whitening in anger. Now the faces of the dead women and children that lay strewn about in the aftermath of Zakarius's ambush was all she could see. She knew Slyvanon poisoned Nemus's mind when he got a hold of him. No matter how hard she tried to convince Nemus that Slyvanon had tricked them all into believing he was dead, the new king did not believe her. He slapped her hard across the face and then banished Karina along with Cyren and Argoth from the castle, left to roam the wilderness at the mercy of wild animals. Karina could smell the odor of death that almost choked her as she, Cyren and Argoth walked out the gate, the look of sheer horror from lifeless eyes of both mothers and children came back to haunt her, as they did every night in her dreams.

One question often remained in Karina's mind: if given the chance, could she kill Zakarius? A part of the woman still believed Nemus was in him. But then the anger bubbled up within as she remembered the slaughtered women and children. She grabbed the claymore with both hands and with a feral scream, flung it at the nearest archery target, with the sword hitting the bullseye.

Nemus is no more, Karina reminded herself. Conjuring up a teal-colored fire ball, she thrust it at another archery target, leaving a scorched stain in the center of the gold circle.

Yes, Zakarius would be as good as dead if they were to ever meet in battle. Just like his army did to the defenseless people in Zargothia, no mercy would be shown to him but only the end of her blade.

* * *

Henry put the last few items into his saddle-bag sitting on his chocolate brown destrier. The destrier neighed as Henry patted it down. All around soldiers were putting items into their saddles too.

"Are you ready to go?" Tracey said.

"Just about." Henry turned to face her. His eyes widened and his mouth opened as he was stunned by Tracey's beautiful appearance today in her tight violet dress. The way the sun's rays hit her hair made it shine like a halo.

"I think you might wanna close your mouth there before you catch a fly," she said with a half grin.

"Wow, you look beautiful…even more so than usual."

"Thanks," she replied, putting her arms around his neck and kissing him on the cheek.

"I know this is probably a dumb question but are you scared?" Tracey asked.

"Yeah, I am. I just hope I don't let anyone down."

"And come back alive," she added.

"Yeah, that too. When do you ride out?"

"About two hours' time. I'm riding in Sir Dreyfus's company."

"Just be careful out there. Remember what Sir Dreyfus said-"

"*Keep your wits about you.* God, if I hear that once more, I'll scream."

"Guy's got a point, though." He smoothed down her hair. "I really wish you'd stay here while the battle's going on. I don't want anything bad to happen to you."

"I'm not going to be that clichéd scared little girl, Henry. I really care about you and I wanna fight beside you. Besides, I can't let you have all the fun," she said with a wink.

"This isn't a videogame, Tracey, it's real life. I don't wanna risk you getting killed."

"I know…and that's sweet. But Sir Dreyfus and Hannorah taught me well. So you got nothing to be worried about."

Henry was able to see past this brave façade she was putting on by the tiny speckle of dread lurking in her eyes.

"Just watch your back at all times, okay? Promise me that."

"I'll be fine. Relax. There's something I wanna give you before you go," Tracey said.

From her pocket, she took out a flat wooden carving of her just from the shoulders up. "This is for you."

"Wow, that's really neat." Henry took it from her, examining the carving's fine detail of her facial features. "Where did you get it?"

"I asked Hannorah to make it for me. She used her magic. She's kind of handy that way."

"Guess so."

"That's to remember me… just in case something does happen," she quickly added to allay his fears, "but it won't, I promise. I'll be fine."

"Thanks. I hope so." He pulled her in and kissed her slowly. Henry wanted this moment to last forever, where they were safe and together, not with thousands of Sadarkians swarming in around them, baying for their blood.

He broke the embrace after a minute. Staring into her eyes, he said, "Just come back in one piece, okay?"

"I will, you gotta have more faith in me."

They both laughed at her statement and then Henry removed her arms from around his neck. "Time for me to go." He put the carving into his pocket.

"Yeah, I got to put on my armor and get my own pack ready."

A tall guard's voice echoed around the stables. "King Argoth's company leaves in twenty minutes. He wants you all in formation at the gates in ten."

"Guess that's my cue to go," Henry said.

"Okay, see you in a day's time." She gave him a quick kiss on the lips and dashed to her room. He watched her leave, feeling a pang of fear for her safety knowing that he would not be able to watch over her like some guardian angel in the battle.

But one thing was for certain: now he was more determined than ever to beat Zakarius and make it back.

Chapter Seven

Last Fight for Freedom

Drizzle fell, moistening the ground outside the walls of Zakarius's castle on which both armies stood in the early morning three days later as an orange horizon streaked the gray, cloudy sky.

The flags of Zargothia stood proud in their bright colors. Argoth's banner of red and gold bearing three insignias, the lion, to represent humans, the sun and moon representing the Volarks and Jenormes.

Henry sensed nervousness amongst soldiers around him. His destrier was restless as it lifted its head up and down in the armored chamfrain. The red and gold flag in his lance stave flapped about. Henry sat in the saddle with a jagged red caparison that was adorned with silver diamonds. Hannorah was beside him on her stallion. She looked pale too, hand resting on her stomach every so often, calming the butterflies Henry thought fluttered in her belly. Trying as much as she could to conceal it, her hands trembled as she held her horse's reins.

Argoth, with his legion of knights, was on the far right flank. Cyren on a tall stallion beside him, wearing silver armor, the Volarkun crest over her right breast. She didn't wear any helmet, only her purple hair was braided, blending in with the purple cloak she wore. Her cloak billowed slightly. Henry, with Argoth, had their own legion of knights on the left. Tracey was with Sir Dreyfus's legion, much to Henry's objections. Argoth explained to him before leaving that he thought this best as she would only serve as a distraction to

Henry. He reckoned the king had a point but he really wanted her to ride in theirs. The boy just hoped that she'd be okay.

In the center were rows of infantry. The first two rows of the vanguard consisted of spearmen. In their right hands they held wooden shields that were long and tapered to a point.

The archers behind them stood firm.

Behind the archers stood the light armored infantry in full-body chainmail from head to toe and white surcoats with long round helmets. In the center of the helmets was a visor in the shape of a cross.

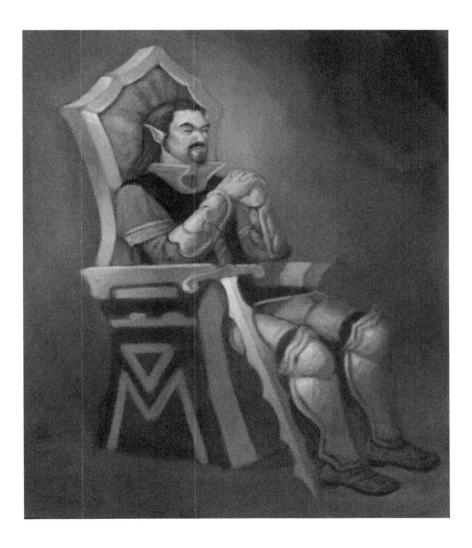

ZAKARIUS ON HIS THRONE

The central rows consisted of heavier armored infantry with metal plates covering their chests, arms and legs. Their weapons were maces and battle-axes.

Behind them were armored knights with oval shields. Argoth's rearguard comprised of Volarkun archers on horseback. Also riding on the Volarkun archers' horses were Jenormes. The small warriors would keep back oncoming attackers with their swords or war hammers.

Zakarius, Slyvanon and General Haynach stood behind the might of their army outside the town's dark gloomy walls. Zakarius wore black armor with the Sadarkian crest emblazoned on his chest and a dark yellow cloak. Every soldier wore black armor with conical helmets. Archers were on both flanks. Acting as the last line of defense were cavalry knights on horseback. Also to Zakarius's far right were two cannon surrounded by a dozen guards.

Henry had wondered how Argoth and Cyren would fare in battle, considering their age. Then he remembered a quick conversation that he had with Dreyfus while riding towards here. The knight told him that Karina had given Cyren and Argoth special oil to rub onto their bodies which would help their muscles be more flexible and a potion for each to drink to give them extra energy and strength to last them a couple of days. Deep down though, Henry knew this fight would be over in a day, whether they won or not.

Argoth readied the front line of his vanguard with the sound of his own trumpet. The front line began to advance.

Henry's heart pounded so hard he feared that it would explode. The boy knew that soon he would be called upon to fight. Henry clutched the coin in his palm and hoped that he, Tracey and his friends would survive this battle. Again he glanced at Hannorah; she still was a little ashen but held onto her hilt, ready to strike at whoever came her way.

Swallowing hard, Hannorah closed then reopened her green eyes. She wore a more determined expression.

From his position in the right flank, Henry saw who he guessed was General Haynach ride to the left side of the Sadarkian front line. Pointing to Argoth's army, he gave the order to charge.

Sadarkians screamed in the charge towards Argoth's army.

The spearmen charged forward, ready to launch at the oncoming attackers. Then a short distance from where the two sides were about to clash, the spearmen stopped, and their spears planted in the ground, creating a wall.

Just as Zakarius's front line was only a few inches away from the wall, the Volarkun archers aimed their crossbows and unleashed a wave of arrows.

Many Sadarkian soldiers fell to the Volark arrows. Half of the front line was on the ground, while the unaffected tried to break down the barrier.

Volarkun archers fired again. More soldiers fell, this time the spearmen drew their swords, delivering fatal blows to those prone and vulnerable on the ground. Those who remained standing fought. The bodies began to pile up on both sides. Henry watched as the Volarks and spearmen fell back.

The cannon were fired, breaking the speared wall. Humans were sent flying with a fountain of viscera as cannon balls ripped through the defenses.

Zakarius's armor-wearing archers advanced. They ran towards their comrades and stopped, the front line kneeling to draw back their bows.

Volarkun archers were given cover by the spearmen's shields. Some Volarks watched as the arrows penetrated the shields along with the men holding them.

Henry looked to his left as he heard Argoth yell, "Send the light armored infantry forward."

Four rows of men almost spanning the width of the field, raced forward; the Volarkun archers fell back to provide covering fire.

Argoth's men in chainmail and white surcoats joined the battle. Sometimes the size of Zakarius's warriors worked to their advantage as they overpowered the humans and their allies, hacking and beating them to a gory, bloody pulp.

* * *

Tracey's lips quivered while watching the battle unfold before her. A number of times she had to look away as Sadarkians were beheading Argoth's men and any other act of savagery committed by both armies. She knew war would not be pretty but seeing it up close like this made it hard for her not to vomit.

I wish this whole war would be over soon, she thought. It had crossed her mind to duck out when things got too busy around her; nobody would notice Tracey sneaking off while they're fighting for their life. But Tracey wouldn't do that to Henry. A pang of jealousy crept into the girl as she thought of Hannorah beside him. It should be Tracey's job to watch her boyfriend's back and not Hannorah's. Just like him, she was mad that Argoth separated them, even argued with Sir Dreyfus over it. She begged him to try and persuade the king to change his mind. Now she understood why. If they fought close together, both would be distracted, looking out for each other.

She petted down her stallion's mane. Tracey named the horse, 'Beauty'. It shook its head and trotted slightly back and forth in nervousness.

"Shh," Tracey said while continuing to rub Beauty's neck. "It's gonna be okay." *I hope.*

***

HENRY GETTING READY FOR BATTLE

The moment had now arrived for King Argoth and Henry to join the battle. Argoth looked at Henry and the boy met the king's gaze. Argoth nodded to him.

Henry nodded back.

With his sword unsheathed, Argoth raised it in the air. "Charrrge!"

A trumpet blared and they charged.

Spurring their horses, Henry and Hannorah galloped forward with Sir Dreyfus into the battle. With the boy's heart thumping faster than ever, Henry's horse pounded down the battlefield and into the abyss of sooty smoke.

When the boy, Hannorah, Tracey and the knights rode out of it, a band of Sadarkians charged straight for them. Taking the lance from the lance rest, Henry gripped it in his hand. Picking out the forerunner of the oncoming group of warriors, Henry catapulted the lance at him, landing it in the soldier's sternum.

* * *

"Fire the cannon," Zakarius ordered.

"Some of our men will be hit if we do that, Your Majesty," General Haynach said.

"Question me again, General, and I shall have your head. Now fire the cannon!"

Haynach carried out the order without further question.

* * *

Cannon felled more soldiers on both sides. The battlefield was now becoming a sea of pink and red blood.

Zakarius's second wave of infantry was launched, clashing with Argoth's forces.

Argoth along with others had been knocked from their horses. Human soldiers fell in and formed a circle to protect their king and queen as both were getting up and being checked for any injuries. A soldier quickly patted down their armor to see if there were any broken bones but Argoth waved him away. Cyren, with both an expression of anger and fear, drew her sword, staying close to her husband.

When the circle of men had broken, fighting Zakarius's knights, the king caught sight of Henry. From the concern on Argoth's face, Henry knew that the man dreaded defeat. Argoth pointed to the cannon for Henry and the boy knew what he wanted him to do: to stop them once and for all.

Henry looked left and right frantically for Hannorah and Tracey. He fought through several soldiers to reach them. When he got to them and they saw him, he said, "You two come with me."

"What, where are we going?" Tracey asked.

"To stop the cannons. Just watch my back," Henry replied.

Damone and Xongrelan rode forward on horseback, Damone swinging his sword holding back any Sadarkians, as did Xongrelan with his battle-axe.

"You guys, over here," Henry shouted at them.

Once it was safe to dismount, Damone and Xongrelan ran to the boy.

"You need us?" Damone asked.

"Yeah. Watch my rear. Tell them, Tracey," Henry said. The girl explained about the mission they had just been given as Henry held the coin in his hands, closing his eyes, mentally wishing to be taken to where Zakarius's deadly siege weapons were. A golden mist swirled around them. They disappeared in a bright flash, appearing five yards from the cannon.

"It worked," Henry gasped.

Guards manning the weapons saw Henry and the others drew their swords and charged towards them.

Henry drew his own sword, slicing off the arm of one soldier, sticking his blade into the neck of another. As others rushed in to replace the fallen, Henry and his friends broke from the skirmish. The two girls along with Damone and Xongrelan stood guard protecting Henry as the boy wished for two grenades, they wavered in the air and he caught them in his left gauntlet.

Setting down the grenades, Henry looked back to see the others barely managing to fend off the reinforcements. Closing his eyes, Henry felt his right arm tremble as the coin's power surged through it. As he opened his eyes, a gold hue enveloped them. With one swift movement of his arm, a strong breeze sent Sadarkian knights hurtling through the air, putting a good distance between them and his friends.

"Hurry, Henry," Tracey shouted.

Once the gold hue coloring his eyes had passed, Henry saw why the girl was concerned. In his peripheral vision he saw more archers turning toward them, arrows being nocked and aimed. Henry picked up both grenades, pulled the pins, throwing a grenade under each cannon barrel.

"Let's go," Henry roared. His four friends fell in beside him. Just as they reappeared back in their original position, a loud explosion rocked the battlefield as the cannon exploded. The barrels split, sending shockwaves of sound across the battlefield, terrifying fighters on both sides before their shrapnel rained pain and death upon the field.

* * *

"No!" Zakarius cried as Henry accomplished his mission. "Damn him! I will not let Argoth beat me. Not now. General, lead the charge. Spare no one."

"Yes, sire." General Haynach sounded the horn. He shook the reins on his horse and surged forward, the soldiers falling in behind him.

* * *

Seeing General Haynach charging towards them with Zakarius's legions, Argoth bellowed, "Archers, stand your ground, cover our retreat. The rest of you, to the woods!"

A long row of archers rushed forward. Aiming their bows into the skies, they let loose their arrows as Argoth's army headed for the woods.

Henry glanced behind him. The silhouettes of many enemy horses and riders could be seen through the smoke.

Two minutes later, Argoth and his army were a good distance inside the forest. Henry knew the king would wait until their pursuers reached a certain point before he'd give the order for his men to split up.

When Henry and the others had reached the designated point, Argoth shouted, "Now!"

* * *

As Haynach and the legions entered the forest, he noticed that the trees were coated with a greasy substance.

As Argoth's army separated, three brown, rider-less horses were heading for Haynach and the soldiers.

In a heartbeat, the horses spread their wings and took flight. The dracorns bellowed fire. The trees below became a ring of fire, trapping the knights in the intense heat. Haynach realized that the greasy substance was animal fat. He knew that a dracorn's fiery breath was just as hot and as lethal as a large bonfire. Argoth must have painted it on each tree bark during the night.

Haynach and his soldiers were trapped in the forest fire.

From behind the bushes, more Volarkun archers emerged, arrows pelting the helpless soldiers. Springing from the bushes were what Haynach thought were mercenaries Argoth had gathered, warriors with only a tunic, and a cloak fastened around their neck but were just as effective as any knight. They didn't wear their usual uniform but disguised who they really were. With little care for their own bodies, they lunged at the enemy, hacking and slashing with abandon.

Soldiers looked around them frantically as their friends fell. Argoth's soldiers in their droves, leaped from the flames. General Haynach was about to retreat back to the safety of the castle when an axe, whirling through the air, found its way to the back of his skull.

The mercenaries set upon the riders who had fallen. Soon all the knights who had entered the woods were dead, casualties of war.

* * *

Zakarius's face grew pale when he saw Haynach and the army running into the trap. It grew paler when Henry, Argoth and his army performed a U-turn with their horses, charging like rogue monsters towards him.

Zakarius turned to the men in the gatehouse and shouted. "Open the gates. Let out the reserve forces."

Once the gates were opened, more black armored knights and general infantry who wore little armor except on their knees and elbows, silver surcoats with black cloaks and conical helmets, poured out.

Zakarius beckoned to a servant who carried a red flag. "Release the dragons."

The servant faced the castle wall, waving his flag excitedly.

* * *

Inside Zakarius's castle, Wernach saw the men race about, building barricades. Pots were filled with boiling hot water along with pigs' and boars' innards to pour down on enemies.

Veran was with him. They made their way to the dungeon where human prisoners were kept.

Unlocking the dungeon's iron door, he and his friend went down the stairs that led to the hallway of cells. Wernach walked to the table where a guard sat. Veran waited at the entrance.

"Argoth's army has almost beaten the main forces. Every soldier available is to go up top to defend the castle. We were ordered to take over watch of the prisoners."

"I received no such order."

"You have now." Wernach stabbed the guard in the jugular with his rapier.

"What the-" the guard at the entrance said, still bewildered by events he lunged for Wernach. Veran took out his own knife, thrusting it twice into the guard's neck. The soldier fell, coughing up blood, quivering on the floor, a pool forming under his head. Wernach drew his sword, finishing the job by embedding its blade into the guard's skull.

Wernach took the black keys from the soldier who he just stabbed and began unlocking cell doors. The prisoners glanced at one another in confusion.

"What is going on?" one of them asked.

"They are not Sadarkians," a man in a lemon tunic replied.

Wernach showed a ruby to the prisoners and rubbed it. He transformed into a human.

"Argoth sent them disguised as Sadarkians to scout the castle and poison the dragons. Karina used the dust from the magic diamond to create the disguises," explained the lemon tunic man.

"We were also sent to free you. We could use every man we can get up top," Veran added.

Wernach continued opening the cells until all were freed. All the prisoners cheered, praising Zymbion above for sending these men to free them. Some hugged each other, while others hugged their rescuers.

Wernach motioned for some calm with his hands before speaking. "All right, all right. Shh, take it easy. Listen." All the prisoners hushed, gathering around him. "Follow me to the armory. We must get weapons if we are to stand a chance of getting out of here alive. We must go there quietly, though."

* * *

Henry forced soldiers back with his shield as he punched and thrust his way past them. Though the number of enemy soldiers was being reduced, more seemed to arrive every minute.

Argoth's men were beginning to fatigue, weaken. Some became frightened, losing their concentration as more black-armored knights surrounded them. They made hasty swipes but were countered with quick, fatal strikes. Cyren was in the thick of it with them, never leaving Argoth's side as they charged at knights together. Her armor now covered in Sadarkian and human blood, cuts along with soot spread across her face.

"Your Majesty, look! Enemy forces are coming from the eastern and western hills," Dreyfus said.

Henry's heart sank upon seeing further masses of Sadarkian knights running down the hills. He noticed that Hannorah and Tracey looked deflated too when they saw them. Zakarius's cavalry was arriving and Henry knew that there was no way Argoth could win this war with the men they had left. Henry's hopes for winning were being squashed. He saw from Argoth's bleak expression that the king recognized the same thing. Cyren looked dejected too but fought on.

A sudden silence descended on the battlefield as a thunderous sound came from the sky: *whomp, whomp, whomp, whomp*. Every soldier from both sides stared at the clouds both in wonder and dread.

Shimmering into view high above both armies were Karina, Jasper and the two airmen on two giant hawks. Flying behind them were five hundred unicorns led by Queen Eusaba. Each hawk's body, including its head, was aquatic blue, their beaks were lemon. Its golden wings had a span of six feet once spread. In its eyes lurked a vicious glare. The large birds plunged the battleground into semi-darkness for a number of seconds with their gigantic shadows while they flew low to the ground.

"Our cavalry has arrived," Argoth announced.

His army sent up a rapturous cheer upon seeing their reinforcements.

Queen Eusaba held her crystal scepter aloft as she commanded her troops. "Unicorns unite!" All at once, their horns glowed sending out a blinding light that affected only Zakarius's army.

Henry saw the giant birds flying over him. Edward waved as Conor manned the turret gun fixed on a wooden platform on the hawk's back that allowed him to move one hundred and eighty degrees. A belt of bullets linked to the side of the barrels, provided a constant feed of ammunition.

Eusaba's troops, landed and transformed into men, they strode into the fray swinging down with their large swords, hacking with fury as they lay waste to more soldiers.

Seizing the opportunity, Argoth's army attacked the blinded knights.

* * *

Karina directed her hawk to fly beside Edward's to pass on instructions to the English pilot.

"Captain, concentrate your firepower on the hills to the east. I will take care of the forces on the west and the soldiers on the battlements as well."

Edward took a glance to his left and raised his left thumb as he looked back at Karina.

Conor swiveled the gun to face the enemy below. The soldiers began firing on them but Conor soon quelled their resistance by pounding them incessantly with rainfalls of bullets.

"How do you like that, you ugly bastards?" the Scot retorted.

Edward grinned and fired his pistol while Conor let loose another string of obscenities. The Oxford airman saw the destruction Karina was causing as the sorceress blasted soldiers with her staff. Jasper dropped balloons containing a blue powder, temporarily blinding any Sadarkian below, allowing

Argoth's forces to attack, and quickly bringing the number of Zakarius's soldiers down.

* * *

Karina's hawk banked to the right after clearing some of the forces from the east. Now she concentrated on reducing the number of soldiers on Zakarius's battlements.

As her hawk approached, archers on the battlements aimed at the giant bird. Using her staff, she pelted them with purple beams of light, knocking ten off. Her attack also damaged some of the wall walks too, preventing reinforcements from replacing their fallen comrades.

While looking down near where Zakarius stood with his final legion, she could see the king pointing to her hawk, ordering more archers to fire at her. Karina held on tight as the beast tilted to the right a little. Arrows whizzed by them with one or two narrowly missing her. The soldiers aimed again but this time Karina was not taking any chances. She shook the reins and her hawk surged forward to the west out of firing range.

* * *

"That blasted sorceress," Zakarius cursed. "Should have killed her years ago when I had the chance!" Zakarius had thought about sending Slyvanon in to use his magic to repair the damaged section of the wall walks but knew there wouldn't be much time. He rubbed his forehead, feeling the effects of a migraine coming on as the number advantage he had held all along now seemed to be dwindling faster than he liked.

Yena - the servant he had ordered to release the dragons - ran to him.

"I ordered you to release the dragons. Where are they?"

"I have received word, sire. They were poisoned, every last one of them," the trembling servant risked the truth.

"Poisoned? How?"

"Someone inside must be working for Argoth," Slyvanon reasoned.

"Blast it. Get out of my sight and make yourself useful," Zakarius snarled at Yena and ducked his head into his hands. He sighed. "It looks like I have to take care of this myself." Drawing his sword, he aimed it at where the two armies fought. "Forrrwarrrrd!"

* * *

Seeing reinforcements arrive, Henry felt a certain amount of relief. The rapid firing of Conor's gun sounded and he saw many soldiers fall.

Suddenly, pulled back off from his horse, Henry realized someone had snuck up behind him while he'd been distracted with what else was going on. The guard wasted no time in pouncing on the boy and squeezing him in a tight bear hug.

"Henry!" He heard Tracey shout. The guard's grip on him suddenly slackened. The boy spun to see Tracey's sword embedded in the soldier's back. She extracted her weapon, watching him keel over, falling on his side.

"Thanks," Henry said but his eyes widened in horror as he saw another soldier sneaking up behind Tracey.

"Tracey watch-" he didn't get a chance to finish his sentence as one of Argoth's knights beheaded the soldier. Tracey thanked the knight before she vomited onto the grass.

"Still think I cannot fight?" the knight asked lifting his visor.

"What are you doing here?" Henry asked surprised to see Daniel. "How did you get here?"

Daniel killed another two attackers before answering. "I snuck out and put on some armor."

Henry figured that was possible, Daniel was tall enough to pass for a knight.

Another trumpet blasted. Zakarius led the charge. The king's yellow cloak flapped about as his stallion and hundreds of others thundered forward. Zakarius hacked any of Argoth's soldiers standing in his way.

* * *

This was the moment Argoth had been waiting for. He knew that with Zakarius's forces mostly concentrating on their king's charge, which meant less would be left back at the castle, especially since Karina cleared the battlements. Twenty paces from either side of the two walls, two siege castles materialized, previously rendered invisible by the coin's magic. The wooden structures were hauled forward by men-at-arms using ropes, the towers were built on wheels to make the task easier.

From the discussions that Dreyfus and Argoth had, Henry knew that two hundred (Volarkun and human soldiers) in total were inside both towers. Fortunately for them, the wall walks at the front of the battlements were all that was damaged; those at the side were not touched. When the towers reached the lower section of the gatehouse wall, a door at the top of each tower was opened. Soldiers ran along both walls. Argoth's soldiers filed into position and readied their bows, eliminating the enemy running up to meet them.

Zakarius's archers ran forward attempting to reduce the numbers but when they tried to fire arrows, they were mowed down by missiles fired by Argoth's archers. When the path was cleared, the soldiers from both towers advanced further into the castle.

* * *

Zakarius looked back for a second. Henry could see a curse slip from his lips. Then he locked eyes on the boy and dismounted. Like a raging boar, Zakarius ran forward, hacking down all Argoth's men who dared fight him while he made his way to Henry.

There were too many of Zakarius's army to get through to reach the king. So Henry knew he needed to call in some air support.

"Cover me," he said to Tracey, Hannorah, Xongrelan and Damone. Touching his shoulder armor, he connected with the coin's power. Looking around he saw Edward and Conor bombarding soldiers to the east. Closing his eyes for a brief second, Henry felt a throbbing sensation in the center of his forehead.

Opening his eyes again, he fought on while telepathically trying to reach Edward, *Captain Johnson, can you hear me?* There was no reply. *Can you hear me, Captain Johnson?* Again nothing. Henry was about to let loose a curse when-

Henry... Henry, is that you?

Yeah, it's me. Hold on. Henry picked up a round, silver metal shield one of Zakarius's reserves had dropped and slammed it hard into a few knights, knocking them down before finishing them off. *I need you to clear the way ahead for me so I can get to Zakarius.*

Where are you?

Look for the gold armor. You won't miss it.

Roger that.

Henry fell in again with his friends as they formed a circle, taking on each enemy as they came. He could hear the *rat-tat-tat-tat* of Conor's turret gun drawing nearer until he saw scores of knights being mowed down with bullets ripping through black armor, making a clear path for Henry. There were less to fight through now.

"Guys, fall in behind me," Henry said. Damone and the others fell in behind him as he battled to reach Zakarius.

Soon they were about ten feet apart, only some men on both sides standing in their way. Once they were killed, Henry and Zakarius stood staring at each other for a few seconds.

It's show time, Henry thought as he ran to meet the king, all fear melting away inside of him.

An area hit by a cannon ball to Henry's right, still billowed some smoke. The small plumes cleared as Henry and Zakarius's swords clashed, generating a little shockwave.

"So we finally meet," Zakarius snarled.

"Why don't we just skip to the part where I kick your ass."

"Let's take this somewhere a little more private," Zakarius head-butted Henry. The boy stumbled back and fell. Zakarius grabbed Henry's leg. Both warriors vanished in a cloud of black smoke.

* * *

Hannorah saw Henry and Zakarius disappearing. Her heart thumped as she wondered what danger Henry would be in. She knew Karina had to be contacted; Argoth seemed too far away to be reached as she'd have to fight through too many to get to him. But contacting Karina through telepathy would be impossible with hundreds of knights bearing down on the girl.

Then an idea struck her. She thought of an invisibility spell Karina had shown her. Laying about twenty feet from her was a stallion that had been killed. Hannorah raced to it, almost retching as she touched it.

"Yemana, tyeros, tirilly," Hannorah roared. A bubble of what seemed like rippling water shimmered around Hannorah for a few seconds before disappearing. The spell had worked. Not only was she invisible, but the bubble would stop anything from hitting her while she was talking to Karina. Now to contact her.

Hannorah sucked in a quick deep breath. The girl shut her eyes for two seconds, connecting with Karina. She opened them again.

Karina... Karina, can you hear me? There was no response at first, only a low almost inaudible mumble. *Karina... please answer me. Hurry!*

The mumble became clear as Karina spoke up. "I am here, Hannorah. What is it?"

Zakarius took Henry somewhere but I do not know where. Can you sense him? A pause lingered for what seemed like thirty seconds. She knew her mentor would scan the battlefield and the castle with her magic to find him. Then Karina answered.

They are in the throne room. Take whoever you can and get there quickly. I will try and get there as fast I can. Be careful.

Hannorah recited the spell, breaking her shield of invisibility. Racing towards Daniel and Tracey, she said, "Follow me!" Both fell in behind her as they raced towards the throne room.

* * *

Henry recoiled once the smoke dissipated. They were now somewhere else. As Henry looked around, it appeared to be a throne room.

We're in the castle? he thought.

Leading up to a large well-crafted wooden throne chair and rolling over three steps that were before it, was a soft, red carpet. Two big metal doors were at the entrance. On either side of the room were balconies with two slanting aisles of wooden seats, kind of like the ones Henry would see Senators sit on on TV when the President was addressing the Senate. A portrait of a Sadarkian king hung above the throne, Henry guessed that it was King Mordoch. Lining both sides of the room were marble columns that had a special metal holder, each one with a lit candle in it. Adorning the walls were crested oval and square-shaped shields.

Henry got up and stood firm, the sword in his right hand. "Why did you bring me here?"

"I did not want any interruptions. I wanted to see how good you are on your own. So let's settle this once and for all."

Henry stepped forward. "Bring it on."

"Believe me, boy, it will be my pleasure." Zakarius held the sword to the right of his face. The light from the candles enhanced the snake-like flames on the blade. Zakarius secured his grip on his hilt. With a feral scream, he charged at Henry.

HENRY AND ZAKARIUS BATTLE

Chapter Eight

Meeting the Father

Sparks flew as the two blades collided. Henry held his blade horizontally. Zakarius swung to the left and right, air movement from the action brushing the boy's ear.

Henry weaved and ducked each swipe.

Zakarius pressed forward with another thrust, Henry again parried. With a well-timed jump, Henry dealt a hard right punch across Zakarius's jaw, sending the king stumbling back.

"Is that the best you've got?" Henry taunted.

Growling his anger, Zakarius charged forward again. Their blades clashed left, right, up, down. Zakarius pushed Henry back. The king took a swipe at Henry's throat but he arched his head just in time. Zakarius thrust again. Henry jumped to the left only for Zakarius's sword to stab the air. Henry caught the blade with his gauntlet, delivering a hard shot to the stomach with the butt of Zakarius's sword. When the king was doubled-over, Henry followed through with an elbow to Zakarius's nose; a *crack* resounded as the blow connected.

Zakarius roared, retreating a few steps. Pink blood oozed from his nose. Spitting out blood, Zakarius pointed his weapon at Henry.

"Argoth's knights taught you well, boy, but not well enough." With a roar he struck again. Henry was forced back by the intensity of each thrust and cut. In a move of brute strength that was timed perfectly, Henry was forced hard into the wall. Zakarius's sword slashed in on Henry's. The two crossed blades were a mere inch from Henry's face.

Henry's eyes widened, his breath labored as they struggled in deadlock. The flame etched on Zakarius's sword glowed, writhing like a snake. The moment of distraction allowed Zakarius to knock the sword from the boy's hands. It clattered along the floor.

Zakarius held his sword with one hand; the other gripped Henry's throat, lifting him off the ground.

The American teen struggled for breath. Stars burst at the end of his sight. His heels smacked the wall as he reached for the floor. His temperature rose as he fought for air.

Zakarius brought the sword back in his left hand, ready to thrust it into Henry's throat.

"Many nights I have dreamt of this moment. I will enjoy snapping your neck and cutting off your head," Zakarius said.

"Snap on... this," Henry brought his knee up with as much force as he could muster.

Zakarius dropped his weapon, folding and clutching his crotch with both hands.

Henry kicked the sword away and landed another blow with his knee to Zakarius's face. Zakarius cried out. More blood pumped out from his broken nose. Henry gasped for air and moved away, but had to put his hand on the wall to steady himself. Bending down to grab his weapon, he heard Zakarius get to his feet.

As they faced one another, Zakarius's face was now a pink, bloody mess. He reached for his weapon. It flew to his palm like an iron filings to an electron magnet.

"That's a nifty trick, but I've got a few of my own." From his palm, Henry thrust forward a golden fireball that slammed into Zakarius's stomach, sending him flying back across the hard floor.

Zakarius shook his head getting slowly to his feet.

Henry, seizing his opportunity, fired another energy ball, hitting Zakarius in the center of his chest. As it connected, it launched Zakarius into the air, sending him back a few inches. Zakarius banged his head off a column as he went down. His sword fell from his grasp, now too far out of reach.

Henry wiped sweat from his forehead. His whole body ached. Henry limped to where Zakarius lay face down, a nasty gash across his temple.

Henry panted as he rolled Zakarius onto his back. "I guess it's time to end this." Henry raised his sword.

Just as Henry was about to bring his weapon down hard on Zakarius, from the corner of his eye, the boy saw the jagged blade flying at him. It burned like a falling meteorite. Jerking his head back, the sword swooshed passed Henry's nose, colliding with his blade. Henry's weapon was knocked out of his hand.

Zakarius sat up, grabbing the boy's neck, bringing the teen face to face with him. Magic pulled Zakarius's sword back to his left hand.

Henry saw Zakarius's nostrils flare as the king thrust his sword through the gap in Henry's breastplate, piercing the young boy's heart.

Henry gasped, unable to form a scream. Staring at the wound in incredulity, he slumped to the floor, breathing his last breath.

Leaning heavily against the column, Zakarius, still in pain, scrambled to his feet.

"I am victorious," he bellowed, his left arm raised in triumph.

* * *

EVEN JASPER ASSISTED IN THE BATTLE

The remainder of the knights coming down from the east and western hills that weren't affected by Karina's or Conor and Edward's bombardment, stood in front of the castle walls. They were now the last line of defense to stop any further advancement.

    Karina saw the reinforcements arrive and knew that if they were to press further, some of the knights would have to be cleared. Her hawk banked to the right and along with the pilots' help, she cleared a space wide enough for some of Argoth's army to get into the castle. Breaking through in a U-formation, she saw the rest of Damone and Xongrelan's cavalry arrive as well, driving back more Sadarkians and making more of a path for them to enter.

    Landing her hawk twenty feet away from the castle walls, Karina threw down a rope and slid down it. The pilots' hawk landed nearby and they dismounted too.

    As they were about to enter, she saw Hannorah, Daniel and Tracey join them.

    "We couldn't get here quicker," Tracey said, almost out of breath, her face covered in bruises. "Too many… to fight through."

"We have not got much time. Come on," Karina urged. Her staff crackled with electricity, a purple hue falling around it. With her staff in the left hand and a sword in her right, she gritted her teeth, leading the charge as she blasted and thrust her way to the throne room. Edward and Conor aided in the advance, firing their weapons she heard them call "pistols" with something inside call "bullets" hitting the forehead of any soldier they aimed at, blood spurting out once the bullet connected, exiting out the back of their head.

Karina, Hannorah and the rest arrived at the throne room. Her stomach churned. She put a hand to it, closing her eyes while taking a deep breath.

"What is wrong?" Hannorah asked.

"Nothing," Karina lied, fearing the worst before pushing open the heavy metal doors that had two round brass handles on them. Once the throne room doors were opened, everyone gasped in shock.

Henry lay face down in an expanding pool of blood. Zakarius stood over him. He slowly turned his head to face them; a smug, victorious grin spreading as his eyes zoned in on Karina's.

"*Nooo*!" Tracey screamed as she fell to her knees, crying inconsolably. Hannorah knelt down to comfort her.

"See your *Savior* now," he taunted before an evil snicker slipped past his lips.

"You bastard!" Edward retorted. He and Conor both aimed their pistols at Zakarius. The outer contours of the king's pupils turned a fiery red as he fixed his gaze on their weapons.

Conor and Edward were wide-eyed, gasping as the pistols melted into dust in their hands, slipping through their fingers.

"You will have to do better than that to kill me," the king said.

Karina knew a direct assault would be futile. Then Jasper's tail rubbed off her left calf. She looked down and saw the cat's head bowed down in mourning. She could feel the sadness emanating from him. Then an idea came to her.

Jasper, can you hear me? she asked telepathically. *If you can, just nod your head once.*

Jasper raised his head, nodding it once.

You still have one balloon. She wiggled her fingers; he now held the top of a balloon in his mouth. *This is what I want you to do when I give the signal.* Karina explained and when she was finished, she wiggled her fingers again making Jasper invisible. She felt the cat brush past her legs as he got into position.

"Karina, you have to do something," Edward whispered.

"I am."

"What? No last word of defiance? Are you that speechless?" Zakarius said, raising his sword in victory. "Imagine Argoth's face when I take this boy's head out into the battlefield. He will be devastated… and it will be oh…so… good." Zakarius's laughter rang in the throne room.

"You are not taking Henry's head anywhere." Karina looked to the left and winked. She could see the outlining of Jasper running towards Zakarius. He dropped the balloon at the king's feet before running back to safety.

"And what are you going to do to stop me? Give up. You have lost. You were always a miserable sore loser, Karina."

Gritting her teeth, Karina charged her staff with magic. "Who said we lost, Zakarius?" She fired a purple beam at the king's feet. It hit the balloon. Blue powder was released into the air. Zakarius coughed and staggered about as he inhaled some of it while more of the powder went into his eyes. They began to water as he tried to clear the blue mist.

Karina drew her sword and ran forward. As she was only a mere inch from Zakarius, she blasted him with a beam which knocked him and sent the king sliding along the ground. Karina released a feral roar as she jumped up, bringing the sword down hard on Zakarius's chest. His mouth was opened in surprise as Karina's blade sunk deep into his heart. Zakarius's eyes rolled back into their sockets before dropping his head.

Panting, Karina staggered back, turning her attention to Henry.

Tracey, Hannorah, Edward and Conor ran to him.

"Is there anything you can do, Karina?" Tracey asked in between each sob. "You gotta save him. You just gotta."

"Aye, can you do anything, lass?" Conor chimed in.

"I think so but hopefully it is not too late." She knelt down beside Henry, gently turning him on his side. Her hand was red with blood as she cleared some from his face. She began to sob thinking of his mother and how that woman would never see her son again if this did not work.

Closing her eyes, concentrating on a mental image of Henry's dead body, Karina felt the magic flowing from her body into Henry's. She knew from the message given to her by Zymbion on Remembrance Bonfire night that human magic might bring Henry back to life when the Elders could not intervene.

Karina's arms trembled from Henry's dead weight as they grew tired and weak with just having enough strength to hold the boy until the last morsel of her power had been transferred.

Karina's face blanched but was also somewhat relieved when she saw the spectral outlining of Henry's golden spirit leave the body and float up.

SLYVANON'S ROOM

Slyvanon watched the battle from afar. When he saw Zakarius and Henry disappear, he scanned the area for them. He found them in the throne room. Taking one of Zakarius's best archers with him, they snuck inside the throne room undetected, hiding behind one of the seats on the balcony to the right.

    Slyvanon cursed under his breath when Zakarius was killed. He knew that there were too many here to fight, even though his own magic rivalled Karina's. Still he did not want to chance taking her on. Gesturing to the archer with his head to follow him, they both stole out silently.

* * *

When Henry opened his eyes, he found himself lying on a bed. The golden armor he wore had disappeared. Instead he wore a white robe.

Where the heck am I? Henry thought.

An old man in bright clothing stepped forward and lowered his hood. The stranger's hair was silver; his beard snow white. An unusual gleam lurked in the man's eyes.

"No need to be afraid, child." The man's voice was as smooth as velvet. "My name is Hamorin."

"Where am I?"

"You are in my domain…in the ethereal." "The ethereal?" Henry asked, confused.

"Yes…where us Elders live. Only special mortals can come here if summoned or…if something else happens to them."

"Wait a second… am I dead?"

"Yes."

Henry's eyes widened. "Oh no. I'm dead… which means no more seeing mom and dad." He jumped off the bed. "No more Joey. No more…. Tracey. Nooo!" He sank to his knees, burying his head in his hands. "No… I can't be dead. That means I let King Argoth and his people down." He cried for another few seconds until he took a deep breath, wiping his eyes.

"You have not failed anyone."

"Wait a second. You said that this place is where the Elders live. Does that mean you're one of them?"

Hamorin nodded in confirmation.

"So, does that mean you're my…?"

"Yes, I am your father, the being who thought of you, and the others helped create you. We each put a worthy quality of our own into your body."

"You're the voice in the movie I saw about Zargothia's history. There's so much I want to ask…but I don't know where to start."

"I had to send you to another world to protect you from Hernacious. I was lucky to escape. He would have been too powerful to take on alone. He took the powers from the dead Elders and stored some of them in the sword you were killed with."

Henry swallowed hard, summoning up the courage to ask his questions. "Why didn't we meet before? Why did you let me think all this time that my folks back home were my real parents?"

"Because I could not risk exposing myself, and if I had appeared to you, you would not have believed me without coming here first."

Henry walked a few paces from where Hamorin stood. He looked at the wall of white light that surrounded them. "You know, I always felt different but could never understand why. Now I do." Henry turned around, pointing at

Hamorin accusingly. "Why didn't you send me some sign? How could you let me go on for seventeen years thinking I was somebody else's son? At least my parents back home cared for me, they *loved* me. They didn't abandon me like you did!" Henry lowered his head and voice. "But now I might never get to see them again…to tell them I love them one last time."

"I am sorry you had to go through this, Henry. But I could not come to you. The time was not-"

"I swear, if you give me that whole, 'the time wasn't right' crap, I'll kick your ass, dad or not."

"It is true, Henry. I am sorry you feel this way, I really am, but we had to do it the way we did. It was for your safety and ours."

"That's crap. You have all these powers and you expect me to believe you couldn't have come, not even once?"

"I could not, Henry. It was too-"

"Dangerous, yeah I got that but still…" His lips began to quiver. "Still, you could've tried." Henry had to turn away as the tears threatened to spill over again. "This all feels like some damn nightmare. I- I-" Henry covered his face as tears streamed down. His shoulders shook as he did this.

Hamorin put his arms around his son, hugged him close.

"I know this is a lot for a boy of seventeen, but everything I did was out of love for you."

"Sure doesn't feel like it. All the lies I was told." Henry's shoulders shook as he sobbed into his father's chest. "All the people I've killed out there… I shouldn't have to do that; I shouldn't have to face that. I should be out enjoying myself, dating, get married and have kids when I get older. This won't happen now." Henry pushed Hamorin away. "And you could have warned me about all this… sent one damn sign!"

"I know… I know." Hamorin's voice had a soothing effect. Henry's crying eased off. Hamorin lifted the boy's chin. He wiped Henry's face. "I hate it that you did not get to live the life you wanted. I am sorry the truth was hidden from you all this time. You might not believe me when I say this but I *do* love you, son. I wish we had more time to spend together but you must return to your people. They need you now. We will meet again soon."

"What? *Return to my people*? In case you haven't noticed, I'm dead. Zakarius stuck his damn sword into my heart!"

"You forget, my son, you are only *part* human. The blood of Elders flows through you which means we can heal you."

"Really?" Hamorin nodded. "Yes! Then what are we waiting for, heal me and send me back." Henry realized that this sounded a little heartless. "Wait, sorry, I didn't mean it to come out that way. I'd like to stay and talk more but… you know…"

"I understand."

Henry took a deep breath before talking again. "Before I go, that movie said that there were five more of you guys. Where are they?"

"Yes. Come out, gentlemen. Meet my son."

Five other Elders in similar clothing emerged from the dazzling light. They nodded their heads in greeting.

"It is an honor to meet you," one said while bringing his two hands together like a monk in prayer.

"Same to you," Henry replied.

A feeling of regret emanated from his celestial father. "Sorry, Henry, but it is time to go. Let's get you back to Zargothia."

"Okay," Henry said. "But when this is all over, can we talk about all this? I've still so many questions."

"If you like." Hamorin nodded.

"Promise?"

"I promise. We have to hurry before your ethereal cord separates from your mortal body. If that happens, you are trapped here forever."

The Elders formed a circle around Henry, each placing a hand on his head, and started chanting.

Henry heard Hamorin's voice in his head.

You may feel dizzy when you go back. I will always be watching over you and always remember that I love you, son.

The world fell away from beneath Henry's feet and he was falling

***.

The light around Henry's body transformed from a bright white to a brilliant gold. In a matter of seconds, Henry's body was back to normal, devoid of any injury and no unnatural glowing. He opened his eyes and sat up.

Karina smiled. Jasper purred. Hannorah sobbed and wiped her eyes. Her face, which was awash with hopelessness and her cheeks marked with tear trails, broke into a broad smile. Tracey, also wiping her eyes, smiled as Henry sat up.

"Oh my head," Henry moaned, the room swaying around him for the first few seconds after opening his eyes.

"Thank God you're alive!" Tracey hugged him tightly, kissing him on the right cheek. Then she recoiled. "Oh, sorry. I didn't hurt you, did I?"

The dizziness had passed. "No... actually, I feel fine." Henry looked inside his armor. Where Zakarius's sword was embedded was healed, even the surface wound had vanished.

"I'm sure glad to have ya back," Jasper said and jumped up on the boy's lap, rubbing his furry head against Henry's chest.

"Master Henry, I am glad the magic worked."

"Thanks Karina. I owe you one."

Jasper leapt off his lap. Karina and Hannorah each caught an arm, helping him up.

A pain soared across his chest, Henry doubled over, and then his head jerked back. An intense amber hue fell over his eyes. He could see armed Sadarkians racing towards the throne room. Karina's concerned voice increased in volume as Henry snapped out of his vision.

"Master Henry? Master Henry, answer me! Are you all right?"

"Yeah, yeah I'm fine. I just had a vision. Sadarkians are coming," Henry said firmly as he stood straight, raising his sword, "Let's finish this." Henry, Hannorah and Karina stood side by side, their weapons drawn as soldiers arrived at the throne room's entrance. "I think it's time you boys took a little trip," Henry said, the ends of his mouth curling in a grin. His blade, charged with the coin's power, sizzled as he aimed it at the soldiers.

A yellow beam shot from Henry's weapon to hit them. They disappeared.

"Where have they gone?" Karina asked.

"Somewhere far from here," Henry replied. "Come on, let's go."

Henry and the others ran out of the throne room to rejoin the skirmish. Together they fought on. Edward and Conor climbed up on their hawk again, killing soldiers from the air, and Argoth's army bravely fighting on the ground, the enemy's numbers were slowly being reduced.

Soon word got out amongst the Sadarkians that Zakarius was dead. In sheer dread, some dropped their weapons and fled; some were killed while others were able to escape into the wilderness.

* * *

For the twelve months that followed, Argoth helped the kings of Eviranna and Nevarom. With their forces combined into one mighty army, the Sadarkians controlling the lands of the Volarks and Jenormes were defeated.

Henry and the others stayed in Little Zargothia as Argoth's masons rebuilt the damaged sections of Zakarius's castle which Argoth had now reclaimed as his own. Once this was completed, everyone returned to their new home to enjoy their newfound freedom.

VICTORY WAS ACHIEVED

Chapter Nine

Homeward Bound

In the early afternoon, Hannorah, Tracey, Edward, Conor, Xongrelan, Damone and Karina were seated (with Jasper sitting on the floor beside her), as they waited for Argoth and Cyren to come. Henry paced the floors of the redecorated throne room. Gone was the portrait of King Mordoch hanging over the king's chair. Instead there hung one of King Argoth and Queen Cyren standing together, looking united, both with swords strapped to their sides. On either side of the room, shields bearing the crests of human, Volarkun and Jenorme royal families adorned the walls. Today was a special day for Henry, as he along with Conor and Edward would be knighted. Henry had asked that Tracey be knighted too as she had put her life on the line but Argoth refused as women were never knighted. Argoth did not leave her empty-handed as he had Hannorah and her spend time with a seamstress to make beautiful silk dresses to take home. She wore a chrome-gold dress today for this occasion. Hannorah wore a cyan one while Karina's dress was a dark navy. Henry, Conor and Edward, in a rare moment of breaking Zargothian tradition, were allowed to wear their own clothes so they chose tuxedos.

"You'll wear the floor out with your pacin'," Conor joked.

"Yeah, sorry, I'm just a little nervous," Henry replied.

"Don't be, lad, you earned it."

"Sergeant MacCall is right, Henry," Edward agreed. "You fought well out there. A knighting is the least you deserve."

"Thanks, guys. That means a lot."

"Please sit down, Henry, you're making me nervous now," Tracey said.

"Sorry." He laughed uneasily while taking his seat.

Henry asked Karina earlier that day why Argoth did not invite other people to witness this. Karina said Argoth preferred only a small crowd because of an incident that happened many years ago. Past kings would have held a ceremony in the castle's large chapel but all that changed when Argothram, Argoth's grandfather, was almost assassinated by a disillusioned nobleman who snuck in a knife in his cloak, throwing it as the former king knighted three soldiers. It struck him three inches above his heart. Kings since then did not want a large crowd. Henry also noticed Daniel was not there. Argoth did not knight him since he was forbidden from fighting.

"I know Daniel and I didn't see eye to eye but still, it sucks that he's not getting knighted," he said to Tracey.

"Yeah, he put a lot on the line too," Tracey added.

Karina overheard them and joined in. "I admire Daniel's courage but he went against his father's wishes. He should not have been out there. Besides, he is too young by Zargothian law to be knighted anyway."

"How come I'm getting knighted then?" Henry asked.

"It is not every day an Elder's son saves us." A warm glow seemed to emanate from Karina's eyes as she smiled.

"Maybe," Henry said. *Still, I can't blame him for not being here. I'd be angry too.*

The throne room doors opened. Two guards entered, each standing at either side of the entrance. They were proceeded by two guards who blasted their trumpets as Argoth and Cyren walked in. Henry and the others stood up. Cyren took her seat but Argoth remained standing.

The king spoke. "A year ago I would never have dreamt that I would be standing here today, back in my castle. This was made possible by you, Henry, and your friends. I will never forget that. So without further ado, Henry, Edward and Conor, please step forward."

They stepped forward, stopping at the foot of the three steps.

Argoth parted the ermine cape draping over his shoulders and drew his sword which he held over Henry's head. The blade first tipped the boy's head. Then the left and right shoulder.

"By the power vested in me by Zymbion himself and on behalf of the people of Zargothia, I knight you, Sir Henry Simmons from the land of America." He moved onto Edward and did the same, "I knight you, Sir Edward Johnson of the land of England." Finally finishing with Conor. "And I knight you, Sir Conor MacCall of Scotland." Argoth put his sword back into the acorn brown leather scabbard. "Arise ye knights for you have earned your titles well." Tracey whooped and cheered along with the others as they applauded. Karina bearing a broad smile wiped a tear from her eye.

Cyren rose from her chair to stand beside Argoth. Each of the new knights kissed her hand as a mark of respect.

When Henry, Edward and Conor were finished, they turned around to be congratulated by their friends. Tracey hugged Henry, giving him a long, passionate kiss.

Later, everyone who was in the throne room celebrated long into the night. With music being played, they danced, ate and for the teenagers, they drank non-alcoholic drinks Argoth had Karina make especially for them.

The next morning, dressed in the clothes they arrived in Zargothia with, Henry and Tracey ate in the banquet hall. They were joined by Hannorah,

Jasper and Daniel a few minutes later. Daniel sat at the far end of the table as the others sat together.

They all stopped eating when Karina walked in.

"Good morning. When you are all finished, I want you all to meet me in the royal gardens in about thirty minutes," Karina instructed.

Later, Henry and Jasper were first to arrive. The two girls came a few moments after.

"Does anybody know why we're here?" Tracey asked.

"Beats me," Henry replied.

"Me too," Hannorah added.

"Wait, isn't Daniel supposed to be here?" Henry said.

"Yes, but Daniel is still mad about not being knighted," Hannorah answered.

Henry saw Hannorah's eyes widen in delight upon seeing Karina approach in a peculiar aqua blue gown that had silver stars sewn on its sleeves.

"I will not keep you all waiting," Karina said, "so let's do what I called you all here for."

"Is this what I think it is?" Hannorah said, her voice bubbling with excitement.

"It is. We are here because I want you all to witness a special ceremony." Karina pointed to the ground. "Hannorah, if you please." Hannorah got down on her two knees.

"Put out your hands, Hannorah." Karina commanded; she complied. The sorceress removed a short, silver dagger from inside her gown and handed it to her. A tiny sparkling diamond in the shape of a silver star was crafted into the weapon's wooden hilt. Karina laid her dagger across Hannorah's two palms. "I have not forgotten about how well you fought in the battle. You proved yourself a worthy apprentice. I now anoint you my Rradoka."

What's a Rradoka? Henry thought. He guessed that Karina must have read his thoughts again when she said,

"She is now a level two apprentice," Karina explained to the others. "The next level is Enchantress."

"Thank you, mistress," Hannorah said.

"That dagger was given to me by my master and now I give it to you."

Hannorah, speechless, eyed Karina's beautiful dagger in amazement until she found the words to utter her gratitude. "I am honored. Thank you."

Nodding her head to the hilt, Karina said, "That star represents a power that must always be used for good. You are my shining star, Hannorah. I have great faith in you."

Henry noticed Hannorah fighting back her tears as she said, "I will serve it, and you, well."

"I know you will." Karina helped her up. Henry and Tracey hugged her.

"Way to go, Hannorah," Jasper said.

"What's the difference between a level one and level two apprentice?" Henry asked.

"A level one apprentice learns the basics of magic but because Hannorah's mother was a witch, she knew more than the average apprentice," Karina answered. "At level two, a Rradoka learns even more spells and how to move objects with their mind."

"Okay. Neat," Henry replied.

"Come, Henry, Tracey and Jasper, it is time we head to Argoth's throne room and send you home." Standing to the side, Karina lifted her hand in the direction of the throne room to let Henry and Tracey lead the way.

Soon all three Foretold Ones stood in the throne room with Queen Cyren, Argoth, Xongrelan and Dreyfus ready to meet them. A small flour sack was given to Tracey that contained the dresses made for her by the seamstress. Hannorah stood by Karina's side. A melancholy atmosphere surrounded them as they were about to leave this world and return to their own. Deep down, Henry was glad to be going back home and he guessed Tracey was too, but he would miss his friends in Zargothia. Plus the two airmen would be returning to the 1940s and he knew they'd never meet again.

Hamorin appeared in Henry's dream the night before and told him that he'd come today to show the way back to their home world.

"It was a pleasure fighting beside you, Henry. Good show, m' lad, good show."

"Gee thanks, Captain," Henry said, shaking his hand. "It was great fighting beside you as well."

"Aye. We'll miss you, wee fella." Conor ruffled the boy's hair.

Edward then shook Tracey's hand. "It was nice meeting you too, Tracey."

"Thanks," she replied.

Conor took her hand. "Ah, come here, lass." He pulled her in. She laughed as he wrapped his arms around her for a quick hug.

"I shall miss you too, Master Henry. It will not be the same without you," Karina said, her words laced with sadness.

"I agree with Karina," Xongrelan said. "But you did bring peace and our freedom so we are eternally grateful for that, boy."

"Goodbye," Hannorah said. She hugged him and Tracey. "I will miss you both too. Especially our chats, Tracey," Hannorah grinned mischievously at the girl.

Henry kissed Cyren's hand. She gave him an algae green rose. "This is a flower given to brave warriors in my world when they return home. It is a mark of respect...and love." She gave the others one too.

"You fought well, Henry. I could not be more proud had you been my son," Argoth said.

"Thank you, Your Majesty. That means a lot."

Argoth removed from his finger a silver ring with an amethyst gem on it. He handed the ring to Henry.

"That's for me?" The teen eyed it in astonishment.

"Yes, Sir Henry, that is for you."

"Awesome," Henry slipped it on his finger. "Don't worry, Your Majesty, I'll take real good care of it. I promise."

"As for you, Captain Johnson and Sergeant MacCall, I have not forgotten you either." Argoth waved at Miralda to come forward. She held in her hands a black velvet cushion. On it were two silver chains with a diamond on each of them. "These are for you."

"That's very kind of you, Your Majesty." Edward took his, putting the chain around his neck, as did Conor and when they were done they gave a perfectly synchronized salute.

Without warning, the room turned cold, mists swirled around them. Soldiers reached for their swords.

"Chill, guys," Henry said to the guards. "It's my dad, Hamorin, the Elder."

The mist that surrounded them was beginning to circle on a fixed point a short distance from where they were standing. It soon dissipated. All that remained was a man, holding a large staff topped with two bull's horns.

"No need to be afraid. I am one of the Elders here to send the Foretold Ones home."

"Hey, Dad," Henry said. It felt strange calling him that when he was only ever used to giving that title to Jack back home. But he felt, although as short as it was, that he bonded with Hamorin enough before his life was restored.

"Henry," Hamorin nodded with a smile of acknowledgement. "Walk with me a moment."

Henry followed the Elder to a quiet spot away from the others.

"I hate not having enough time to talk to you. I would love to go with you but I cannot. I am needed here."

"So we're not gonna have that chat you promised now, huh?"

"No, but we will. I swear to you we will."

Disheartened, Henry lowered his head. "Yeah... whatever."

"Henry-"

"Just send me home, Dad." Henry was about to walk away when Hamorin caught his right arm.

"Please, just hear me out." Henry sighed and waited. "I know you are disappointed. It hurts me that I can never be the kind of father you want. I am not human, I cannot be that kind of mortal parent, but that never stops me from loving you as much as any parent can possibly love their child. I cannot spread myself too thinly between worlds; that would give Hernacious an opportunity to kill me too."

Henry looked to his feet, unable to meet his father's gaze. Hamorin lifted the boy's chin.

"Someday we will be together. You have grown up to be a fine boy and a great warrior. A father could not ask for anything more."

"Thank you," Henry replied in a slightly happier tone but he still had a slight frown.

"I know you are sad but believe me, there is no other way. Oh, one more thing."

"Uh-huh."

Hamorin motioned his head in Tracey's direction. "Breaking that spell was the right thing to do. You will not be needing it anymore anyway," Hamorin said with a devilish grin. "Let's return to the others. Do you have the coin?"

"Yeah." Henry held it in his hand.

"Good. Give it to me." Taking a dagger from within his robe, he said, "Do not be alarmed. This will not hurt." Hamorin slit a line along the boy's palm. Blood spilled out onto the floor. Positioning the coin in the flow, Hamorin spoke again. "It is only through your blood the portal to your own home world will open."

The cut on Henry's hand healed as a portal was created.

"The first to leave will be Captain Edward and Sergeant Conor. Once you step through, you will be back at your base. Please step forward, the gateway will not remain open for long."

The two men waved goodbye to everyone before they stepped through the violet gateway. They disappeared.

Henry and Tracey stared at the portal but it wasn't their time yet to go home.

Jasper was next to leave. He leapt into the portal, but not before saying. "Catch you later, Henry."

Hamorin placed a hand on Henry's right arm.

"You have served the Elders and your people well. Time to go home and be free."

"What about the coin? Do I take that with me?"

"No. That will stay with us. If we need you, it will find you again. Go now."

Henry said his farewells to Karina, Argoth, Cyren, Dreyfus and Hannorah.

"I can't believe we've to go back in that thing," Tracey said.

"Don't worry, it mightn't be as bad this time," Henry bluffed. *At least I hope not.*

Just as he and Tracey were about to step through the portal, he took one last look at his Zargothian friends.

**THE PORTAL OPENS FOR HENRY AND TRACEY AS
HENRY YELLS FOR TRACEY TO GRAB HOLD OF HIM**

Tracey held onto his arm tightly as they entered it. She closed her eyes, muttering a prayer. After they took another step, they were swallowed up by the vortex. In a matter of seconds, Henry and Tracey were outside the dance hall.

"Oh thank God, we're home," Tracey exclaimed, hugging Henry, relief pouring out of every fiber in her body.

"Yeah, it's good to be back." Henry felt something in his jacket. The cell phone that was broken by Sid Connors was now inside his pocket. He pressed a button and the screen lit up.

"Cool. My phone's working again." He looked up to the skies. "Thanks, guys."

"I think it's time we went home," Tracey said.

"You got that right." Henry punched in the number for a cab his mom had given him before going to the prom. The lady from the cab company told him it would be there in twenty minutes.

"Look, Henry, about what happened in Zargothia," Tracey said.

"Don't worry, that stays between us. It's not like I was gonna blog about it. I mean, can you imagine what people would think?"

"I… wasn't talking just about that… I meant… about us."

"Look, it's okay. I understand if you want to keep quiet about it."

"Oh no." She smiled while hooking her arm with his. "I have no intention of keeping quiet about us."

"You mean… you want everyone to know?"

"I guess a part of me was a little shallow in not wanting to be with you before… all this happened. But now that I've seen the real you, I don't care what people think. I want the world to know you're my guy. Are you okay with that?"

"Yeah… duh! Wait, what about Sid? Won't he be mad about this?"

"Leave Sid to me. I'll take care of him."

"So, what are you going to tell your dad about those dresses?"

"I'll try and sneak them up to the room without him seeing me. But let's not worry about that." She pulled Henry close to her again. "In the meantime while we're waiting for the cab…"

They hugged and kissed again and again until their ride home arrived.

Tracey was first to be dropped off. On the journey to his house, Henry reflected on her amazing kisses and everything that happened in Zargothia.

As the cab stopped outside his house, Henry was full of mixed emotions. He now knew that the people in his home were not his real parents, but what Karina had told him was still in his mind. If they loved him and treated him right, that should be enough for any boy. He also knew he should be glad to be alive to see them again.

"Hey, kid, take all night if you want. I'll just keep the meter runnin'," the cab driver said sarcastically.

"How much?"

"That's twenty bucks." The chubby driver took the money. Henry got out of the cab.

The curtains were drawn in the sitting room but through the little slit, he could see that Jack, the man who he once thought of as "Dad", was watching TV. Before entering the house, he put the ring from Argoth into the inside pocket of his jacket along with Cyren's rose.

As soon as he closed the front door, he heard Jack calling him, "Hey, slugger, how was the prom?"

Henry went into the living-room and stood beside where Jack sat on the couch. "It was great. We had fun." Henry was about to leave when he turned and bent over to hug his father in the tightest of embraces.

"Whoa, kiddo, someone put something in your drink?" Jack joked.

"No… just felt like doing it. That's all."

"Hey, I'm not complaining." Jack patted Henry twice on the back.

Henry walked into the kitchen, where his mother was reading a newspaper. She looked at her watch as he entered. "You're home early, honey. Everything all right?"

"Yeah. I'm kind of beat. Tracey had me out dancing a lot."

"Oh, okay."

"I think I might just go to bed."

"Are you sure you're okay?"

"I'm just tired, that's all." Henry was outside the kitchen when he thought of something. "Mom, I know I don't say this much but…I love you."

"Aw, that's sweet, baby." Suzanne put down the paper and kissed him.

When Henry reached his room, he fell back, relishing the feeling of being in his own bed again.

It's good to be home, Henry thought.

* * *

On Monday morning, Henry was on his way to school. He was about to pass Mr. Anderson's when a faint but recognizable voice called to him from behind his neighbor's bush.

"Pssst. Hey, Henry, over here."

Henry walked into the garden. Jasper sat behind one of the old man's plants. He squatted to talk to the cat.

"Hi, Jasper. You're still able to talk here?"

"Yeah I know. Ain't it cool?"

"Er… I guess so." Henry looked at Mr. Anderson's porch window to see if the man was coming. The last thing he wanted was to be caught talking to a cat. The old man was not in sight so Henry continued. "When did you find out you could still talk?"

"I think it was about two days ago. I was chased by a dog and I screamed. Lucky for me, Anderson was upstairs and didn't hear me. Nobody knows I can talk except you."

"Wow. You must be happy."

"I sure am." Jasper cocked his head up high as his tail tapped the ground. "For a cat like me, being able to talk has its advantages, you know."

"How?"

"You know Ms. Williams, the woman that minds me?"

"Sorta."

"Well she's a mean old hag so I decided to get even with her. So yesterday I snuck into her house and hid under her bed. When she was praying, I pretended to be God and warned her that if she was mean to me again, she'd spend eternity in hell being attacked by cats," Jasper chuckled.

Henry raised an eyebrow in astonishment. "Are you serious?"

"Uh-huh. She cried like a baby and promised to never be mean to me again." Jasper rolled over in devilish laughter. He stopped after a few seconds. "Sorry. I'm okay now."

"That was mean."

"Maybe, but she had it comin'."

Checking his watch, Henry knew that he would miss the bus if he stayed talking. "Okay, Jas', I gotta go. Catch ya later. No more mean pranks, all right?"

"Sure thing, Henry. See ya 'round."

Henry walked to the bus stop, grinning at Jasper's mischievous behavior.

By afternoon, Henry was still getting so used to his old routine it was like he'd never been away. He never thought that the ringing of the school start of day bell would be music to his ears.

Just as Henry was about to unlock his locker, Brad Thompson walked by and shouldered him. Henry's head hit the locker. "Ow."

"Oh I'm sorry," Brad said, sniggering.

Henry was more than a little tempted to kick Brad's butt but he had done enough fighting in Zargothia.

Tracey stopped as she was passing by, "Catch you later in the cafeteria?"

"You bet."

"Looking forward to it." She winked and waved goodbye.

He smiled proudly before making his way to the toilets.

As Henry washed his hands, he saw Joey enter.

"Joey, man, good to see you."

Joey wore an expression of uncertainty. "Er… you too." The boy shook his head in puzzlement. "Is it true what I heard?"

"What did you hear?"

"Rumors are going around that you and Tracey kissed outside the dance hall Friday night."

"Sure is."

"How did you manage that?"

"Guess I got lucky."

"Lucky? Man, you hit the friggin' jackpot!" Both boys chortled at Joey's remark. "Look, dude, I'm just glad for ya."

"Thanks, Joey, that means a lot."

"I also heard Sid did a number on you Friday night. You all right?"

"Yes he did and a whole lot more happened." Henry cursed under his breath. He did not mean to say the last few words.

Joey and Henry each took a tray as they queued for lunch at the cafeteria.

"What do you mean by 'a whole lot more happened'?"

"Oh nothing. You wouldn't believe me even if I told you."

"Try me."

"Wait a sec'." Henry had waited until the lady behind the counter had given him his lunch portion. While Joey was receiving his, Henry scanned the tables for two empty seats. There were some near an emergency exit door. A table was vacant. This was perfect for Henry because if he was about to tell Joey what really happened, he didn't want anybody sitting next to him.

"So, what happened after Sid hit you?" Joey sat, ready to wolf down the lunch.

"I'm telling you, you're not going to believe me."

"Like I said, try me."

"Fine, but don't say I told you so and *don't* tell anyone else."

"I won't, man, just come on and tell me."

With his white straw, Henry stabbed a hole in the carton of orange juice. Henry looked left and right, leaning in closer. "It all began when I found this really cool gold coin…"

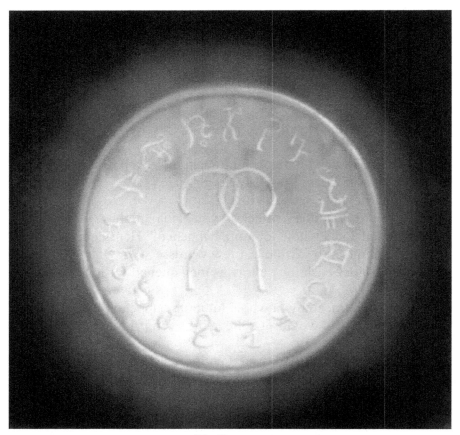

Epilogue

THIRTEEN MONTHS LATER: To the far north of Zargothia, two figures, a man and Slyvanon, walked through a blinding blizzard. They traveled over many hills, valleys and mountains to reach their destination, which was a cave. The man in a polar bear fur coat led his companion. They trudged through heavy snowfall. Both of them shivered as a frosty chill swirled around them.

The man put a wisp of his overgrown, long hair behind his ear as he thought he saw a fire up ahead.

"I think there's light just beyond us," he shouted above the howling wind.

Slyvanon followed him as they walked further on, shielding their eyes from the large snowflakes.

They stopped at the cave mouth; the man swept away cobwebs with his sword. When the way was cleared, Slyvanon went forward. "This time I will lead the way. These caves are very treacherous."

The cave was brightly lit with torches on the wall. The ground was dry, painted golden by the firelight. They made their way through the winding labyrinth. Stopping at a long, narrow walkway acting as a bridge connecting one path to another. Both men looked at it nervously; one wrong step or stumble and you would fall far below to certain death. Slyvanon turned to his companion.

"I believe what we came for is just beyond this."

"Then lead the way, my friend." Slyvanon was first to cross.

Together, they wandered through another labyrinth until they had reached what they were looking for.

The man smiled with delight. A glance over at his friend revealed that Slyvanon was overawed too as his jaw dropped a little and his eyes grew wide in excitement.

The two travelers were now in a large, round room. Before them was a crack along the cave floor leading to a towering rock.

"Behind that rock is the weapon you seek," Slyvanon told his companion.

Lifting back his hood, the pinched features of a once handsome man, grinned with malevolent gratification. With this weapon he could take his revenge on Argoth at last.

THE END

Well, What Did You Think?

We'd love to hear your feedback on *The Lost Son*. All reviews help get a novel like this noticed more. Reviews also lets the author know what fans like and don't like and what they want more/less of.

So reach out today and leave your review on either Amazon or Goodreads.

Thank you again for reading *The Lost Son*.

ABOUT THE AUTHOR

Aidan Lucid began writing in 2002 after having a religious experience. Since then, his works have appeared in national and international poetry anthologies, magazines and e-zines. Lucid first began working on *The Zargothian Saga trilogy* while recovering from a horrific accident in 2005. Over the years Aidan has been perfecting the story and is now ready to share it with the world. Mr. Lucid is working on book two, but in his spare time he likes to meditate, listen to music and go to the movies with his wife, Claire.

Subscribe Today and Be Notified of:

- Book Releases
- Promotions
- Competitions
- New Merchandise (t-shirts, mugs etc.)

Go to: www.thezargothiansaga.com/mailing_list.php and subscribe.

CONNECT WITH AIDAN ON:

https://www.facebook.com/Aidan-Lucids-The-Zargothian-Saga-212119345506612/

https://twitter.com/TheZargothian

https://www.instagram.com/zargothianauthor/

Made in the USA
Columbia, SC
20 December 2020